# two
# marriages

# two
# marriages

*novellas*

**PHILLIP LOPATE**

Other Press · New York

Production Editor: Yvonne E. Cárdenas

Text design: Alexis Morley

This book was set in Adobe Garamond by Alpha Design & Composition of Pittsfield, New Hampshire.

10 9 8 7 6 5 4 3 2 1

Library of Congress Cataloging-in-Publication Data

Lopate, Phillip, 1943-
  [Stoic's marriage]
  Two marriages / Phillip Lopate.
      p. cm.
  ISBN 978-1-59051-298-2 (acid-free paper) 1. Married people—Fiction.
2. Marriage—Fiction. 3. Domestic fiction. I. Lopate, Phillip, 1943- Eleanor.
II. Title.
  PS3562.O66S76 2008
  813'.54—dc22

                                                        2008008083

Publisher's Note: This is a work of fiction. Names, characters, places, and incidents either are the product of the author's imagination or are used fictitiously, and any resemblance to actual persons, living or dead, events, or locales is entirely coincidental.

# CONTENTS

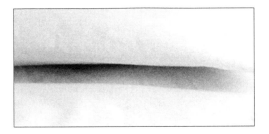

# The Stoic's Marriage

*a novella*

PART ONE

MAY 14

I would like to record here, in this brand-new notebook of twenty-two lines per page, with my new Rollerball pen, the story of my marriage as it unfolds. Why? Because a good marriage deserves to be examined as well as commemorated, it requires alertness, vigilance. All unhappy marriages are actually alike (*pace* Tolstoy), the two partners endlessly miserable because they fail to communicate, and the wellsprings of mutual affection dried up, replaced by petty malice. But each happy marriage is at once a miracle and a complex mechanism, like a Swiss clock whose successful inner workings, once analyzed, could conceivably offer hope to conjugal sufferers everywhere.

Of course it may be that there is nothing to analyze, I am simply lucky, having stumbled upon a paragon for a wife. Rita is a jewel, a tired metaphor, I admit, but clichés become so only because they convey a grain of truth (itself a cliché), and by comparing my wife to a jewel, I simply mean she is radiant, beautiful, kind, affectionate, skillful, exciting, and many-faceted. If I dote on her good points, so be it; of all possible flaws, uxoriousness is the one I most cheerfully own. What is the point of laboring to find imperfections in a woman where none exist? Just to reassure the jaded literary palate that mistakenly assumes you must mix in some bad with good to draw a credible portrait? But supposing there is no bad? I would rather take the risk of boring my readers, or inviting their disbelief, than to calumniate my wife by ascribing to her imaginary flaws.

Myself, I have faults aplenty, enough to sustain the interest of any narrative. I am insecure, timid, either too lazy or perfectionist to accomplish anything with my modest intellectual gifts, overly sensitive and quick to take offense, surprisingly cruel on occasion, a procrastinator, selfish, petulant, introverted, melancholic, and now, on top of all that, thanks to my newfound marital happiness, complacent. How to avoid the spiritual sloth of self-satisfaction? That is a new problem for me. Will it placate the reader somewhat if I confess I have known little joy in life, before this uncharacteristic plunge into bliss? I will go further: I have always regarded myself as having a stunted capacity for happiness. Just for that reason, I have cultivated resignation in the face of what seemed inevitable disappointment, hence my attraction to Stoicism. But that ancient philosophy and my study of Stoicism are matters too convoluted to talk about here just yet, especially in a marriage manual! Besides, I hear Rita coming in downstairs, so I will put this journal away until tomorrow.


MAY 17

I was not able to get to this diary the last two days, because of errands, domestic details, and whatnot, and besides, I told you I was lazy. Happiness alone eats up much of my time, saps my will to communicate with others, even future readers of this diary. Yesterday I was looking over at Rita as she sat beside me on the couch, sewing. She was wearing a red cotton skirt with a white lotus pattern, and a white blouse with red ribbon that bunched or cinched at the neck, and she had a camellia in her hair. I should mention Rita is from the Philippines, and has gorgeous straight black hair reaching almost to the small of her back. Her Philippine background offers a fascinating blend, for me, of the familiar and the exotic. Since both my parents were born in Spain (Salamanca, to be precise, where my father was a professor of law at that famous university), even though I grew up in Brooklyn, I find we have much in common: Philippine culture also has a strong Spanish Catholic base, the rituals are similar, the people very family-oriented. And yet there is an Asian tinge in Filipino women, their almond eyes, slender curvaceous figures, which I find irresistibly attractive. Morally, though one shouldn't generalize, of course, Spaniards tend to be overwhelmed with guilt, especially in carnal matters, while Filipinos have a more easygoing, free-flowing approach to sex, which I think of as the South Pacific sea-breeze influence. Another "Asian" quality in Rita is her self-sufficiency, her delicacy, her unhurried equanimity, if I may be permitted to indulge a little longer this lamentable stereotyping, which, however, as I said earlier about clichés, may contain a grain of truth, unless that is simply another rationalization for lazy thinking. In any case, I was looking over at Rita on the couch yesterday, in the late afternoon, and I was so amazed at her beauty that I thought, this can't be my wife! How did I merit the love of this unaffected, sweet, astonishingly pretty, naturally elegant woman, with such round yet chiseled cheekbones, and with that adorable dimpled smile? For a second I even wondered if she were a laser projection, so unrealistic did my good fortune seem to me. You will smile when I tell you that I actually placed my hand on her ankle, just to make sure she was real. She gave me a tender look and returned to her sewing. Then I squeezed her foot to make doubly sure. Yes, she was real all right, unless laser technology has made amazing strides and now includes a tactile dimension, for when I squeezed her foot, she let out an ow!, which no laser projection could do, although there are those dolls, come to think of it, that make a similar moan when you bend them at the waist. Now here is the part I find peculiar: in the midst of exulting at my good luck, I suddenly felt heavyhearted, disconsolate, don't ask me why. Maybe my feeling of laser estrangement came from doubting not *her* reality but my own. What was *I* doing in this picture, I, clumsy Gordon, with my roly-poly belly and thinning, wiry hair and inky beard and glasses? How can such a goddess be my wife?


MAY 30

I think it would be helpful to recount the stages by which we got to this point, Rita and I, the origins of our affection, our courtship, and our marriage. It is a delightful story, one I love to review in minutest detail, though it does have its painful aspects, since Rita came into my life at about the same time my mother departed from it. These two images, Mother on her deathbed and Rita's miraculous arrival, are linked in my brain, much as horse and man combine to make a centaur, to use a ridiculous analogy.

Let me back up a bit. I need to explain that I am an only child. My mother doted on me, as did my teachers, the nuns, everyone, heaven knows why. I am one of those who grew from a brilliant boy into a commonplace man, the old story of the wunderkind who discovers as soon as he leaves childhood's protected circumstances for the larger world that he is in fact nothing special. Not only did I lack an original perspective, I also lacked the "fire in the belly," to use that abominable phrase applied to politicians and artists, which might have allowed me to impose my will on the world regardless of limited talents. A disappointment, I suspect, to my parents, I was on the whole a good son. After my father passed away, I tried to ease my mother's sorrow by looking in on her as much as possible, especially after she became ill. She had been the best of all mothers when I was a boy, a sacrificing angel, but in her old age she became, why not admit it, quarrelsome, demanding, and difficult. She refused to be relocated to a nursing home or even an assisted-living community, which I can understand, but since she was patently unable to take care of herself, and kept falling down and breaking her hip, or forgetting that she had left something on the stove, I had to move back into my mother's house, the same house where I had been raised, to take care of her. Here I was, a bachelor in my late forties, approaching fifty, once again living with my mother. I felt myself to be an object of condescension, and the implication I saw (or imagined, let us be fair) in people's eyes was that I was an overgrown mama's boy or closeted homosexual, as many people assume all aging bachelors to be. Of course, people are free to think what they choose. But if you were in my shoes, loving your incapacitated elderly mother, you might very well have done the same thing I did. It is a sad commentary on our age that taking filial responsibility for one's infirm parent should be seen as neurotic.

To make matters worse, I myself felt that by moving back home I was in some sense regressing, so that any faint smirk I detected on others' faces was matched by my own inner smirk. Let me note in passing that all my life I've sensed I was being laughed at. I don't speak here in a paranoid manner; I simply mean that people tend to regard me as an amusing distraction, not to be taken absolutely seriously. It has something to do with my being pudgy, I believe, not fat exactly, but chunky (which is how I got the childhood nickname Gordo), and American culture equates being overweight with being clownish. Any ability to project myself as a romantic lead has been compromised by my belly: most of the pretty women I pursued quickly decided I was not infatuation material. I would never be the love of their life, so why blame them for their giving me the gate? Those women who *were* crazy about me (there have been a few) saw me as a kind of huggy bear, and I could not recognize my gloomy self in their adorable-panda misperceptions. Foolishly, perhaps, I felt suffocated by their undifferentiated approval, as if it was evidence of not being taken seriously enough. My mother, of course, took me very seriously, I was her only child—too seriously, you might say. Now Rita, my wife, takes me seriously, but not too seriously, she is able to laugh at me—I wonder if a part of her wasn't always laughing at me, which is fine, all the better, I would not hold it against her if she *was* laughing at me, since we are all ridiculous, myself more than most. What I like is that she is affectionate but does not smother me with gush. She has a restraint, a reserve, an instinct for privacy, which suits me. I often sense I am approaching her diagonally, that is, I am facing her head-on and she is turned to the side. I am reminded when I look at her of that Gauguin painting where the woman is holding the slice of watermelon. A good deal of her charm lies in the graceful way her shoulders and neck carry her beautiful head. She lifts her head like a doe, and as you approach her, you see one eye, not both. I am speaking metaphorically, of course. I often see both her eyes at once, but there remains this impression of a one-eyed doe, I don't know how to explain it any better, forgive me.

Partly I like to approach her from the side or from behind, because I am crazy about her skin. She has amazingly smooth, unblemished brown skin, a glowing cocoa color, with a cinnamon tinge. The underside of her arm is white and smooth. And her smell! I could write pages just about that smell, with its hint of jasmine and coconut, and the sheen on her skin, its suppleness to the touch. The other day she had on an orange shift, very simple, gathered at the waist, that stopped just above her ankles (she was wearing some high-heeled sandals with sage-leaf decorations), that left her shoulders bare. The combination of that tangerine color against her light brown skin was delicious—all the more so because I would never have predicted those two shades would go well together.


JUNE 8

I see, reading over my last entry, that I did not get very far in recounting the circumstances of our courtship. I am going to have to be more disciplined in bringing these entries to a narrative point. The problem is, I am torn between shaping this diary as a publishable account, which means throwing in all sorts of tiresome background information I already know but readers won't, and exploring for just my own amusement those day-to-day enchantments of life with Rita that lead me into a thicket of digression or, worse, inane nonsense, such as that comparison of her to a one-eyed doe. Really! No wonder I never accomplished much with my previous literary efforts, those contrived sestinas, poems in Latin, and abandoned Chekhovian short stories of my youth.

When Mother started failing, after her last chemotherapy treatment for bone marrow cancer, I bought her a special adjustable bed, the kind they use in hospitals, and stocked her room with a portable commode, a wheelchair, mountains of fresh sheets, pillows, and towels, and a bell. I also set about finding a team of nurses who could administer round-the-clock palliative care. One of the nurses at St. Barnabas, the hospital where Mother had gone for treatment, was a sharp Filipino woman named Gloria, who ran her own little business on the side, a sort of medical booking agency supplying at-home professional care. These nurses brought their brisk buoyant manner into our home, and mostly Mother loathed them, she disparaged them constantly. The pillows were an especial source of grievance, because the sicker she became, the fussier, and they had to be arranged just so, which sometimes took all morning. I kept trying to humor Mother, while feeling sorry for these women, who struck me as doing a decent job, maybe not perfect, but competent. On top of all that, you can't imagine how costly such a nursing staff turned out to be! I'm not saying we didn't have the money, but I was growing alarmed by these staggering monthly bills, thinking that if Mother was to endure, at this level of care, for several more years, it might bankrupt us.

The compromise I arrived at with Gloria was that we would employ a combination of nurses and less expensive, unlicensed attendants. As it happened, the one helper Mother could stand was a pretty attendant named (you guessed it) Rita. She was newly arrived in America, on a tourist visa, and she still had that island way of walking, that sensual sashay of the hips from side to side that conveyed an unhurried pace, in other words, the lower half of her body had not yet grown numb to her, as happens in advanced capitalist societies. She had straight, shiny black hair almost down to her waist, with an enticingly voluptuous figure (the Filipino costumes she wore outlined her body with startling accuracy), long thin shapely legs like a model's, and a composed, harmoniously symmetrical face, smoldering brown eyes, full lips which would most charmingly and unexpectedly break into a playful, dimpled smile. . . . I see I am rapidly descending into mush, as often happens when the average person with no literary flair attempts to describe, feature by feature, a beauty's beauty. Let me try again. Here is what I noticed: her face was at once youthful and wise, she looked at first to be only in her mid-twenties (I later learned she was thirty-six), but clearly was no stranger to hardship, poverty, some species of trouble, which she had absorbed with equanimity, like a palm tree buffeted but not broken by tropical storms. (Ugh! Ridiculous.)

My mother, as I say, liked her. "Get me Rita," she would moan when someone else was on call. She refused to let anyone else bathe her, or comb her hair, or help with the niceties of toilette that women, even at death's door, insist upon. Rita would tease her with made-up stories, the way one might a child. They would invent gossip about the doctor or the mailman, and I would sometimes come upon them giggling like two sisters, in their own little world. You can't imagine what a relief it was to see my mother lighthearted, even for five minutes a day. This attendant, this Rita, had the gift of a tranquil spirit: she brought happiness and cheer to everyone, with her dazzling smile.

As she ministered to my mother, I could not help being aware of her alluring presence. I was, in spite of myself, aroused. I would follow her with my eyes, inadvertently, and sometimes she would catch me looking at her and smile almost as though giving me permission to admire her. As though she knew I was having erections just by looking at her. Let us be honest, sickrooms attract an erotic current. All that interminable waiting, that grim attention to the invalid's body despair, provokes a perverse counter-response, a will to thrive and embrace beauty. We, the healthy, form a stronger bond, even if we were but strangers a day ago, than is possible between the one entering death's black waters and those of us watching on the shore. Our complicit glances make us akin to criminal accomplices, or else it is that we share guilt from not being able to alter the inevitable. In any case, sitting in my chair beside the sickbed, holding my mother's liver-spotted, bony hand, I began to have remarkably vivid fantasies of taking this young woman in my arms and ravishing her, at the very moment I should have been devoting my every thought to the one who had brought me into this world. . . .

It had been my mother's expressed wish not to return to the hospital, no matter how badly her condition deteriorated. I honored her desire to die at home, which struck me as very European. My mother had that air, so common in Spanish ladies, of being resigned to suffering and surprised at nothing. As she slipped into and out of consciousness, I became less troubled that she might notice me looking at Rita. In her prime, my mother could be very jealous: she often disapproved of the women I dated, but her jealousy went further, she grew cross if you shifted your attention from her momentarily, or daydreamed while she was talking to you, as I did too often when I was a boy. But one time she did wake up, just as my eyes were trailing helplessly after Rita, and the corners of her lips flickered in a semi-grin. I thought about that enigmatic smile of Mother's on our wedding day. I fancied it her way of giving us her blessing in advance, as she lay dying. In retrospect, knowing my mother, it could have as easily been a sneer, meaning: "I knew you'd fail me in the end. Men are such dolts!" But why be cynical? I prefer to think Mama was acquiescing in my future marital happiness.

One night, toward the end of that long struggle, I felt the heat between Rita's body and my body whenever we happened to pass each other in the narrow space around my mother's bed. It troubled me. I went out into the hallway to cool off. Ten or fifteen minutes later, Rita came out of the bedroom, signaling with a gesture that Mother was sleeping soundly. I looked into her eyes with great intensity, sweating profusely, wishing that by some miracle she could read my mind and, in that way, intuit my passion for her, so that I would not have to embarrass either of us by speaking it aloud. As she drew alongside me to pass in the hallway, I—touched her shoulder. Just that, that single, timid, ambiguous gesture was all I could bring myself to do, and I was well aware that the gesture could have been equally read as comradely, rather than as expressing yearning and desire, which is perhaps why I chose it. I will never forget what happened next. She signaled me to follow her. We went into the guest room, where the night attendant generally slept, down the hall from the sickroom. She sat on the bed and began calmly unbuttoning her dress, a simple cotton dress of light-green-and-white stripes. She took my burning hand and placed it on her bra.

I dislike reading about others' sexual acts, so I will spare you a description of ours. Suffice it to say that what followed was physically and emotionally perfect for me, and left me stunned with gratitude. Her touch was uncannily comforting yet arousing, so much so that I could not help wondering if she was acting merely out of pity for me, or out of some deep, compassionate understanding of life's sadness. It also crossed my mind that she may have felt she had no choice, in the way that a chambermaid might accept an employer's unwanted embraces in the midst of making the bed. On the other hand, I had not used any force, I had merely touched her shoulder, and she was the one who led me to her room. When it was over, she looked up at me with an expression of such sleepy contentment, nuzzled happily against my arm, that I could no longer doubt her affection for me. How that desire for me had taken root in her, at what point it had crystallized, I am still not sure. It remains mysterious, her making that first move; but since in this life we often draw strength from mystery, I prefer to leave it that way.

JUNE 15

My hand suffered a cramp from the last entry, which is why I have had to forgo writing several days in this diary. I must keep the entries shorter. I was pushing myself too hard, rushing to get through the backstory of our courtship so that I could concentrate on recording the day-to-day exchanges between us, which are the real nectar of my life. I may have overdone it. I have a habit of tightening the muscles in my neck when I write, and that could easily lead to a pinched nerve or carpal tunnel syndrome. Complicating the picture is my stoical tendency to endure any bodily discomfort without complaint, telling myself it doesn't matter, until such time as it literally whacks me over the head and I can no longer ignore it, which is not the healthiest approach to pain.

I was sitting with Rita yesterday morning on the back porch overlooking the garden, our sweet little breakfast nook, when I forced myself to tell my wife about the pain in my shoulder, something I almost never do, it being against my Stoic principles. She immediately went into the kitchen, prepared a cold compress for me, got me two aspirin, and began massaging my shoulders. I was so touched with her concern that I took her on my lap (I forgot to mention that we were both wearing morning robes) and slipped my hand onto her nipple. Rita looked around with a nervous smile to see if any neighbors were watching us. Then, as always, she offered her breasts for me to suckle.

"Your breasts are so beautiful," I said.

"Every woman has them," she replied.

"Yes, but yours are . . ." my voice suddenly sounded husky to me, and I could not think of the right adjective to apply, as I stroked her nipple dreamily, feeling the dark brown integument enlarging under my fingers, "extraordinary. And *you* are so deliciously gorgeous, every bit of you."

"Oh, me, I'm just average-looking," she said.

I was taken aback. Could it be that Rita does not really know how beautiful she is? Was she being routinely modest, or are women from her part of the Philippines so sensational that she considers herself just an average specimen? That I find hard to believe. Judging from the rest of Gloria's Filipino nurse team, which had several attractive members, Rita was clearly the standout. Oh, I know that women can be insecure about their appearance, and even supermodels find minuscule defects when examining themselves before full-length mirrors. But in my experience, a beautiful woman always knows she is beautiful. It is part of her manner, the way she tilts her head, her whole gestural vocabulary, so to speak. Rita conveys grace in every moment, but whether it is an artless attainment or a self-confident awareness of her own beauty, who knows? More to the point, what would I gain by convincing her she is a knockout? I might spoil her, and make her conceited or tyrannical. Still, it makes me lonely to worship a divinity who so little understands what all the fuss is about. If I could get her to accept my opinion of how stunning her beauty is, we could both share rapturously in it. I am talking drivel, my pen is leading me into follies, so I will quit for the day.

JUNE 17

Rita admitted to me last night that people told her she resembles a certain popular Filipino actress from her childhood, Vilma Santos, who I gather was very beautiful, though she herself does not take the comparison seriously. To go back to my story: after the first time, from that point on we were often in each other's arms. Sometimes a day would pass when I was too distracted by my mother's condition to approach Rita, and then the fever would come over me again and I would have to be, forgive me for putting it this crudely, inside her again. She never refused me. To this day she never has. You can't imagine how different that is from my experiences with other women. I can remember times when a woman with whom I was involved would suddenly close up like a mollusk, and I would have to beg, cajole, persuade, coax, apologize, grovel, for weeks! Rita does not put me through any of that humiliation, she is there for me day and night. I am almost inclined to define happiness as being madly attracted to someone who will let you make love to her whenever you wish. Can it really be that simple? Can I possibly be so shallow? I knew so little about real happiness before meeting Rita that I am in no position to generalize for others.

Where were we? I was at the point of telling about my mother's death, which is probably why I started digressing. (Other than that I am always digressing.) No, I don't feel like writing about my mother's death, at least not today. What is important for our purposes here is that, after the funeral, I asked Rita if she would stay on in the house to help out, and she kindly agreed. A few months later, two to be exact, I asked her to marry me. I wanted to honor our love in the traditional way, and to bring her, if possible, emotionally closer to me, to have her at my side always. And let's be honest, to give her security: she was in the country on a short-term visa, and in this way I could help her obtain her green card for citizenship. So I proposed; it made perfect sense in every respect, romantically and logistically.

To my surprise, she said, "Why can't we go on the same way we have been?" I said I wanted to do the proper thing, to marry her, I didn't want her for my mistress, I wanted her for my wife. She asked for a few days to think it over. A few days seemed impossible, I could not have stood the suspense, and insisted she give me her answer in twenty-four hours, not to be imperious, but because I feared she might turn me down if she had a lot of time to consider. Another factor, I admit now, was that her hesitation wounded my vanity. I had acted from what I thought a bountiful impulse to rescue her, however fatuous that sounds in retrospect, and had expected her to be, well, if not ecstatic, then at least pleased, and I was offended when she seemed, how to put it, pensive, moody. A cloud seemed to pass over her. (You must understand that I had been a bachelor for forty-eight years, had had little experience asking for anyone's hand, and perhaps as a consequence had come to overvalue my own hand.)

During the next day, I heard Rita discussing it on the phone in Tagalog, and regretted (not for the last time) my ignorance of that language. When we had a moment alone, I begged her to tell me the nature of her doubts, so that I could at least have a chance to counter them. She said she needed only a little more time to think, she would give me her answer in the morning. The next morning she accepted, radiantly. We got married almost exactly a half-year ago. And she has been my happiness ever since.

JUNE 18

I return to where we left off yesterday. Given my present connubial satisfaction and willingness to act the part of a husband, a question naturally arises: Why *did* I wait so long, well into my late forties, to get married? Not only have I often asked that question of myself, others have asked it for me. The conventional wisdom was that I was afraid of intimacy. Of course, what man is not afraid of intimacy? But I always believed that if I met a woman whom I honestly trusted and loved, I would be able to overcome that finally surmountable

fear. It is not lost on me that my mother had long dreamed of seeing me married, and it was only after she passed away that I found
myself walking down the aisle. Was it therefore spite on my part
that refused to give her the satisfaction of seeing me settled, or the
opposite, instinctual tact, which read her unconscious or unspoken
wish as preferring that I remain single while she was still alive? Or
did it have nothing to do with my mother, but only with the circumstances of luck, timing, meeting the right person when I did, at
a point when I was finally grown-up enough to accept love?

These are speculative, hence unanswerable questions, and I
would prefer to do some gardening, as it is a perfect day for it.

(Later) My zinnias and lilies have been coming up nicely. The
cosmos are especially full, the snapdragons turning out fine, it's
too early for the impatiens. I am a little worried about my Japanese maple, which seems a little droopy. Could I possibly have been
overwatering it? I will get David to take a look; he is a young gay
man who runs a little nursery business nearby and who tends my
garden whenever I go away. I am also thinking of planting an herb
garden again, though the last one didn't do so well. I need to start
deadheading a few things.


JUNE 23

When we first got married, Rita thought she should go back to
work as a home-care attendant for Gloria. She wanted to earn her
own money in order to send most of it back to her mother in the
Philippines. I did not like the idea of my wife taking buses and

subways around Brooklyn by herself in the early-morning hours, and frankly, I have enough capital to take care of both of us, and additionally provide a monthly stipend for her mother, so it makes no sense for her to run herself ragged, tiring herself out for a minimum wage. I would never have stopped Rita from the practice of some calling or craft, some significant form of self-expression, believe me, but I saw no reason for her to be emptying bedpans and fluffing sick people's pillows just to bring in a little extra cash. Besides, for selfish reasons, I wanted to keep her around as much as possible, as it makes me happy just to be with her.

Tonight Rita prepared me a delicious traditional Filipino meal of stewed pork on rice mixed with raisins and nuts, a salad of green mango slices with tomatoes and onions, and some sort of eggplant dish (she is brilliant at varying her treatment of eggplant). At first, when we began living together, she was reluctant to cook me Filipino meals, thinking I would find it a "poor people's cuisine," and as a result she made a lot of Italian pasta dishes, and steak and potatoes, all extremely tasty, but I convinced her that since she had been cooking Filipino-style all her life, why not put that knowledge to good use? I am game to try new things. Not that every Filipino dish she cooks is to my taste, but on the whole, this sort of fare is working out beautifully.

JULY 3

We are going to Nevis tomorrow for a few weeks, to get away from an infernal hot spell and celebrate our first half-anniversary. I am dying to flee the city, and all these squashed pugnacious ghetto faces. Nevertheless, a part of me is reluctant to detach myself from the house. We live in a large, rambling, Georgian-style corner house in Dyker Heights, on Eleventh Avenue, that has eleven rooms, most of them barely used. A local giveaway paper once ran a picture of this house, catching in the same frame the stone statues of the huntress Diana, the griffin, the sphinx, and the lion ascending the front steps, and the caption underneath labeled it with some exaggeration a "mansion," it is simply a well-built, commodious house, three stories high, I suppose you could call it a "south Brooklyn villa," oxymoronic as that sounds. My parents bought the house at a time when Brooklyn was in a real estate slump and its properties much undervalued (they have since shot up astronomically, I don't need to tell you). My father, who, as I may have mentioned, was a professor of law at the University of Salamanca, where Unamuno himself taught and was rector (though before my father's time), having emigrated to this country, found he could not practice at the bar here without undergoing legal studies anew, so he redirected himself, starting a surgical instrument business in Queens, which proved very successful, especially because of a metal stent he devised to prop open heart arteries that is still used widely in hospitals. When his business took off, he fell in love with this house and bought it. Many of our neighbors, mostly Italian, live in more modest two-family bungalows with brick or aluminum siding, ours is one of the larger homes on the avenue, but, as we were the first Hispanic family to penetrate what has otherwise been an Italian neighborhood, we felt reluctant to call attention to our-

selves. Our neighbors, on the other hand, have had no such shy-
ness trumpeting their house-pride. You may have even heard of
this neighborhood, Dyker Heights, which has a reputation for
stately homes that go all-out every Christmas with gaudy holiday
decorations. I find this Christmas kitsch frenzy mildly irritating,
the joke has worn thin, but it would be too ostentatious to dis-
sent, so I go along with it, stringing a dozen strands of lights and
antique ornaments as my father did before me.

About my father: He was a good, honorable, dignified, resourceful man, I say this not out of filial piety but out of strict
observation. He had that skepticism and austerity that is typical
of Castilians, and allows them to abide whatever harsh circumstances Life inflicts on them. I know he would have wanted me to
take over the business he started. When he died, very young, in
his late fifties, of a sudden aneurysm that took us all by surprise, I
had just graduated from college, a classics major, unsure what
practical path to follow. Somehow I could not see myself running
a factory. Not that I felt superior to such work, quite the opposite; it was more that his factory workers intimidated me, so that
I kept imagining these skilled artisans ignoring my orders. While
I hesitated, interminably as is my wont, trying to make up my
mind, my mother stepped in and sold the business, for quite a bit
of money, to a large medical supplies corporation. We needn't go
into specific figures: enough money so that, if I am sensible and
don't suddenly become addicted to gambling tables, I need never
hold down a regular job. The freedom to pursue one's intellectual
interests without financial pressure can be a mixed blessing, at least

it has been so in my case; a stronger man might have profited unreservedly from the same opportunity. But we will leave that subject for another day.

Getting back to the house, today I asked Rita if she thought we should extend the deck above the garden in our backyard. She seemed noncommittal. I was trying in an indirect way to broach a more delicate subject: Were there adjustments she might want to make to have the place feel more like her own, to expunge at long last the ghost of my mother, with her heavy, dark, somewhat gloomy taste for mahogany, that style that might be called Hispano-Biedermeier? Since every bride, I am told, has strong ideas about interior decoration, I was trying to ferret out Rita's preferences in this regard.

"But Gordo, I like your house," she said.

"I understand that you like it. I'm glad that you like it. You may still feel you want to stamp it with your personality. This *was* my mother's house, after all, and the decor has some of her fussy, old-lady qualities."

"But I loved your mother. I like feeling her around us still."

It was the perfect response, I was so happy to hear her say that, nevertheless I pressed on, just to make sure. "I feel the same way, but I was wondering if it was selfish of me to want to keep everything more or less the way it was. You may want to turn over a new leaf."

"Oh," Rita said, smiling, "it's not necessary. I'm content to keep it this way."

"I mean, for instance, you might want a sewing room, since you like to sew and knit."

"I can knit on the couch. That way I am near you."

"All right, good," I said, dropping the matter. How can you argue with an angel?

Originally I had figured I would sell this property after my mother died and put the family furnishings in storage. But then good fortune sent me Rita, and she liked the house, and I began seeing it through her eyes, not as a white elephant I was eager to rid myself of, but as a charmingly ornate love nest, and, silly as it sounds, I am sometimes frightened that if we were ever to leave this residence, the spell would be broken, she would come to her senses and realize she couldn't possibly love me, she must have taken me for someone else. Under a new lighting scheme and in a less enchanted environment, she would be forced to consider me more critically. I should ask myself, in the interests of honesty, whether the same would apply for me: whether, if we moved elsewhere, I would stop loving her, given my former fickle tendencies. In my bachelor days, I would have the experience of being dazzled by a date as she swept into Café Luxembourg, let us say, her washed blond hair bobbing and her freshly applied lipstick glistening, her cheeks giving off a rosy glow. But then, as the evening progressed and her lipstick wore off, replaced by grease from the meal, and her hair wilted under the hot lights, and her pancake makeup wore off, revealing a more splotched complexion, I would suddenly perceive her as rather ordinary, not some glamorous, starlit apparition. Rita's beauty, however, is of a different kind. It is a deeper, more sculptural, shadowy beauty, less contingent on the artistry of illusion, I cannot imagine ever tiring of it, regardless of whatever longitude or latitude I might take her off to. So it is far more probable that I am leery of extracting her from this house because, without its helpful evocations, she might see *me* as a pale, pasty-faced, chubby man, someone to pass on the street without a second look. I think about this, I suppose, because we are about to take this trip, to go on vacation to Nevis. Traveling sometimes puts strains on a couple's affections.

JULY 6

We are on Nevis, a Caribbean island formerly part of the British West Indies, where Alexander Hamilton was born. It lies across a narrow strait from Saint Kitts, with which it comprises a self-governing state (along with Anguilla). I knew nothing about the place two weeks ago, but it was recommended to me by my travel agent. He has booked us into a lavish resort, which has everything you can imagine, and which effectively shields us from the actual life of the island indigenes. I suppose I ought to feel guilty, but in fact I enjoy being waited on hand and foot, and the delicious meals, the palm trees, the milky white sands and beautiful, warm azure waters, the reggae band music at night, the heavy mixed drinks, all make this what they call a "no-brainer." I do feel my brain shutting down, as the stoic in me gives way to the sybarite. The only mental activity I have permitted myself is that of continuing to make my way through Trollope's novels (I am at the start of the Palliser series, *Can You Forgive Her?*, which so far is very good). I have even forbidden myself the discipline of keeping up my diary, this entry being the one exception. Besides, how could I have written in it before, with Rita at my side every minute, until this morning, when she deserted me for a horseback-riding lesson? I am glad for the chance to be alone, to scribble a few lines in my diary, but I wish she could have gone off with a less handsome guide. This fellow André is a very dashing, capable black man in his thirties, who is employed by the resort as an all-purpose athletic instructor, and who dresses in crisp whites and has sparkling white teeth. We first met him yesterday when he was riding his horse along the beach. Rita was admiring the horse, and André was admiring Rita. She had on a brightly colored sarong over her one-piece purple bathing suit. The upshot was, he offered to give her a riding lesson this morning. They have been gone two hours and I hope she will return soon.

AUGUST 1

We are back in the city after a relaxing, uneventful time at the seashore. I dare not call Nevis "vacation," since I was not exactly working before we left. It was, in any case, a vacation from diary-keeping, with that one exception.

A question that keeps besetting me is: Am I writing this diary for outside readers, or only for myself? If the latter, I have no need to explain that my father started a surgical instrument business, since I am well aware of that fact and unlikely to forget it. But if I am writing for a general audience, I must identify each new person who comes into these pages, providing sufficient context to clarify the events I am recording. I don't see how a general audience can hope to follow, much less profit from, this diary the way I've been going at it so far, leaping from subject to subject, shuttling between past and present. If I am to continue to entertain the fantasy of publication, I will have to go easy on myself and consider what I have been doing an initial first draft, part of the basic research process, a collection of random notes that may someday be given narrative shape and logical order, but not yet, as St. Augustine says about relinquishing sin.

There exists a fourth possibility, that I am writing it for an audience of one who does not yet exist, namely, my future doddering self, forgetful and on the brink of senility, who will come across this notebook and find in it a precious Rosetta Stone, unlocking memories of the past, perhaps even reigniting his/my capacity for memory itself. So, I will continue to enter those situating facts just to be on the safe side, and it cannot hurt to reiterate them.

For instance, this morning I received a phone call from Gabe. Now, who is Gabe? you ask ("you" being either the general reader or my future doddering self). Gabe is one of my oldest friends: we were in graduate school together, though I dropped out before finishing my dissertation and he went on to pursue an academic career and achieve the summit of that profession, namely, tenure. Gabe asked me if I wanted to teach a course next fall at the Free School, where he is chair of the philosophy department. He was in a jam because one of his regular instructors had at the last minute taken a post in Cincinnati. Still, I was flattered. Of course I would be only an adjunct, the pay would be minimal, but it would give me a chance to develop an introductory course on Stoicism. I realize the Free School is a trendy educational supermarket for New Age types who flit from one spiritual anodyne and/or discipline to another, yet precisely for that reason, the prospect of exposing those seekers to this sober philosophy of classical antiquity amuses me. Before I had even gotten off the phone, I was beginning to organize a syllabus in my mind. The question I pondered was: Should I arrange the readings chronologically or thematically? If chronologically, then the students would march from Early Stoicism, starting with Zeno and Chrysippus, through the innovations of Panaetius and Posidonius, and then the Roman period, from which the fullest texts are available, which might make for a somewhat superficial, historically top-heavy survey. If I was to group the readings around topics such as Virtue, Nature, Happiness, the Problem of Evil, Illness, Friendship, Exile, Death, and the Consolations of Philosophy, which does appeal to me, I would have to photocopy an enormous amount of pages, in effect creating my own textbook, which seems too much work. In the end I decided that I would concentrate on the major figures of the Roman Imperial period, Seneca, Marcus Aurelius, Epictetus, of course, maybe even Plutarch (though he's hardly a Stoic in the strict sense, he would make a good contrast). That way the students would have to buy only five or six books, mostly paperbacks. I am told undergraduates today don't like to read that much.

I myself went to a good Jesuit high school, where Latin was emphasized, and without meaning to boast, I have to say I showed a marked aptitude for that language. One of the Brothers introduced me to Epictetus, as a Stoic in the early Christian era who had affinities with the Church Fathers. I liked the fact that Epictetus had been a freed slave, and I found myself immediately attracted to his realistic sayings (which did not strike me as particularly Christian). Unable as I was to hold on to my childhood faith, by the age of twelve I had stopped believing in the Trinity, though I told no one at the time, not wishing to hurt my mother's feelings. Not that she was such a believer herself, but she continued going to church, more to socialize than to commune with God. As for my father, I have the impression he was always an agnostic, though he kept his doubts largely to himself, supporting my mother in her insistence that I get a good Catholic education at an all-boys school, just as he supported all her decisions regarding my upbringing, whether he secretly agreed with them or not. Epictetus says somewhere in the *Enchiridion*: "Ask not that events should happen as you will, but let your will be that events should happen as they do, and you shall have peace." To accept what is dealt you, to love your fate (*amor fati*) instead of railing against it, became my ideal and remains so. In that sense, I think it was fortunate that I was sent to a good Jesuit high school. From that point on, I took to Stoicism in private as my spiritual discipline, my "substitute religion," you might say.

Around twenty years ago, when I turned thirty, I even published a little book, *A Slave's Wisdom: The Sayings of Epictetus*. It was meant to be one of those "impulse buys" kept near the cash register, along with cat cartoons, Bloomsbury Circle calendars, or *Sonnets from the Portuguese*, and actually it sold fairly well—

or would have, if I had had the patience to devise a more reliable distribution method. Each time a bookstore sold out and reordered, I resented having to package a new set with bubble wrap, take it to the post office, then follow up, getting them to send me a check for the previous order. I liked producing the book, arranging the texts, choosing the typefaces, selecting the end papers, approving a cover design and a colophon, but I did not like selling it.

The one good thing that came out of that adventure was that it led to the establishment of the Epictetus Society, a group of like-minded amateur enthusiasts who met in my Greenwich Village duplex on Charles Street for years, twelve years, to be precise, to study classic Stoic texts. Eventually the group broke up, not from dissension but from the usual attrition, some members moved away, others became distracted with family cares, and besides, it had run its course, it had done what it meant to do. I still harbor fantasies of starting a scholarly journal, to be called something like *The Stoical Review* or *Epictetus Quarterly*, I haven't made up my mind what to name it. It will probably never happen. If it did, I would have to get Rita's approval first. For that matter, I will have to discuss Gabe's proposal about the course with her, either tomorrow or soon after that.

AUGUST 3

I have still not broached the subject of my possibly teaching with Rita. For some reason, asking her frightens me. I don't mean I'm afraid of Rita, or her response, I'm sure she'll say it's fine. So then why am I averse to bringing it up with her? Perhaps I am worried that it will disturb the equilibrium between us. There is the thought in the back of my mind that Rita may distrust the proposition because it came from Gabe. I sense a chill, a distance, an excessive politeness, between my old friend and my wife, which Rita, intuitive as she is, must have picked up by now. In fact, she already told me, "Your friend Gabriel doesn't like me."

"Not at all," I reassured her. "He's just awkward around women, especially beautiful women." That part is true. Gabe has been married twice, and the second time ended traumatically, he came home from classes one day, without suspecting anything wrong with his marriage, to find a note on the dining-room table from his very pretty wife saying she was leaving him, she had fallen in love and, worse, with another woman. "Why 'worse'?" my mother asked me at the time, when I told her. She had known Gabe for years by then, certainly well enough to comment on his situation. I remember my mother saying she could never understand why a man will take it doubly hard if he is left for a woman, since in her opinion another male would be direct competition, but he needn't feel so bad if his wife discovered she was a lesbian. I was amused by my mother's comment, because she could be so proper, even prudish, but she also had a worldly side, which surfaced at odd moments like this and took me by surprise. I tried to put into words why I sympathized with Gabe's feeling that that sort of betrayal might feel worse than the other. To be left for a woman brought into the open the contempt that a man suspects every woman harbors secretly for men in general, for the whole phallic mystique, and leaves him feeling unmanned. My mother snorted at this response, which displayed, she thought, my own childishly macho viewpoint, when in fact I was only trying to share an objective insight into male vulnerability. I saw that there was no point pursuing that line of reasoning, so I turned to another that interested me more, on the radical doubt of appearances. If you thought you knew someone you loved, knew what their affections and desires were, and discovered that you had had them all wrong, it might throw into confusion your entire relationship with the material world. This is what Proust was getting at with Albertine, or Shakespeare, when Troilus sees his lover cuckolding him and says, "This is, and is not, Cressida." Meaning, she could not be *his* Cressida, as he knew his Cressida to be very different, so she must be another woman with the identical face and body, what we would now call a clone.

In any case, Gabe rarely goes out on dates now, and has become circumspect around women, especially women he finds very attractive. He told me, after meeting Rita the first time, "She is one hot number." I suspect this is what underlies his reserve in her presence. There is also a certain jealousy that an old friend might experience when he sees his pal suddenly fall in love and be carried away. I don't mean to suggest a homoerotic tie between Gabe and me by the word "jealousy" (though there would be nothing wrong with that), I am simply describing an understandable hurt when the old friendship claims are forced to yield to those of conjugal domesticity. It often happened to me in the past, seeing my friends get married, that I too would suffer a pang of loss.

But if I am to be completely honest in this diary, I have to record another possibility, namely, that Gabe disapproves of Rita because he thinks she's not intellectual enough for me. As though two hearts couldn't beat in unison if their masters had not read the same books! Such snobbish, prejudiced, elitist notions make my blood boil.

Still, I have to admit that a seed of that very same prejudice lodges in me, and so it is not just Gabe we are speaking of here. There is something that vexes me about Rita, which I am almost too embarrassed to set down in writing. And here we come at last to the heart of my hesitation about telling her I have been asked to teach a course on Stoicism. Rita has still never read my *Slave's Wisdom: The Sayings of Epictetus.* I must admit it hurts my feelings. She packed it obligingly on our honeymoon, started to read it on the plane, and fell asleep! She looked so adorable napping that I instantly forgave her. I was so smitten with her on that trip that she could do no wrong. Later, after we got home, I would leave the little book on the coffee table, hoping she would return to it. To her credit, she did pick it up a few times—I know, because, when I examined it surreptitiously, I noticed different pages would have their corners folded down. But the progress was slow, she never seemed to get past page 25, and one day I was disheartened to see that she actually seemed to be going backward! After that I returned the book to the bookcase. Since my books are alphabetized by author, she would have no trouble finding it again, were she ever inspired to do so.

I realize full well the irony of my being unable to accept Rita's lack of interest in my book, which runs counter to all Epictetus' teachings. "Why then are you vexed?" to quote Epictetus. He would have us master that which is in our power, such as moral choice and self-governance, not externals. We must learn to be philosophical when external reality (i.e., another person) does not comply with our wishes. I knew when I married Rita that she was not an intellectual, much less a classics scholar, but she had more than enough practical intelligence to make up for it, and I loved her all the more insofar as she was not like one of those disputatious, emotionally thwarted academic women who would show up at our Epictetus Society meetings and rattle the group's well-being with long, corrosive arguments. Rita has life-wisdom aplenty. She has no need to read Epictetus, she has him in her bones, for God's sake!

I must simply get over all this petty, egotistical foolishness.


AUGUST 10

I finally told Rita about Gabe asking that I teach a course for him, and as expected, she had no problem with it. So now I am starting to prepare the syllabus.

In going over texts for my syllabus, I find myself thinking about my uncle Antonio, whom I associate with my interest in this field, as a kind of symbol or living embodiment of Stoicism. He was my father's older brother and, like him, an anti-Fascist, a refugee from Franco's Spain, but he had none of my father's nose for business. He ran a shoe repair shop well into his eighties. Even after he had reached retirement age, he would still come in each morning at 7:30, except for Sundays, and work at the machines, or, after he became too arthritic to handle them, check that his assistant was doing a good job. As a kid I loved to hang out in my uncle's shoe repair shop during vacations or after school, bringing my homework. It was a very traditional shop, with a counter for the customers to deposit their shoes, and a few red, cushion-cracked chairs where they could sit and wait for him to put on a heel or shine up a pair, if they were in a hurry, meanwhile glancing at a copy of a tabloid newspaper, either the *Daily News* or the *Post*, and it had the pleasantly acrid smell of glue, leather, and dust, and of course my uncle in the back, hammering away. He was a squat, thick-necked man, with massive shoulders slightly hunch-backed from constant stooping, and with a fringed head of hair around a bald spot, like a monk's tonsure. Nothing fazed him. His attitude seemed to be: Life is a piece of shoe leather; if it pinches, you widen it by adding a strip, if it's too roomy, you put in a wedge or a pad until it feels snug, if your belt doesn't fit, you punch in an extra hole, if the heel is too high, you cut it down.

A customer would come in with an old pair of winter boots, say. She would ask, phrasing the question with deep, frowning concern, as to the Delphic oracle, "Should I bother to get new soles and heels put on them, or just throw them away?" My uncle would inspect them and say, "Don't throw them away. Leave. I put new heels on. The soles still good for a few months, see?" he'd demonstrate, bending them back as if the customer actually knew what a viable sole looked like. The point I am making is that he always tried to save his customers money, and never charged them for a repair job that wasn't strictly necessary. In fact, he undercharged them. Toward the end of his life I used to scold him for hewing to decades-old prices which were out of touch with the rising cost of living. He would shrug and give me an impish grin. He seemed to have a Platonic idea of how much a thing should cost, and he would not charge beyond that amount, regardless of inflation. Epictetus says, "Do you accordingly accept the material and work it up," and that could have been my uncle's motto. Accept the material that life brings you and work with it. How often have I envied Uncle Antonio his inner certainty, his self-sufficiency! I even, ludicrous as this may sound, fantasized taking over his shoe repair shop after he died. I imagined burying myself happily there, relinquishing all other ambitions, working steadily with my shoulders bent over the last, and if I had had the least manual dexterity, I might have. But, given my clumsiness, I knew I would be forever banging my thumb with the hammer, or piercing a finger with the sewing machine needle, it would be one disaster after another.

Uncle Antonio would have really appreciated Rita. She too is clever with her hands. I sometimes imagine them meeting, my wife with her teasing, sweetly melodic voice and he, gruff, taciturn. Come to think of it, they would have made a good couple, putting aside their fifty-year age differential, because Rita is very down-to-earth, as was my uncle. How trying she must find me, with my head in the clouds! She never criticizes me for it, though I sense her being careful around me, a bit, at times. We had an electrician over the other day to fix the wall switches, a Filipino guy named Mike De Jesus, and I couldn't help seeing how effortlessly she got on with him, how casually they communicated about the work to be done. I know she would never betray me, I only mean to say that she is such a womanly woman, and this electrician Mike has such a bull's physique bursting out of his sleeveless "wife-beater" undershirt that, from a purely Darwinian perspective, she seemed better matched with him than with me. Or so it crossed my mind at the time.

AUGUST 20

One attribute of Rita's that delights me is her playfulness. She will make up funny voices, get the shoes by our bedside talking to each other, suddenly invest inanimate objects with personalities and concoct instant playlets between them. In bed, too, after our lovemaking, she will purr away in cat language, meowing all her words, and I cannot stop laughing. I've taken to calling her "Kitty" from these mincing little dialogues. Rita will jest even during the early stages of foreplay, but not me. When my passion is aroused I become solemn as a donkey, I stroke her and grunt, no talking allowed. But once we are finished, and resting, I encourage her to do her cat voices.

Happy as I am these days with Rita by my side, it makes me happier still to recall our first times together. My mind reverts often to our courtship period. Sometimes I ask her, "What were you thinking that time my mother did such-and-such?" or "When you first came here, what did you make of me?" I am always trying to get her to put into words her old first impressions, but Rita is evasive about her past judgments, partly, I think, because she so wholeheartedly lives in the present. It even seems painful for her to analyze old feelings, or I gather as much from the shadow crossing her face whenever I ask her to do so, and since I hate to cause her any discomfort, I end up sparing her further embarrassing questions. If Rita is not introspective, I am too much so, and would much prefer being more like her. I analyze merely to fill a vacuum, it is an old mechanical habit, like whittling, I don't like doing it but I can't stop myself.

Having said all that, I would still like to know in much more detail the particulars of Rita's past. Her generalized responses to inquiries are frustrating. I have only the vaguest notion, even now, of her background, her parents, her childhood, her education, her work history. I know she was obviously not well-off, she keeps saying she left the Philippines because "there was no money," but I don't know whether that was always the case or whether a sudden decline in finances compelled her to leave. It sounds as if her family was lower-middle-class, comfortably so at times, from certain references she has dropped about vacations in childhood, in any case scraping by, then torpedoed by inflation and the national recession. She says she took a course in accounting at night school but was forced to drop her studies, I'm not sure why—to help out her parents, I assume. As for her previous romantic history, she giggles and will tell me nothing.


## AUGUST 27

Is this to be a book? Everyone these days writes books. I have no desire to add to the world's rubbish with my incontinent scribbles. Part of the reason I hit on the scheme of compiling Epictetus' sayings in the first place was that it would not require me to strike a presumptuously authorial pose. I would be the compiler, the drudge, leaving it to others to interpret and write scholarly nonsense. Even a critical bibliography of Epictetus scholarship, which I considered for a long while, struck me as offering too great a temptation to prattle. Only in this diary do I allow myself to babble on the page, and that is probably because I am giving up hope it will ever be published. So I may as well have my say, as no one else will ever be forced to read it.

This morning I went outside to run an errand, and I bumped into Lucia, a neighbor who lives across the street. Just to be polite I crossed the street and said hello, against my real wishes, since I was in a hurry to get to the store and Lucia can talk your ear off. She is a widow in her early fifties, a few years older than I am, a short stocky Italian woman who wears what looks to me like the same faded housedress for weeks on end, although to be honest, they could be a set of similar housedresses, whose differences in pattern and color

I am too inattentive to notice. On balmy days she sits outside in a lawn chair in front of her stoop and watches the comings and goings of the block, always with the same Sicilian scowl on her face. It's a look of peasant mistrust that says: The whole world is out to cheat me, to put one over on me, but I'm onto them.

"A beautiful day, isn't it?" I said cheerfully, to circumvent her usual sourness.

"These pigeons are making me sick," she said. She pointed up to the second-floor window ledge of her house, and then to her stoop, which was unquestionably defaced by white pigeon poop. "What can you do? Some idiot on this block started feeding them"— she looked around conspiratorially—"that moron *Gladys*, and then they end up coming here and shitting all over me."

I looked up at the three pigeons squatting plumply on her ledge. "You've got a problem. Maybe you should call an exterminator."

"I called Pest Control. And they said they couldn't put poison out there unless it was in an enclosed box. That's the new City Council rule. Can you imagine such bullshit? The poor pigeons, God forbid you should lay a hand on them! Then they told me I have to put metal spikes up there to keep them away. And not only there, but on every window ledge! On all the floors, because if you do it just on the top floor, they move to the lower ones. And the exterminator has to lower a scaffold from the roof, it's a two-man job, and the whole thing comes to fifteen hundred dollars. Can you believe that, fifteen hundred dollars?! And on top of that, Gino down the block tells me it won't even work, because the pigeons are too smart, they figure out a way to roost on the spikes."

"So what are you going to do?" I ask, just to be polite.

"I don't know. I'm screwed no matter what I do," she says in her martyred tone. Then she starts telling me about one of her tenants who doesn't put the garbage out properly, he puts the soda cans in with the paper, even though she's explained to him a dozen times already about the recycling, and she once got a fine from the sanitation department for that, and she doesn't want to have to pay a fine again, so she has to get up early and rebag the garbage, and it makes her furious. Lucia's always got a reason to be furious. She is never without a long list of grievances about her tenants, the neighbors, the city, which is going to the dogs, her health problems . . . Maybe I mentioned this peculiarity of mine, maybe not: I dislike listening to complaints. To me, it makes no sense whining about one's lot, it accomplishes nothing, it's undignified, and moreover, it shows a lack of perspective on the greater stock of suffering in the world, like in Africa, the Sudan, and the Middle East. But that is my rational response, and I'm prepared to admit there may also be an irrational component in my antipathy to complaints. As soon as people start complaining, I can barely listen, my mind wanders, I get a queasy stomach, I break into a sweat, I want to run. What does this mean exactly, that I am intrinsically unsympathetic to the plight of others? No, not to their plight, to their whining about it! But, one may counter, since a good percentage of all conversation is taken up by complaints—with some individuals, like Lucia, maybe the figure reaches as high as 80 percent—aren't I being inhuman by disdaining such a large part of human discourse? I'm afraid so, I am. Whence stems this intolerance of mine? I wonder. No idea. My mind draws a blank. I know that I associate complaining (a horrifying admission, but I'm trying to be honest here) with the female sex. My father, my uncle Antonio, they never complained. Maybe this association started with my mother, whose lamentations I perceived as a form of seduction, a way of breaking me down, forcing me to surrender to her will. My hostility to complaint may thus reflect an inability to embrace my weaker, "feminine" side, as they say, or an Oedipal panic, label it however you want, the fact remains, I do not like expressions of self-pity. Pity may be a noble sentiment, but self-pity is a despicable one.

Rita is not a complainer. She has no self-pity. What I love about her is that, given the opportunity to be contented, she takes it! Rarer than one might suspect is this ability to convert potential contentment into its real form. Rita has an acceptance of things, or else an extraordinary self-restraint, I'm not sure which; in any case, I look upon her as an exception to the surfeit of resentment, discontent, and complaint I encounter everywhere else. And I love her, I can't tell you how much, because of this remarkable pleasantness, which is the moral equivalent of her physical beauty. In the past, I seem to have always gotten involved with women who complained a lot and were depressed, so much so that I began to speculate that maybe all women are depressed. Shameful to admit, even to myself in a private diary, that I had such a misogynistic thought, but you have to understand that it came from my actual dating experiences. Then I met Rita and saw how wrong I had been to generalize in that way, for here was a woman who embraced life cheerfully, and was anything but depressed, and it made me love her all the more for saving me from continuing to entertain such a misogynistic hypothesis.

I realize that Rita probably doesn't love me as much as I love her, but it doesn't matter, just so long as she doesn't complain, criticize, or sulk all the time. The fact that I love her more than she does me is justified, because I'm not as lovable as she is.

To get back to Lucia, it's not even that she is self-pitying, but that on top of it she's resentful. She hates to see other people happy. And if I am being scrupulously honest, I have to admit a twinge of guilt every time I'm around that woman, as though I've let her down. This may sound crazy on my part, but I get the feeling Lucia was—setting her cap for me. That widow with the housedresses used to greet me with a flirtatious sparkle in her eyes, and once I got hitched to Rita, Lucia's tone turned bitter. Out of jealousy, racism, who knows what, she disapproves of Rita. One time when I was talking to her and Rita came walking toward us, with her island smile and swaying hips, Lucia caught my fond expression and rolled her eyes in unmistakable disgust. That look of primal mistrust came over her porcine face.

## LABOR DAY

The summer is slipping away, the last hot days before it turns to autumn, which always makes me feel a bit hollow. Everyone is out in the street today, chatting up a storm. I know I'm supposed to feel, "What a great block this is, where neighbor looks out for neighbor, and burglars know to stay away, and everyone is friendly," but somehow I can't help thinking it's all a performance. I get a lonely ache inside me when I see my neighbors in their holiday strut.

Despite my having grown up on this block, I have always felt estranged from my neighbors. Part of it had to do with the old Italian/Spanish tension, but it's also undoubtedly my fault, because I'm unable to "hang out," as they say. Since I don't like gossip or complaint, I have very little small talk, let's amend that: no small talk. It is torture for me to stand around on a summer day "shooting the breeze," I keep thinking I'd rather go inside and read a book, or prepare my syllabus. Ever since I was a child, the kids on the block called me "Professor" because I wore glasses, and so it has remained, with my neighbors thinking I'm an intellectual snob who looks down on them, and I thinking they're contemptuous of me as an unmanly nerd. But I had hoped that, with Rita, all that would change. I guess I put too much stock in Rita's ability to win them over. Oh, everybody likes her, how could they not, except for a few women, led by Lucia, who cluck over nothing. And some of the men think they're being funny by drooling over her. I understand, they're just envious of me. Like Gino, the block's aging Romeo, who works as a bank security guard, today he had the nerve to say, seeing Rita walk away in a tight dress, "I wouldn't mind a piece of that."

In the old days you would fight a duel if someone spoke of your wife so insolently. I wanted to smack his face, but I was afraid he would get the better of me, as he used to box in the

Police Athletic League. I did force myself to say, "Gino, show some respect."

"What? It's a compliment!"

Not wanting to prolong this offensive conversation, I quickly went inside. So in the end I confirmed their prejudice of me by not acting like a real man (whatever *that* means). Then again, should I have slapped my friend Gabe when he called Rita "a hot number"? What a strange figure of speech! What could be its derivation? And what does it mean, exactly, a hot number? I picture number 5 jumping up inside a kettle on the fire, like in the old Walt Disney "Silly Symphony" cartoons.

SEPTEMBER 5

Lately I've been irritable. I think because my birthday was approaching (it was yesterday). The onset of another birthday always sets off an expectation that I'm going to be disappointed, that others are not going to come through, which I suppose goes back to childhood. When I was nine, I had been hankering for a chemistry set for my birthday, and I told my mother, who said she would get me something different, because a birthday present had to be a "surprise." I was so glum about not getting my wish that, when I opened my present and discovered it was in fact the chemistry set, I burst into tears. Angry at my poor mother for making me suffer disappointment unnecessarily, and even more, for lying to me, I wouldn't forgive her, even though she got me exactly what I wanted. Anticipatory chagrin still clouds my psyche around birthday time.

Yesterday I asked Rita, "Do you want to go out dancing somewhere tomorrow night, to a nightclub or a movie?"

"No, I'm not in the mood. I'd rather stay home," she said.

I dropped the subject. I knew she knew it was my birthday, but she might not think the birthday of a middle-aged man deserving of much consideration—why should she, after all, forty-nine is not an important birthday, who could blame her for not making a bigger fuss of it? The more I tried to appease myself with such thoughts, the more upset I became. As much as I was annoyed at her for ignoring my birthday, I was also annoyed at myself for being so childish. Yesterday morning, when I woke up, I cut myself shaving. It was as though I were deliberately punishing myself for harboring unreasonable expectations of the day. Then I banged my finger by accident in the sock drawer. This drawer is precariously balanced, having lost one of its knobs, and has become difficult to close. "Damned drawer," I cursed. "I hate that drawer!" My fury at this inanimate object was accompanied by the infantile thought that I should not have to open such a difficult drawer on my birthday, a loving wife would have gotten my socks out for me. Rita looked over my bruised finger, held it under cold water, put a Band-Aid on it, but otherwise seemed distressingly unperturbed by my boo-boo. (I am making fun of myself now, though at the time I really meant it.)

I took myself off to the Brooklyn Public Library to work on my Stoicism course, which meets for the first time next week. I also wanted to get away from Rita, whose failure to wish me a proper happy birthday had upset me beyond reasonable measure.

I noted inwardly the paradox of my being unable to apply stoical principles to such a trivial upset; but for once, this mental chastening did not soothe my nerves—if anything, the opposite. What was at the bottom of my dissatisfaction, truly? I asked myself. The answer that flashed through my mind surprised me: It was the sudden suspicion, which had been festering, unbeknownst to my conscious mind, inside me for some time, that Rita did not love me. She tolerated me, she did not actually love me.

When I got home, Rita greeted me at the door with a mischievous expression. I walked briskly past her, and a dozen people jumped up from behind chairs and yelled "Surprise!" For a moment I just stood there, wanting to burst into rage, the way I had when I was nine years old, for having been toyed with and lied to. Then a silly grin spread over my face. So Rita loved me, after all! Rita was an angel, I was the ingrate! How I would have loved to take her into the bedroom and cover her with kisses! But the guests had to be attended to, so I put on a mask of extroverted sociability, which was difficult to sustain. To be honest, I did not have such a great time at my surprise party. (In the Philippines they call it an *asalto*, which sounds almost like "assault.") Part of it was that I don't like surprises. Also, Rita had invited everyone on the block, Gino, Lucia, even that old cretin Nino, who lives at the other end of the street, the whole gang, in short, and I can never feel at ease around my neighbors. A pity she didn't know my friends well enough to invite them. It was my fault, because I had not yet introduced her to the old Stoical Society crowd, and I had lost touch with many of them over the years. I was glad to see Gabe there in the background, looking constrained, but at least she had made the effort to contact him, despite any previous bad feeling between them. Maybe now Gabe will appreciate what an extraordinary wife I have. She had made a wonderful spread, with roast pig and rice on banana fronds, and a bowl of *camote* tops, traditional Filipino hors d'oeuvres, and a fruit salad of mangoes, avocado, pineapple, and some delicious cakes with vanilla icing.

SEPTEMBER 6

This old idiocy of mine, this sudden conviction that I am unloved, all my life I have been bedeviled by these suspicions, to an astonishing extent, for a man of my intelligence, I have allowed myself to be entangled in that stupid, lachrymose question "Does she truly love me?" as if it were a philosophical conundrum of the deepest importance. I don't doubt I tormented some women who did love me, and even turned them away in the end, by questioning too often the substantiality of their affections. You don't have to be a genius to figure out that this uncertainty arises from my own insecurity and self-dislike, which will not permit me to believe anyone could possibly love me.

But this explanation, accurate as far as it goes, does not go far enough. For now I see I was asking the wrong question. I have been obsessing over these rejections to divert attention from the real question: Could I myself love? This shift from passively receiving love to actively giving it was what I wanted most, and secretly doubted most I could ever muster. Did I even love my mother? I am not sure. I needed her, yet often I experienced her as a burden. Let us say for the sake of argument I did love her. Did I love any woman besides my mother? When I consider my bachelor years, I can summon memories of the pain various women put me through, some pleasures as well, but rarely can I recollect a deep feeling of love on my part for any of them. The joy that Rita brings into my life comes from the fact that *I* can finally love, freely and unreservedly. That is such a relief. And now I know she feels the same way about me.

SEPTEMBER 9

"What would you think if I cut off my hair?" Rita said to me this morning.

"Oh, don't do that," I said, "I love your hair long."

"But I had it such a long time this way. It's such a nuisance to take care of."

"It would make me sad if you cut it off."

"Not all of it, just some. So it comes to just about here." She gestured to a point below her ears.

"Rita, please don't," I said, groaning. "For my sake."

"Would you stop loving me if I cut it short?" she asked, with a dimpled, coquettish grin.

"You know that that's impossible."

"Then I won't."

"Good."

SEPTEMBER 28

I was in a funk yesterday, brought on by a silly quarrel with Rita. I still don't entirely understand what set it off, but I hope that by writing down exactly what happened I can make more sense of it.

The fight started yesterday afternoon. I was going through my mail in the dining room, and Rita joined me and began talking about St. Bernadette's, the Catholic church a few blocks away. She has started attending Mass each Sunday, as was her habit in the Philippines. I have nothing against her doing so, and in fact it makes me happy to see her get ready Sunday mornings in her best outfits, with hat and gloves. I don't accompany her myself, it would be hypocritical of me to go to church, but I respect anyone else's religious beliefs. She was telling me how funny she finds the local priest, Father Francis, and the little Italian ladies who surround him. She was performing for me, I sensed, her imitations of the group were lively, and I always enjoy listening to her, she has that melodic voice and accent, yet I felt a pull to open the rest of the mail—whenever I get mail, I can't help it, I just have to go through it right away without interruption, so I continued listening to her while opening a letter from the Free School, which happened to be the official notification of my appointment as an adjunct instructor. I looked up to see Rita frowning. She was wearing a lime-green silk blouse with a lacy border, you know that fashion women have nowadays of wearing articles of clothing that suggest negligees, slips, pajamas? This blouse was of that genre, and over it she wore a corduroy jacket of slightly darker green shade, all very fetching. And blue jeans, lightly faded, chemical-washed. Oh, I almost forgot to mention the red elastic holding her hair in place, a "squinchy" I think it's called, I kept thinking about that bold cherry accent when the rest of her outfit was green and blue, I liked that jot of red, it made me wonder how she had arrived at that choice. The blue jeans I was less crazy about, they were not my favorite pair, and anyway, to confess something really bizarre about myself, I've never liked blue jeans. I realize the whole world wears them (except myself), and Rita, with her shape, looks particularly good in jeans, but still, they suggest to me a conformist uniform, like millions of Chinese wearing blue military jackets, and I mistrust the faux-proletarian air of those who fancy them, the way investment bankers come home and change into a pair of jeans and think they're being devil-may-care. I prefer Rita in a skirt or tailored slacks. Anyway, I saw she was frowning, so I stopped opening the mail and gave her my full attention, listening to her mimic the way Father Francis performed the Mass. She was saying she would prefer to go to a Filipino church in New Jersey, which her friends attended, and where Sunday afternoon Mass is held in Tagalog. I nodded, commenting that that made perfect sense. In truth, I was not entirely happy with the prospect of losing her each Sunday for a big chunk of the day. Still, I could use the time to prepare my week's classes. I began thinking about Zeno and the readings I was assigning next week, and before I knew it, I had jumped up to write a note to myself about a lecture.

"Sorry I'm boring you," Rita said tartly.

"No, I was—I had a thought about my course and I wanted to write it down before I forget. I'm sorry. Can you continue with what you were saying?"

"Why should I? You're not even listening. You're so bored with me you think of something else, and then you expect me to keep chattering away."

"I wasn't bored. I was listening attentively, in fact." This wasn't strictly true, but it wasn't a total lie either. My mind had wandered off in the middle of listening attentively. But I could tell she was miffed. She was not going to be placated any time soon.

Over the next few hours, we kept our distance, and I had time to brood over the spat from many angles. Did it bother her that I did not have the same interest in going to Mass as she did? Possibly. Did she think I looked down on her for her interest in church affairs? Possibly, but I doubted it. Had she sensed my reservation about her blue jeans? Unlikely. Did she jealously resent my interest in the mail, like a rival for her attentions, luring me away? It seemed pertinent that she had gotten angry just as I was opening the letter from the college, and I remembered my hesitation about telling her when Gabe first made the offer. Of course she could not be expected to know whom the letter was from, but I couldn't help wondering if her annoyance was a sign that she didn't like my teaching this course for Gabe, or else that the whole subject of Stoicism was starting to bore her to death. Maybe she thought *I* was bored because *she* was bored, as often happens with married couples, one mate projects his or her feelings onto the other.

## SEPTEMBER 29

Around eight this evening, Rita turned on an easy-listening jazz station and sat with her legs curled up in an armchair. Ordinarily, I have no use for easy-listening jazz, with its interminably warbling saxophone, but Rita seems to like it. Besides, as I have come to realize, when she listens to this kind of music, it puts her in a sexy mood. So I curbed the urge to flee its banal sonorities for my study, where I could have put on a Bach cello sonata (I am going through a Pablo Casals/Bach phase lately), and sat in the living room alongside her, pretending to dig the relaxed, mellow sounds of Kenny G. . . . My reward is that we made love after dinner. Everything is fine between us. Rita is sleeping in the next room, and I've come in here to enter this denouement to the episode in my diary. Surely, even in the happiest of marriages there are arguments, and it may be useful to others, should I ever whip this diary into publishable shape, to record how they can arise, seemingly from nowhere, and how picayune they can appear in retrospect, if you don't hold grudges, or take them too personally, or accord them undue importance.

## OCTOBER 2

The weather has been absolutely beautiful these last few days, magnificent days on the cusp of early fall, and in consequence the garden has been calling to me, demanding more and more of my attention. I've begun to plant a few bulbs for next spring. As I plant

I work out the lectures in my head. It's getting to be below 55 degrees at night, I have to start bringing in the geraniums and a few of the more cold-sensitive perennials, and putting down mulch for winter covering. I am thinking of moving the locust tree from the front of the house to the back. It would be a lot of work, but maybe worth it, since the front doesn't get enough direct sun. Then I could plant a cherry tree in the front; I've always liked them. I don't think I'm going to do an herb garden again; too much trouble. Instead of an herb garden, I could put in a little fountain, or a pond with one or two carp. But how would the carp survive when the pond froze over in winter? They must adapt somehow. I'm pretty sure they stay outdoors all winter in Japan.

OCTOBER 14

I have been busy teaching my course, occupied with this and that, not much time to write in this diary the last few weeks. The course seemed to have gotten off to a good start. There was a decent enrollment, I handed out the syllabus the first week and gave an overall talk on the ground we would cover. The students, a variegated bunch ranging from college dropout kids returning to the friendlier confines of the Free School, to army veterans and people with serious day jobs finishing up their degrees, to retirees taking classes as a hobby, seemed reasonably enthusiastic. I began by assigning them some Zeno, with a few Seneca *Letters*, just to give them a preliminary taste. The second and third weeks did not go as well. Discussion lagged, they were passive and moping, I got the impression Seneca sailed over their heads, if in fact they had even done the reading. Maybe they were turned off by his sententiousness. I tried to point out his craggy charm with some examples, but they seemed unconvinced. Next week, Marcus Aurelius. I have found that even people who don't like any other Stoics are captivated by the *Meditations*. He's very approachable, or so I hope. Marcus Aurelius to the rescue!

After the third class, feeling a bit crestfallen, I popped into Gabe's office with the hope he would cheer me up. I was thinking that he has so much experience teaching this student body, he might have a few pointers for me. We went out for a drink at a local tavern. He listened to my report with a mild expression, he has a sort of Kewpie-doll mouth with arched wings at the tip, and I found myself staring at his lips, thinking how odd, how sweet this feature looked on a man. He does have a docile, almost effeminate quality, and I wondered if this trait had factored into Gabe's wife's leaving him.

"Give it time," he said. "Sometimes it takes awhile for them to come around to the non-contemporary writers." Then he hesitated, as if he wanted to say more but was afraid to offend me.

We have been friends long enough, so I prodded him: "What? What were you going to say?"

"The problem could be with the subject matter."

"I don't understand."

"With Stoicism, I mean. It doesn't work. It's humanly speaking impossible."

I had expected Gabe to criticize my pedagogic approach, which I was certainly willing to grant might be faulty, as I had done so little teaching recently, not since I was a graduate student. I was disconcerted when he took this other, more sweeping tack.

"You were the one who suggested I teach a course on Stoicism," I said.

"I know, but I did that because you were familiar with the material."

"So how do you mean, it doesn't work?"

"Stoicism doesn't work because people can't discipline their souls to the extent it requires," Gabe said. "I don't think it's natural, I don't think it's human, its demands are excessive."

"It's certainly *human*. Billions of sufferers around the world practice unconscious stoicism every moment."

"Unconscious, yes. But as soon as you try to elevate it to a conscious, intentional, ethical system, it doesn't pan out. You can't say, 'I'm really upset, my—wife just left me, but on the other hand, I have these little homilies with which to comfort my soul.' It sure didn't work for me."

"They're not homilies. They're truths."

"You know what I mean. 'Death has no sting, because we were nothing before we were born and after we die we'll return to nothingness'—that sort of thing. Or 'It is silly to want your wife and children to live forever, for that means you want what is not in your control to be in your control.' That sort of bullshit no longer rings true."

"They're no more homilies or bullshit than any other spiritual wisdom. They're no more homilies or bullshit than the teachings of Buddha." I was feeling under attack, and so I said this last remark spitefully, because I knew that Gabe, who had done his dissertation on Wittgenstein, had moved further and further away from logical positivism and had been increasingly drawn to Buddhism in recent years. "If you want to talk about inhuman, you can talk about Buddhist religion. The idea that we should rid ourselves of all human attachment, that's not inhuman?"

"Buddhism is a psychology, not a religion," he corrected, mildly.

"Tell that to the Buddhist monks who immolated themselves, obviously not just for a psychology!" I said, raising my voice. Actually, I have great respect for Buddhism, and had no idea why I was carrying on so. Obviously I felt threatened. I looked around at the waiter and the near tables to see if anyone else had heard me. "The point I'm making is that Buddhism offers an ideal, just as Stoicism does. Yes, it's hard to attain that ideal, but that doesn't make it irrelevant."

"Okay," he said, as much to calm me down as to agree.

"And in any case, Stoicism and Buddhism overlap a great deal," I offered. "Wouldn't you say so?"

"I agree."

"Scratch a Buddhist, you'll find a Stoic."

"Up to a point, yes," he said. "But Stoicism won't do in the end. It's a philosophy of moderation and restraint. It lacks a visionary dimension. It doesn't speak to the great energy and beauty flowing through Creation, which we all hunger to be part of." Gabe smiled with his Kewpie-doll lips, as though to signal his awareness of how high-flown his words must sound. Yet he was not in any way taking them back, underneath he was dead serious. My poor friend had been converted to some cosmic-energy vision without my noticing it. He had always had a soft, mushy side, even as a graduate student, sneaking off to rock concerts in search of Dionysian release.

On the way home I felt sorry for him, knowing that life, with all its "great energy and beauty flowing through Creation," will probably never come through, for a man like Gabriel, enough to suit his rhapsodic hungers. Any more than it will for me, I suppose. We're both too dry, too prudent or stuck in "moderation," as he puts it. The closest I will ever get to such energy and beauty is Rita. She is my own private version of the divine spirit in the universe, if anything is.

OCTOBER 17

Rita has started going to that Philippine church in Bergenfield, New Jersey, on Sundays. She comes home excited, having reconnected with a group of acquaintances from her old neighborhood, the San Juan district in Manila. They're also doing square dancing Sunday nights, with a professional caller from Tennessee. She invited me to come along, but frankly I have no desire to hang out in the suburbs of New Jersey, I can't bear those shopping malls, and the dances take place in the back room of a cavernous brew 'n' burger joint. What sort of fun would that be for me, sitting for hours in the midst of a group speaking nothing but Ta-galog, not understanding a word, and then lining up to do square dancing, which I hated as a boy? Oh well, it could be worse, at least she's enjoying herself. Yet why a lovely woman from the Philippines should be so taken with this ersatz-Appalachian folk dance is beyond me. She says they also practice the Texas Two-Step—as if that were further inducement for me to join! Now Rita wants to buy a pair of boots and a whole cowgirl outfit. I fear she is as susceptible to American kitsch as, say, someone from Borneo who has not yet built up immunities to the common cold.

NOVEMBER 2

I am thinking of expanding my *Slave's Wisdom* and republishing it, or even doing a new translation of the entire Epictetus. I dis-like the dry Victorianism of the Loeb series, and some of the more recent translations strike me as too colloquial. An author in a for-eign language is so dependent on his translator's skill, and Epictetus has never been served in that respect as well as Marcus Aurelius or Seneca, which may explain why he lags behind them in renown. Some classicists would argue that the best translators have been drawn to Marcus Aurelius and Seneca right off the bat because they were better stylists than Epictetus (or his disciple Arrian, who set down his sayings—Epictetus himself wrote nothing), but I don't agree. I would like to champion Epictetus, to try my hand at it, at least. I know my Greek has never been as good as my Latin, but I still think it worth attempting. These scholarly ambitions must be stirring again in me because I'm being left alone a lot. Recently Rita has been disappearing during the day. She gets dressed in the morning to go out, and comes home around six or seven. I have no idea what she does with herself all that time. She says she takes the bus into New Jersey to visit friends. If only she knew how to drive, she could use our car, but there are still some complications over her green card and getting a driver's license, even if she wanted to take lessons, which she doesn't seem to, she says she prefers the bus. I worry about her coming home late on the Port Authority buses. And what is the attraction of those godforsaken malls, these fake consumer villages like Woodbury Common, which she and her friends prefer? It seems ridiculous for her to be living in one of the greatest cities in the world and, with all her free time, not exploring the treasures of Manhattan, like the Metropolitan Museum or the Frick. Or the fancy stores along Fifth Avenue, if shopping is her thing. What is the point of relocating to the New York area and then ignoring the vibrant center of town? I have noticed many Filipinos seem leery of Manhattan, more comfortable in suburban malls, I don't know whether it's because the suburbs reflect better what they're familiar with in the Philippines, low-scale buildings perhaps, or because malls are more focused on shopping than city streets. When we first started seeing each other, and I took Rita into town for a show or a first-class restaurant, I noticed she would get a startled look on her face, almost like fear, in the midst of crowds. I thought she was over that. Perhaps she only got better at hiding it for my sake. She must feel utterly dislocated, my poor darling, it must be an enormous strain to feel her way into this strange metropolis, and New York is difficult even for Americans who visit it from elsewhere. I must give her time, time to adjust. I only wish she would come home already, so that I could show her how understanding I can be.

NOVEMBER II

I am beginning to develop a superstitious relationship to this diary. I am afraid to write anything unpleasant in it, lest that condition become fixed and locked into place. For instance, I recorded in the last entry that Rita was spending more time away from home, thinking that by writing this down, through a kind of reverse magic I could get her to stay put, but instead, she keeps going off and disappearing during the day, and I wonder if I have jinxed myself by writing down what I did. This makes no sense, I realize. I am not ordinarily superstitious, it is only when I start to worry and have no easy explanations that my mind gets stuck on an obsessive track, despite all my efforts to stay calm. I see now I had wildly underestimated the adjustments involved in immigration. Now that she has a moment to catch her breath, she is trying to reconcile those two worlds, the Philippines and the States, Tagalog and English. It's all perfectly understandable.

NOVEMBER 15

Where does Rita go during the day? She says she is shopping with friends, but she doesn't bring home any packages. I asked her about it once, and she said she was "just looking," that it was fun for her to look, she doesn't need to buy. Perhaps this whole world of American consumer goods is still so new and entrancing to her that she can entertain herself merely by wandering around suburban shopping malls all day. She must be up to something. Since I avoid shopping malls like the plague, I can't imagine anyone else finding them amusing, though objectively I know that millions do. But there is something fishy going on. I can't help connecting Rita's mental preoccupation recently with these day excursions. Does she have a lover? (I'm almost afraid to write these words down!)

I have fantasized spying on her, trailing after her from a suitable distance, but how could I manage it? I would have to sneak into the subway behind her and follow her to the Port Authority bus terminal. That part is doable, but then I would have to get into the same bus as Rita, and she would certainly spot me. Unless I kept my car parked near the terminal and drove behind the bus. I could find out from the bus schedule beforehand what bus she normally takes, and be waiting with my car outside the terminal, a discreet distance away. The only problem with that is, if she was lying and not going to Woodbury Common or New Jersey but somewhere else, I would be stuck all day at the off-ramp while she was gallivanting around. No, I would have to follow her from the moment she left the house and into the subway, for several days in a row, to learn her exact schedule, her routine, and only then could I synchronize the part of trailing her by having a car parked near the terminal. It's too much trouble, too risky, surely she would spot me in one of the stores, and then she would get justifiably angry at me: "You don't trust me, you're insane with jealousy, you want to keep me chained like a prisoner," etc., etc. And she would be right. Besides, it's not in my nature to shadow her, I'm too timid. In the past, my timidity was a problem with women, who respond best to the conqueror type, no matter what they tell you. But it wasn't just a problem with women, since my male acquaintances also would upbraid me for not standing up for my opinions, even when I found theirs dubious. Why I pretend to go along with everyone's opinions I don't understand, unless it is a childish desire to please and smooth things over (in response perhaps to my late mother's temper). The upshot is, I am too timid, I question my own point of view too much. "You're probably right," or some such cowardly expression, springs from my lips ten times a day. At the moment I always think the other person probably *is* right and seeing more sharply than I can. Now how did I get into this digression? Oh yes, I see above: too timid to tail Rita.

NOVEMBER 17

Does she have a lover? Where does she go every day? If she is shopping, why doesn't she bring home any boxes? I am tempted to go through her credit card receipts, but I don't know where she keeps them. In any case, it would be an unforgivable invasion of her privacy. Rita has her own bank account with a reserve of funds, $25,000, which I gave her so that she wouldn't feel so dependent on me. I instructed my bank to keep it around that figure, and to draw on funds from my account when it dipped below. As a result, now I have no way of knowing what she is up to.

All these thoughts buzz around my head endlessly, boring me to death, and the worst of this situation is that I am becoming mentally impoverished, like all obsessive jealous types. There is no intellectual nourishment in jealousy. I never even thought myself capable of jealousy. Yes, I had a few incidents back when I was younger—one time when I spied on a girlfriend as she chatted with a musician in the cab of his truck, another time when I pretended to stalk an ex-lover for half a day, though she never even found out. Minor stuff; for the most part, I felt as if I was trying on the mask of jealousy, never really believing in it. Perhaps the reason I didn't is that I was never truly in love before. I look at Rita, her tender, sympathetic brown eyes, and think, It couldn't be! Then the buzzing in my brain resumes.

NOVEMBER 22

I was in midtown, running an errand, when I passed a storefront with a big sign that said The Spy Shop. In the window were cameras, listening devices. On an impulse, I stepped inside. It seemed a prosperous establishment: I had no idea espionage technology had grown into such a large retail business. I was trembling while I stood waiting for a salesman to speak to. When one was free, he asked me what sort of intelligence-gathering I was interested in doing. I said I wasn't sure, maybe he could tell me what was available in the way of eavesdropping devices. Ashamed, I kept the information about my problem vague, and consequently must have sounded like an idiot. In the end, I realized that what I wanted was not equipment but the services of a private detective. As it happened, the salesman knew of one and gave me his card. "Dominick Caputo" said the name on the card; his offices were a few blocks south of Herald Square in Koreatown. I thought it would be insane of me to look up this detective, just as I had thought it had been crazy to enter the Spy Shop in the first place. But the urge to know got the better of me. I told myself that it was curiosity, not jealousy: I had always wondered what a real private detective's office looked like. No doubt it would be nothing like the ones in the movies, with blinking neon windows across the street and a whiskey bottle in the desk.

That much I had right. Dominick Caputo's office was on the second floor of a brownstone, above a photography studio, you reached it by climbing an old-fashioned set of metal stairs. Caputo himself was a large, gregarious, oxlike man with a comb-over, who stared into a computer, he was sitting in an ergonomic swivel chair that seemed too small for him, and this must have contributed to my overall impression of him as outsized. Plus he extended his hand like a swollen beef salami. I immediately wanted to run, to flee down the metal steps, but it felt as if I had no choice except to go through with the interview. I know it is lame to say that I felt I was in the grip of a dream, I hate it when others use that excuse, but there was something somnambulistic about the experience. Perhaps it was the preternatural calm I felt after those first moments of panic. I had to admit, this fellow Caputo had a reassuring effect, he listened to my concern about Rita's comings and goings with a steady, professional attentiveness, making sympathetic grunts and taking notes. I almost had the feeling that the problem was solved merely by telling it to a stranger. I would have been happy to shake his hand good-bye and never see him again, but he was not about to let that happen.

"It's probably nothing, I'm just being alarmist," I said.

"Oh yeah? I know these people, I was stationed in the Philippines, they'd sell out their grandmother for ten cents. You can boff the whole family for a hundred bucks, including the dog."

I was shocked, even nauseated by the vulgar prejudice of this man's speech, so much so I was tempted to slap his face. I should have. But truly garish vulgarity and ignorance have a way of silencing me. They put me at a loss for words. In my mind's eye I could see myself reaching over and smacking him, defending the honor of my wife and her native land, but I was deterred by several thoughts: (1) He was much larger than I; (2) I did want to find out what Rita was up to, and by hiring a private detective who had no inclination to give her the benefit of the doubt, I stood a better chance of learning the truth; (3) How could I blame him for casting aspersions on my wife's virtue, when that was what had brought me to him in the first place? If anything, I should have slapped my own face. I was appalled by this man's crudity, but a part of me, to be perfectly frank, admired his maleness, his confident virility, which made me want to follow his lead. I have always been excessively in awe of men who conveyed the impression that they knew what it meant to live in the real world. They have a kind of hypnotic effect on me. So I found myself making out a check to Caputo, a "retainer," as they say in movies. In a week's time, he said, he would report back to me what he had found by trailing my wife. If nothing else, I have taken an action, however misguided, and that part feels good.

## NOVEMBER 25

I am taking elaborate measures to hide this diary, ever since the appointment with D.C. Now it is inside my Latin dictionary; I know Rita would never dream of looking there. A dozen times a day I have been on the point of telephoning D.C. and calling off the arrangement. I am so appalled at myself for hiring him. It's really unforgivable, one of the most reprehensible things I have ever done. What bothers me most is my own duplicity. I much prefer to be straightforward, I would have even thought it's not in my nature to hide a big secret from Rita and go on with our daily routines, hypocritically pretending nothing is wrong. I am discovering that duplicity has its appeals, its voluptuous allure, maybe not addictive, but tantalizing.

## DECEMBER I

Well, the nightmare is over. I feel so relieved. Yesterday I went into Caputo's office to listen to his report. He had photographs, detailed records, tapes, hour by hour. Just as Rita said, she had been taking the bus into New Jersey and shopping at the Woodbury Common mall with several Filipino women. They were all doing their Christmas shopping. Rather early, it seems to me: I usually think of the Christmas season as beginning after December 1, but these women take it so seriously it becomes almost a half-year process. Rita herself bought a number of gifts, nothing very expensive, a quilted bathrobe, children's pajamas, lots of makeup, an electric shaver, a basketball, a set of headphones, a robot toy, Barbie dolls, baby clothes, boys' shirts, things of that order. I assume they were for her relatives back home, her aunts and uncles, nieces and nephews. She dropped off the packages at a friend's house. On another day she went back to that friend's house and wrapped the packages and mailed them at the post office. They were all going overseas to the Philippines. A boring report, nothing remotely juicy. Rita has no lover. My need to misconstrue her as Jezebel, betraying me in the arms of another man, says much more about my own sick imagination and primitive mistrust of women than it says anything about her. At bottom, I just have trouble believing that a woman as beautiful and desirable as Rita could be content being mine alone. This is the last time, I solemnly promise, I will ever doubt her.

DECEMBER 10

My neighbors in Dyker Heights are going nuts with their Christmas decorations. Everyone is putting on their lawns those wire-sculpture reindeer, and the giant inflatable Santa Claus figures that wave in the wind, and the chunky Jack Frost snowmen, the candy canes, the toy soldiers that stand at attention like Beefeaters (though what they have to do with Christmas I have no idea), the religious crèches, the Madonnas and baby Jesuses (surprisingly rare compared to the secular holiday symbols), and of course colored lights, dangling from the roof of every house, that flash on and off at night. The local TV news crews have started to arrive, and the sightseers from other neighborhoods, who drive by with cretinous slowness, up one street then down another.

Rita has a yen to join in the decorating madness. She has been talking to the neighbors about where they buy their decorations, who are the best suppliers, electricians, and so on. She is thinking of hiring that fellow Mike De Jesus, that handsome Filipino electrician who worked on the house this summer. Not that I will ever doubt her again, it's him I don't trust alone in the house with her. I told her we already have a set of modest lights, kept in the basement, which I usually string by myself. But she wants our display to be commensurate with the neighborhood—a blazing commercial for the Christmas spirit. That idea holds no appeal for me, nor do I relish the prospect of shelling out thousands of dollars for such kitsch. Still, I find it difficult to resist Rita's adorable importuning. Besides, I owe her, for having secretly doubted her fidelity, so I expect I will compromise and indulge her holiday-decorating wishes, within reason.

You might say I am taking lessons from her in the art of being human. Part of the reason I married Rita was to draw me into the human community, so that I could behave more appropriately, more like a normal person. I have always felt abnormal compared to most people in my counterintuitive reaction to everyday cues. I thought I had grown at peace with this isolation, until I met Rita. I have appointed her, not entirely facetiously, my teacher in humanity. She has a kind, generous, and, for that matter, conventional reaction to everyday things, she will ooh and aah at a puppy in the pet store window, she will get misty-eyed on the subject of Christmas. I see the point of all that now. I could have avoided much misery in my life if I had just gone along with the expected response. It's true, Christmas never meant much to me, even as a boy, because my scholarly austere father, coming from Spain (the university town of Salamanca), frowned on the ostentatious consumerist displays of American society around Christmas time. My mother insisted on a tree, "for the boy," though it was more for herself, since I found tree trimming crushingly dull and I could never get it right, my mother had very precise ideas about how each ornament should be hung (the big red balls buried deep in the branches, for instance), and I was bound to break one of her favorite ornaments, which made her livid, so that in the end I merely gave up and watched her. I will never forget the tedium of sitting there hour after hour, keeping her company, while she surveyed the best angle from which to hang each spangle, star, tinsel strand, and angel. After my father died, we never got another Christmas tree, which was curious, since he was the one who had always denigrated the custom as heathen and you would think Mother would have indulged herself to the fullest in it after he was gone. Perhaps she did it only to annoy him. Anyway, Rita wants a tree. I will humor her to that extent, but not all the other nonsense, all that over-the-top decoration of the exterior façade of our house.

## DECEMBER 15

We have settled for an inflatable globe in the front yard, blown up by means of an electric pump. A recumbent Santa, who, I like to imagine, is sleeping off a hangover, goes from a completely prone, horizontal position to a standing posture in only ten to fifteen minutes, along with a tree and a snowman, which pop up alongside him, while snow falls relentlessly in the background, like an isinglass souvenir. We got the expandable Santa fairly cheap from Home Depot, though the extra lights, the flying angel with trumpet, and the tree itself, along with several boxes of ornaments, padded the bill. But Rita is pleased, so I am.

## DECEMBER 20

"Should I go on a diet?" I ask Rita, looking dubiously at my potbelly.

"No, I love that belly of yours. Don't you dare! If you go on a diet you'll look thin and drawn, and really, really old. I want you to have a big, big belly, even bigger than Santa Claus." She put her arms around my stomach, then lowered her ear down next to it, as though she were listening for sounds of a fetus. "You're my Gordo," she said. "I love you this way, my soft pillow."

## DECEMBER 28

On Christmas Day, Rita made me a feast of traditional holiday foods, including a whole fried carp, some Filipino tamales, a sort of quiche with chicken, pork, potatoes, carrots, and onions, and a variety of delicious rice cakes. I was stuffed! We exchanged and unwrapped our presents. And now I am looking forward to spending a quiet New Year's Eve at home with my wife, contemplating our good fortune. It has been an amazing year. It even makes me dizzy to think of these past twelve months as one chronological unit. First getting married, then adjusting to the ups and downs of intimacy, even passing through that little crisis of jealousy, the return to academic teaching, I will cherish the full gamut of memories, good and bad. I have so much for which to be grateful. After decades of steeling myself to accept disappointment with a stiff upper lip, I am improbably and at last being giddily rewarded with marital happiness.

PART TWO

JANUARY 15

A few days ago Rita told me that her cousin Hector had just arrived in the States. She seems less than delighted with the news—annoyed, in fact. He is hanging around their friends in New Jersey, hoping to start looking for work, and she wants to bring him over to our house so that I can meet him and see if maybe there is anything I can do to help him find a job. I had a hard time figuring out what she was getting at.

"Do you want me to hire him as a gardener or a handyman?" I asked her.

"No, he isn't good at those things."

"What does he know how to do? Does he have any skills?"

She gave me her dubious dimpled smile. "He's useless, like a big overgrown child. Sweet, but hopeless when it comes to practical things."

"I don't get what I'm supposed to do for him, then—"

"You're so clever, I'm sure you'll think of something. Just talk to him. Give him some advice."

I bowed to her excessive faith in me.

We arranged for him to come over the next afternoon.

Hector arrived wearing a basketball T-shirt with Michael Jordan embossed in orange letters, a pair of gym pants, gray Nike sneakers with yellow trim, and a Miami Heat athletic jacket, probably made of polyester, in any case much too thin for New York winters. He is a small, wimpy fellow, with a patchy attempt at a mustache, very unassuming, grins shyly when you look at him. To give him his due, he's fairly good-looking, in a boyish sort of way. It's hard to believe he's the same age as Rita, she seems so much more worldly and responsible. She addresses him in Tagalog in a tart, snappish voice, like an older sister. I have not seen this side of Rita before: the one that grows bossy and impatient with spineless men.

Hector speaks English passably well, though he doesn't stray far from present tense. Also, I keep forgetting a good many Filipinos grow up speaking English, so it is not that much of an accomplishment. He was eager to talk to me about Michael Jordan, Madonna, Shaquille O'Neal, and other American pop and sports icons. Not exactly my area of expertise, but I was willing to employ what scant knowledge I had about these universal figures of global entertainment. I have the impression that for Hector it is enough just to have made it to the homeland of superstars for riches to rain down on him.

He wanted to know what television shows I liked. I started to answer that I didn't watch much television, but Rita said something sharp in Tagalog, and he looked abashed. He also smiled at me in a conspiratorial manner, as though to say, "We've both felt her lash, haven't we?" Maybe it was his attempt at male bonding. Though he didn't have much to say after that reprimand, he was also in no hurry to leave. He seems to have a vast capacity to sit around like a sheepdog, waiting for the next meal to be served.

I tried to get him to explain in what way they are related. The lineage is complicated, partly because Rita's father started a number of families, in and out of wedlock. These extended Filipino families can be as complicated as a soap opera.

## JANUARY 18

I had an errand in the city today: I went in to see my stockbroker. Apparently the value of my portfolio has dropped considerably. Everyone has lost a great deal of money in the recent market downturn, my broker reassures me (as though that were a consolation). The smartest players have lost the most, he says. Since we lost only something like $50,000, I conclude I am not so bright, and take heart from the fact.

When I came home, I found Hector sitting on my couch, watching television. Rita was out buying groceries. The sight of that wispy-mustached boy-man in his gym outfit, lounging around in my living room, disturbed me. As though anticipating my displeasure (which I tried hard to conceal), he turned off the television immediately once I came in.

"Mr. Gordon," he said, screwing up his courage, "may I ask you something?"

My blood chilled at the prospect. I had to catch myself and ask why this innocuous, deferential idler provoked such irritation in me. Jung's shadow theory posits that we hate in others what we cannot bear in ourselves. If so, I must be seeing my own passivity, underdevelopment, or placating tendencies writ large in Hector. Perhaps I was also unfairly shifting onto him my earlier chagrin about the stock losses.

"Please be my guest," I said.

It turned out he wanted to ask my advice about getting a job. It was the same vague request Rita had made earlier, and I wondered if she had put him up to this talk. In the midst of my fruitless efforts to elicit information about what sort of work he felt inclined or qualified to do, during which he manifested no ambition, no vocational drive, no governing passions or interests, an inspiration struck me. I would ask Niko, the owner of the Greek diner two blocks away, to try him out as a waiter or short-order cook.

"Do you think you might like to work in a diner?" I asked. Hector seemed less than thrilled with the idea, but was willing to give it a shot. He could hardly say otherwise, having no other prospects.

When Rita came home from the supermarket, I told her of our plan. She was very pleased, insisting he go for an interview as soon as possible. He became animated as well by the prospect of becoming a diner employee, almost as if she were breathing new life into him by her own vitality and energy.


JANUARY 20

Yesterday I walked Hector over to Niko's Diner and introduced him to the boss around 10:30, after the breakfast meal. To my surprise, Niko said he would try him out right away. He installed Hector behind the counter and began giving him prep jobs to do: slicing tomatoes, replacing mayonnaise tubs. I left, not wanting Hector to be made self-conscious by my witnessing of his receiving instruction.

At three o'clock Hector returned to our house in a huff, his whole manner truculent and resentful. Niko had told him to go home. He had paid him fifty dollars and sent him on his way.

"What happened?" I asked.

"That man is very unfair and even yelling at me. He tells me I am 'slow'! First he tells me do one thing, then he tells me do something else. I can't work like that, pressure, pressure all the time."

"But maybe after a few days you would get into a proper rhythm . . ."

"Nobody can talk to me like that. I quit!" he said proudly. From his tone, it sounded as though this was not the first time he had uttered those words.


JANUARY 21

Late in the afternoon I popped into Niko's. After beating around the bush, I asked, "Can you tell me what happened between you and Hector?"

"That boy don't want to work. He does something, then he sits. Takes a break every ten minutes. You give him an order, he don't want to do it. I got no time for bums like that."

## JANUARY 23

Today I went for a long walk, from my neighborhood all the way to Prospect Park and the Brooklyn Public Library. I am about to start teaching a second semester for Gabe, and I wanted to clear my mind. I have found that the regular rhythm of strolling vigorously generates a free-flowing mental relaxation, while the presence of refreshing exterior stimuli promotes mental clarity. It was snowing, not hard, just a bit, and the temperature bracingly chilly but not too cold, which formed an invigorating backdrop to the introductory lecture I was composing in my mind.

When I came home, I found Hector smoking on the porch in front of my house. Immediately my sense of well-being dissolved, my good mood vanished. I nodded to him and walked inside. I did not feel like engaging the guy in conversation, after his failure at the diner. To be honest, I was a little annoyed at the idea of his becoming a regular visitor.

Rita came into the house a few minutes later. She looked miffed. "What's the matter," she said, "you don't say hello to Hector? He thinks you gave him the brush-off."

"I just wasn't in a talkative mood."

"It's nothing to do with talkative. Don't pretend your mind is engaged in 'higher things.' It's just being rude. You don't say hello, you walk by him like a robot. He's a member of my family, so it's being rude to me."

"Sorry. You're right."

"Don't shut me up by saying 'Sorry'!"

"I mean it sincerely. You're right, I'm sorry, I won't do it again."

"You act arrogant, superior, and everyone has to get out of your way." Rita did an imitation of me stumbling past people, shoving them out of my path. "You are very—abrupt, the way you move. It's insulting."

I was at a loss how to reply. I had no idea she held such negative thoughts about me. Rita has never complained before about the way I move. Nor do I think it true that my physical movements are especially abrupt. But perhaps when I offend her, anything I do becomes magnified and appears brusque or robotic. Thinking that she was being unreasonable, yet preferring not to argue with her, I took a deep breath and said to myself, Don't engage her when she's angry. Let her calm down. I held my tongue, hoping that my restraint would restore tranquility, and glanced over at the list of articles on the cover of the latest *New York Review of Books*, wishing I could open it and immerse myself in its contents.

"Oh, and now you give me the silent treatment!" she said.

"Rita, I'm not giving you any treatment. I'm just baffled as to why you're suddenly so angry at me."

"I said why, because you are being rude. You're so—you're so unpredictable in your—your body language, the way you move, it's so abrupt that it frightens me."

"*I* frighten you?" I asked incredulously.

"Yes!" She held her ground. "I never know what you're going to do next."

"I'm sorry you feel that way. I had no intention of scaring you."

I put my arms around Rita to mollify her, though with intentional (perhaps sarcastic) slowness, so that she would not flinch, would not misinterpret my affection as an oncoming blow. She held herself stiffly in my embrace. She was not ready to make up yet. In fact, I had the hunch she had been looking for an excuse to be angry—that this whole fear of my "abruptness" had been manufactured by her. The more I pondered her charge about my alleged herky-jerky movements, the more disturbing it became. After all, there are few aspects of one's character more essential, more unchangeable than the way one traverses space. To disapprove of a person's gait is to reject his very being. Underneath her criticism, I wondered, was she intimating that she didn't like the way I made love? Was I too precipitous in entering her? Not enough foreplay? I did not think this to be the case. Often when we were making love, it was Rita who would urge that I enter her, not dally any longer at the preliminaries, and after she had reached her climax, she would urge me to come as well. Our sexual relations had always taken place in a charmed circle, with contentment on both sides. I concluded that this was not about sexual dissatisfaction. Perhaps she had been with men who hit her. I've known women who were physically abused and forever after kept a wary eye on men's fists. The impulse to probe Rita on her past relations with men is strong, but I sense it would be a mistake to question her just now, when we are not getting along. I will wait her out. She will tell me in her own good time what all this is about.

FEBRUARY 4

Maybe Rita is right that I am arrogant. I always used to think the opposite, that I was too self-effacing. But I am getting ahead of myself. Here is what happened. After I had finished teaching Wednesday (the new class is going much better, by the way), I ran into an old schoolmate of mine from Sacred Heart, a fellow named Louis Osario. It turned out he was taking a course at the Free School, something to do with economics, he works at a bank nearby and wants to get into high finance. What are the chances that someone with whom you went to high school would be walking down a college hallway at the exact same moment you were going in the other direction thirty years later? He was the first to recognize me, I admit I did not recognize him right away, I was in my usual daydreamy state. After we had both expressed astonishment, we went out for a drink. It turned into one of those friendly but awkward encounters between two old acquaintances, now strangers, casting about for points in common. I don't know if I was the one at fault, or he, but the conversation started to dry up, so I brought myself to ask him what I was secretly dying to know: "How did I strike you in those days, Louis?"

"You? You were a brain. Half the words you used went over my head. You loved to stand in front of the class and expound. The nuns loved you."

"What else? You can be honest," I said.

He responded suddenly, with a vengeful gleam: "I also thought you were snooty, you know, an arrogant prick." It was something to see this middle-aged bank officer transformed into a spiteful, resentful schoolboy for one honest instant. Curiously, I had remembered those days quite differently, for me they were filled with social humiliation, living in mortal fear that tough boys, the Louis Osarios of this world, would beat me up in the schoolyard, hence my efforts to ingratiate myself with them, or better yet, to try to be as invisible as possible in their presence. Now it turned out that *I* was perceived as the threat, by their mistaking my diffident reserve for arrogance.

When I got home I was still digesting this odd encounter, so I told Rita about it. She agreed with him. "You *are* arrogant. You think you're better than everyone."

"How do I act arrogantly?" I demanded.

"Like the other day, when those ladies from the Jehovah's Witnesses ring the bell, you closed the door in their faces."

"It's true I was a bit hasty in closing the door, but that's because I was on the phone to my broker and I didn't want to be impolite to him by putting him on hold, so I ended up being impolite to the Jehovah's Witnesses. Give me another example, besides the Jehovah's Witnesses."

"You're always 'hasty' with people you think are not on your level. Not everyone can be a Classics professor," she said, drawing the words out sarcastically.

"Okay, give me another example of this arrogance of mine."

"Everyone on this block is afraid of you!" Rita asserted.

I found that impossible to believe. No one feared me on this block. She kept repeating her assertion, and I kept demanding proof, so she brought up an incident that must have happened several months ago. Nino, the old man who lives at the end of the block, a little guy with a curved spine, a bit touched in the head, who always speaks in a gargled voice, rang my doorbell to inform me that my car needed to be moved, because of alternate-side-of-the-street parking, and I told him I was aware of it, I had intended to get to it in a moment—and closed the door in his face. (Why? I have no idea. I've never liked Nino: there's your answer.) He then went and complained to my wife that I had been "grouchy," and the result is that now she is convinced I am this monster terrifying the neighbors with my superiority complex. It's almost laughable, this inclination on Rita's part to protect the world against my alleged domination. What's not laughable is that I feel my marriage suddenly turning into a wreck, I don't know how it started or why, because truthfully I don't think I've changed that much, I'm behaving exactly the same way as when Rita doted on me and I could do no wrong.

FEBRUARY 7

I am still in the doghouse. Every little thing I do, Rita finds fault with, from my tying up newspapers for recycling to my buying fruit at the supermarket. The skin of one apple I chose was bruised, and now she does not trust me to pick out the fruit properly. I can't believe this is the same woman I asked to marry me, I have the feeling some evil spirit has invaded her body, some harsh, complaining witch. The one and only consolation is that Hector, that jerk, has stopped hanging around here for the moment, he must have gotten the message by himself, or else he was told to stay away. But Rita seems in a permanent snit, and I don't know how to gentle her out of it.

The other problem is—I'm embarrassed to write it down, for fear of jinxing myself—that we've not been making love this past month, not at all. I realize women, or men, for that matter, can get distracted by stress, fall into periods of low libido, menstruation cycles may play a part, but I keep looking for a signal. Usually, if we're going to do it, she will give me a certain coquettish smile, or signal by the way she gets ready for bed. It's hard to put into words exactly. I then usually say to her, "Do you want to fool around?" which is our code for sex, and she will nod, but generally she signals me first. Last night I didn't get any sign from her and I began touching her, and she grunted and wrinkled up her nose. "What?" I asked.

"Not tonight. I'm too tired," she said.

I kissed her on the cheek, so she wouldn't think I was pressuring her further, and she patted my leg reassuringly. There was something patronizing in that gesture, as though I were a little child making a fuss because he couldn't get an ice cream cone, there was an impersonal tenderness in that pat, a forbearance even, that I found insulting. I wanted to let it go, which would have been the wisest thing to do, yet I couldn't, the mental equivalent of a gas bubble of petulant heartburn was working its way through me and needed to be burped up.

"You don't seem at all interested in making love lately," I said.

"I'm sorry, I just don't."

"Don't what?"

"Don't care that much about it."

"Why is that?"

"I don't know." She yawned. "I guess it just doesn't mean as much to me as it does to you."

"You mean tonight, or in general?"

She shrugged. "Maybe in general." That was all she would say. Not the answer I had expected, or wanted, quite the contrary. I turned away and tried to go to sleep, but my mind wouldn't shut off. It made no sense to me, her statement. From the start, our first night of ecstatic jointure, Rita has always seemed an unusually passionate woman, free in her amorous expressiveness. Now I am starting to wonder if that was all a lie, just a way of ensnaring me. I doubt anyone could be that good an actress. More likely, she is undergoing a temporary cooling-off period, which deceptively feels to her, for the moment, like something that has always been true. I know married couples cannot expect to sustain their newlywed passion, and am fine with that. But we have been married less than a year, it seems too early for the fires to bank.

FEBRUARY 12

I had lunch yesterday with Edith, an old flame of mine. About once a year we get together. Though our affair ended badly (mostly my doing), it was all so far in the past, more than twenty years ago, that there are no hard feelings anymore. There are virtually no feelings at all, but we try to keep up the pretense that we have evolved into friends. Ex-lovers seem able only to consider each other enemies or, if positively inclined, friends: rarely is the option of benevolent indifference allowed expression. I do like Edith, up to a point, and am curious about the way her life has progressed. When I first went out with her, she was a struggling freelance journalist, pretty, moody, dark, morose, intense, with jet-black hair and a challenging manner ("What do you mean?" she would demand). Now she is cheerfully middle-aged, her figure more matronly, thirty pounds heavier, with salt-and-pepper hair cropped short, and dressing the part of a professional academic. She teaches sociology at N.Y.U.; the restaurant where we met was a few blocks from her office, near Washington Square in the Village. It seems I am always the one to come into Manhattan and meet on her territory, rather than the other way around. My accommodating her in this way is part of an unspoken debt I can never seem to pay off—I assume for our breakup ages ago, but maybe just for being a man, or for being comfortably well-off. Though she herself is not starving, she has a way of persistently trying to put me on the defensive about social class: I think it is fair to say she regards me as a spoiled, self-deluded rich kid, not without a certain rumpled appeal.

Edith has one trait which makes me afraid of her or, I should say, of trusting her. Sometimes when we haven't seen each other for a while I forget about this peculiar mannerism, but then in the course of conversation it springs up and I remember what it is that makes me nervous in her presence. I am speaking about her tendency to pounce rabidly on any sign of difficulty I am having with another person. As soon as she smells blood (particularly between me and a woman), she will want to hear everything about the problem, which in itself would not be bad—I understand the impulse to revel in the melodrama of human conflict, and the desire to ferret out all the gory details—but what annoys me is that she invariably takes the other person's side in any disagreement I am having, and uses my own testimony against me.

Understand, I do not expect my friends to act as a collective supportive mirror. They do well to point out my errors. But they should at least begin with a few drops of sympathy toward *me,* whereas Edith always sees it first from the perspective of the other person, whom I have ostensibly wounded. I have the sense she is referring every situation back to our ancient breakup, whether or not it applies. Knowing all this, I still allowed myself to be drawn into a description of my recent troubles with Rita. They are so much on my mind that I couldn't avoid speaking of them, and besides, I needed to hear a woman's point of view. Edith has never met Rita (I did not invite any exes to our wedding), but she has formed her own impression of my wife, and I daresay, from the ironic, skeptical faces she pulls, it seems a dubious one. First of all, she knows Rita is beautiful, and as someone who was once quite a looker herself and then, at a certain age, could no longer count on men's gazes following her, Edith tends to be antagonistic, though I'm not sure she's even aware of it, toward young, desirable women. That antagonism does not stop her none-theless from seeing Rita as the victim of my insensitivity. She re-proaches me for, in effect, buying a mail-order bride, someone I imported to be my sex slave! In spite of the fact that Rita was already working in this country when we met, and that our car-nal relations were consensual, Edith continues to see my mar-riage as an instance of the imperialist West exploiting the Third World's natural resources.

"How long did you know your wife before you proposed to her?" she asked me over our coffee and dessert, in a pouncing sort of way.

"Three months," I admitted.

"You see? You know nothing about her! You treat her like a domestic servant who sleeps in your bed."

I explained that we had a cleaning woman in once a week, and I had offered to have her come every day, but Rita insisted she wanted to take care of the house.

"You're not getting my point. How well do you understand this woman's *soul*? Do you even think she has a soul?"

"Of course she has a soul," I said, "or would, if any of us had. I'm not sure I have a soul."

Edith shot me an irritated look. "You don't realize your wife has a *mind*, a consciousness, as complex and teeming as yours," she said. "That she is *real*." Then she gave me a lecture about men objectifying women, and my own past sins in this regard—a sort of Introduction to Feminism 101. Edith said she would e-mail me her reading list of classic feminist texts. Her syllabus.

FEBRUARY 13

The day before Valentine's Day.

I keep turning over everything Edith said to me, and answering her in my head, or experimenting with taking her point of view. I don't doubt that Rita has a mind as complex as mine, but I don't have the same access to hers as I do to my own, and surely never will. Is Rita real to me? Of course she's real. But what if there are unsuspected depths to my solipsism that question her full, existential reality, and see her only as an instrument of my needs? Emerson wisely said, "We must treat all people as if they are real, because who knows? Perhaps they are."

Of the two charges, that I am a sexist and an imperialist, the first, I believe, has some merit, the second, none. I simply can't see myself as a colonialist with gunboats streaming into Third World harbors, exploiting the natives. Maybe I'm being too literal-minded here. Still, Rita came to New York of her own accord. She slept with me the first time of her own accord. To compare me to Cortés or Clive of India seems a stretch. The second accusation, that I am a male chauvinist, is a different matter. Probably all men are—heterosexual men, anyway, I cannot speak for gays. True, the lecture Edith gave me the other day contained nothing new, I'd heard it many times before, but this time, I don't know why, it touched a chord. Maybe I was finally ready to hear it. Suppose the recent problems I have been having with Rita do stem from my being supercilious and lording it over her, or from not taking her seriously enough (*A Doll's House* all over again), that explanation actually makes me optimistic. I can change my behavior, I can learn new tricks, old dog that I am, especially if it will help win back Rita's love.

FEBRUARY 27

These last two weeks, in addition to marking student papers, I've been reading several books on Edith's syllabus: Mary Wollstonecraft's *A Vindication of the Rights of Women*, Simone de Beauvoir's *The Second Sex*, and Elizabeth Cady Stanton's speeches collected in a volume called *The Solitude of Self.* They have left me excited and, I must confess, deeply queasy. I am spinning from the gauntlet they have thrown down. I always suspected I knew nothing about women, but that never shook my complacency before. Now I realize that I have acted unfairly and in fact abominably toward women all my life. I have condescended toward them, I have never regarded them as my intellectual equals, I have dismissed their anguish as mere operatic hysteria, and all this, out of the most banal of prejudices, that garden-variety sexism which props up Western (and often non-Western) patriarchal societies.

My poor mother, what I would give to speak to her, to beg her pardon. She must have been so lonely those last few years of her life, and even more so in the face of my lack of empathy and understanding. If I was a dutiful son in taking care of her, I did not go that extra mile and try to enter her mental space, imaginatively speaking. And Rita! How little I have understood *her* inner life, the fullness of her reality, as well as her need to be respected. No wonder she has started to despise me.

How is it I never read these books before? With feminism so much in the air when I was a graduate student (I would even call it the dominant ideology of my generation, Marxism's replacement), I must have mistakenly thought I knew all about it without having to read its essential texts. Mine was cocktail-party knowledge, the kind I would deplore if someone began talking about the Stoics with the same shallowness. As a follower of Stoicism, I must have believed I had an automatic pass to feminism. True, the Stoics argued that women were equally capable of virtue as men, and Musonius believed there was no contradiction between doing philosophy and engaging in child-rearing. Fine, but it hardly exonerates me. I can say it clearly now: I did not read the classics of feminism because they threatened me, they threatened my masculine privilege.

MARCH 2

Last night, after supper, while we were still at the dining table, I began speaking to Rita about the injustices women have faced throughout the world. I tried to recap some of the main ideas I had been reading in Wollstonecraft, de Beauvoir, and Elizabeth Cady Stanton, which had so stimulated me. By doing so, I had the vague hope of igniting a common spark between us, an ideological agreement, even (I shudder to admit) some gratitude on her part for my being sympathetic to her sex. But instead she seemed bored, picking at her food, politely listening.

"What do you think?" I asked, pausing as I felt my throat go dry. I had been talking on and on, without getting any response.

"I need to do the dishes." She was eyeing the dishwasher with interest.

"I'll do them. What are you thinking?"

"About what?"

"About what I've been saying tonight?" I asked.

"It's rubbish," Rita said. She began clearing away the dishes.

"In what way is it rubbish?"

"I don't feel oppressed. I don't think women always have it harder than men. Sometimes they are just lazy. They expect to be pampered, and they look to the man to do everything for them. Then, no matter what the man does, it's never enough. Especially American women, the less they work, the more they say they are 'oppressed.' I hear them complaining about their husbands in the grocery store. They meet for coffee at the corner diner. They spend all day having coffee. Yowling, like she-cats." And she imitated the sound of a feline whose tail has been stepped on.

I laughed. "Come here, Kitty." Then I pulled Rita onto my lap.

"I need to do the dishes first. . . . I don't want us to get cockroaches."

"But later . . ."

She seemed perfectly willing, as in the old days, and we went up to the bedroom. It was wonderful. Enfolding Rita, I felt I held a kingdom in my arms. It was the return of our happiness, mixed with that strange sadness that comes of getting what one most wants. Perhaps another example of the chemistry set.

MARCH 3

I am still trying to figure out Rita's negative response to feminism. Some of her resistance may have been in response to my presentation, she may have found it presumptuous for me as a man to be raising these issues, or else found my style too dry, too professorial, as she sometimes does. Edith would say Rita's rejection of feminist ideas shows merely that she is not yet liberated and has internalized the dominant patriarchal values of her oppressors. I wonder. Could it be that Rita has seen more of the world than Edith, or understood it more complexly? I can appreciate how, from her perspective as a Filipino woman who pulled herself up by her bootstraps, she might regard the complaints of middle-class American women as self-indulgent whining. I can't help but admire Rita's nobility in refusing to blame others for any problems in life. Of course I see how convenient it is for me to latch onto her unwillingness to think herself oppressed, in that it lets me off the male-chauvinist hook. To abandon so cavalierly my feminist convictions that women are unjustly treated would be intellectually dishonest on my part. Does that mean I have no intellectual integrity? Probably not, because the truth is, as long as Rita has sex with me I am happy, and I no longer feel quite the same urgency to interrogate my thinking for any masculinist errors.

MARCH 7

Another satisfying, soul-lifting night of love; I don't mean to boast. Afterward, Rita looked to me like the women in Gauguin paintings. She has their impassive gaze, their rounded comeliness, and their (how else to put it?) carnal self-possession. Such women ground the universe of plants and suns, their dignified sensuality amounts to an ontological certainty. Yet Gauguin entitles his masterpiece with a series of unanswered questions: "Whence do we come? What are we? Where are we going?" Why pose such questions against the foreground of their stately poise? Are we meant to think that these Tahitian women are secretly uncertain, or that shallow man, faced with the enigma of female depth, is inevitably thrown into a tizzy of self-doubt? Myself, I do think that Woman is the crown of creation. It sounds unfashionable or even sexist to say so, but there is no harm recording it here, in my private diary. Balanchine thought the same.

I have been puzzling a bit over Gauguin's work, how I used to dislike it when I was a college freshman, dismissing it as "ornamental," I suppose, because its unembarrassed voluptuousness was too intimidating to my Catholic-boy, still-virginal self. I preferred in adolescence the tormented anorexic erotica of Egon Schiele, which now holds no interest for me. Now I much prefer that marvelous Gauguin painting of the dark native woman lying on her stomach nude. How can you get any more sensual than that? All of Gauguin's muddy browns, those ripe, morbid purples and greens, applied flatly, gleam with the austere aureate lushness of a Russian icon. It's interesting that around the same time as Gauguin was painting in the South Seas, Robert Louis Stevenson went to Samoa to die. Well, perhaps he went to live, but a part of him knew he was dying, those last five years in Valima. So am I dying as well? Is there not some deadly nightshade, sickly bloom sprouting in this late marriage of mine? I'm talking rubbish here, my pen is getting carried away with its arabesques, don't listen. But seriously, why do I sometimes get the feeling everything will end badly between us? It's because Rita is hiding something from me. Are the stony, masked faces of Gauguin's women truly imperturbable, truly sage, or are they holding back some awful secret from their men? They know too much, and their shoulders stoop from the burden of understanding, while their men are so ignorant that they barely register on our retinas.

MARCH 10

Today we had our annual appointment with the examiner from the INS, the citizenship and immigration service. It was his job to determine, by our answers to his questions, whether our marriage is a true, valid one, which of course it is, and not merely a way to evade the United States immigration laws. He asked us whether we had met through an international marriage broker and, if not, how we came to know each other, what drew us together, what our living and sleeping arrangements were at present, what we did together in our spare time, whether we had any children or were planning to, whether we had arguments and if so what kind, whether there was any evidence of domestic violence, or whether either of us had in the past committed or been convicted of homicide, manslaughter, rape, sexual abuse, incest, torture, drug trafficking, peonage, holding hostage, involuntary servitude, slave trade, kidnapping, abduction, and so on and so forth. The man was reading from a prepared list, and we both responded to his questions good-naturedly, finding no reason to take personal offense. I was curious to see how Rita would answer the questions regarding our courtship—how she would tell it from her angle. I found her demeanor adorable, as she overcame her modesty and talked about her love for me. "He was so good and kind. How can you not love this man? And I feel for him, because his mother was dying." As she spoke, she crossed and recrossed her tan legs. I found myself captivated by the little mole by the side of her left eye, wanting to kiss it, lick it, bite it! From there, I fell into a fugue state and began imagining myself touching her body, different parts of it, her toes, her thighs, especially one little fold near the inside of her thigh. . . . Our answers must have been satisfactory, because the examiner concluded the session with a smile and told us we would be hearing from the government in a few months; sometimes it takes longer, if there is a backup of paperwork. Rita's permanent residence status is still conditional, of course, but after we have been married the full two years, she should get her citizenship card without any trouble, I would think.

MARCH 12

My diary notebook was running out of pages, so I bought a new notebook, black, leather-bound, pocket-sized. (As you can see, I am writing my first entry in it now.) According to the pretentious packaging which came with it, "Moleskine is the legendary notebook used by European artists and thinkers for the past two centuries, from Van Gogh to Picasso, from Ernest Hemingway to Bruce Chatwin." I don't expect it to make me as fine a writer as Chatwin or Hemingway, but I like the way I can slip it so easily into my jacket pocket, without even leaving a bulge. If Rita was to come into the room while I was jotting down something in this diary, I could palm it completely with one hand, without her seeing me, and drop it in my blazer pocket. The bigger question is why I bother continuing to keep this journal. I can no longer pretend that my marriage is perfect, exemplary, without problems. I still have the feeling Rita withholds a significant part of herself, however happy she makes me when we are together. I am probably just being paranoid, surrendering to those ridiculous old fears of being cheated, cuckolded, betrayed in love. I understand how childish all this jealous suspicion sounds, or *would* sound were I to show it to a disinterested reader, but I can't help charting the flow of conjugal feelings, it's become a habit, and now one difficult to break, it would seem. Like a hypochondriac taking his temperature. So then why do I keep up this diary—and for whom? Possibly I am still recording it for that senile, doddering fool into whom I am fast metamorphosing, my future self, who will doubtless find this all very fascinating. . . . I see myself in a nursing home, Rita coming to visit me, looking lovely in a white summer hat, bending over my wheelchair to kiss me on the forehead. . . . I slip this black Moleskine notebook, which I have been rereading, into my pocket, unbeknownst to her.

MARCH 15

Rita has been off and about lately. I can't help thinking about last November, when the same thing happened. In addition to her being physically away a lot, there is her mental absence when she is here, a sort of preoccupation pulling her toward some other, undecipherable realm. As the refrain in that song from *Gigi* goes: "She is *not* thinking of me." Last night she came home late. I asked her where she had been, and she said she was visiting her cousin Hector in New Jersey, helping him set up house. He has rented a room in the basement of some Filipinos' house, and sometimes he comes upstairs to the living room to join the family watching TV.

"How does he pay the rent?" I asked.

"He works a few days a week for the man who owns the house. The man runs a pizza parlor, and Hector delivers pizzas and sweeps up."

"A Filipino pizza parlor? Does he like doing that?"

"So far it's all right, he says, better than other jobs. His boss lets him borrow his car because you need a car for pizza delivery.

The only thing he doesn't like is delivering at night. He's afraid
he will get robbed in a bad neighborhood."

"Does he have a big territory to cover?"

"About a five-mile area."

"How did you help him set up house?"

"I cleaned the room, I hung curtains. That sort of thing," she
said. "I'm tired. I'm going to bed."

MARCH 17

I have been rereading Thucydides, for the fifth time. Whenever I
get truly upset, I reach for Thucydides, and his rugged, soldierly,
soberly realistic perspective, what one may call the long view, has
a calming effect on me. Gibbon has the same effect on me, except I am not always in the mood for untangling his lengthy sentences. Rita is gone tonight, and I am lying on the couch reading
Thucydides. When I was a bachelor, one of my favorite things to
do was to get home from a party around midnight, say, and stay up
reading until three in the morning, finishing a book I was engrossed
in, a biography or nineteenth-century novel, the last two hundred
pages, with no one to tell me to put out the light. Sometimes I would
fall asleep on the couch afterward, still in my party clothes, and who
was there to stop me? But what had been a mark of freedom in bachelor days becomes a forlorn necessity, merely a way to eat up time,
when waiting for your wife to come home, listening every moment
for her footsteps and her key in the lock.

MARCH 26

Tonight marked a climactic episode in my life, one to which my whole prior existence has been tending. What do I mean by saying everything has been leading up to this? I mean that I have lived my whole life under the shadow, the fear, the astrological sign, you might say, of betrayal. It had always seemed a phantom, and now that it is real, there is a certain satisfaction that comes of the nightmare made concrete. "You see, I was right to be afraid." In the end I brought it on myself, like one yelling in a ravine and causing an avalanche to fall on and bury him. But I am getting ahead of myself. Let me try to relate what happened in its proper order. There is bound to be some comfort in the pure pursuit of linear chronology. If I can't remember exactly what was said, I can still convey the way the conversation went. We were in the kitchen, Rita and I, having a piece of pie. It was blueberry pie, quite good, not too sweet, with little stems or seeds in it, which gave it a more authentic, less processed taste. I will never eat blueberry pie with such innocence again. It was 9:30 at night. I began by asking Rita if she had something to tell me. She said no. Then I said, "We need to talk about your past," or words to that effect.

"Why?" she asked.

"Because I have the feeling we can never achieve true intimacy until you tell me who you are." (This was where I made my first mistake.)

"You know very well who I am. What you see here is me," said Rita, gesturing toward her bodice.

"Can you deny that you are holding back something?" I said.

"You are the one who is hard to know," she said. "I am a plain ordinary girl. But no one knows what's going on in that big head of yours."

I was not buying the flattery. "Baloney," I said. I told her I had kept no major secrets from her, whereas I still had the impression that she was always holding back something important. "Can you deny it?" I said, starting to sound like an inspector. "Tell me what you're holding back. Let's get it all out in the open. Why the hesitation?"

"Maybe I don't tell you things because I'm afraid you'll get angry."

"I promise you I won't get angry."

"You can't promise that. No one can."

She was right—but I would not give her the benefit of agreeing aloud. "Don't be afraid," I said. "What are you going to tell me, that I was not your first lover? I realize there were probably many men before me."

"Not so many. Just a few," she said. "I think this conversation has gone too far."

"No, not this time, Rita. Okay, so you've had a few lovers. So how bad can it be? Just say it and get it over with. You've got to tell me."

"Give me a few minutes! Don't rush me."

Rita smoothed down her skirt, and studied her hands, her long tapering fingers. Then she went into the bathroom. I heard her pee. She ran the water in the basin and came back, droplets of water shining in her hair. I assume she had doused her face with cold water.

"I have something to tell you," she said, with determination. "I have four children, back in the Philippines. One is Entoy, he is nineteen; then there is Conrado, who's almost eighteen; next is Nonoy, he's fourteen; and the last is my little girl, Baby May. She's still practically an infant, two years old." I felt an electric shock shoot through me. At the same time, as with any secret, once it is out in the open, you have the sense you already knew it, from the negative space left by the silences that had preceded disclosure.

"Who is taking care of them?" I asked.

"My mother," she said. "But she is getting too old to raise them. Especially the little one. My mother has problems with her legs, and she can't keep up with Baby May. So" and she seemed to gulp, "I would like to bring my children here—just the two youngest, Nonoy and Baby May. Entoy is already on his own, he is going into the army, and Conrado is also going to be too old for the derivative visa. . . ."

"To live with us?"

"Yes, to live with us. If you are willing, you can apply for visas for them to come over, it's called an alien relative visa."

I said nothing. I could have sat silent for a long while, months, years, decades, eons of geological time. The only comfort I felt at that moment, and it was tenuous, derived from my inability or unwillingness to open my mouth.

"Please say yes. You are my last hope."

"Who is their father?"

Rita herself fell silent now for a long while. "Hector," she finally brought out.

"Wait a minute. So you married Hector and then got a divorce?"

"No, we never get divorced. Let me explain." So she explained. They were living in a small house in Manila, a shack really, made of bamboo and corrugated iron and plywood, all six of them sleeping together in one big room, pallet by pallet, and she had her mother living with her, too, and her uncle and his whole family were in another part of the room. And there was no money coming in. There was no money. She kept repeating that. She told me I probably couldn't imagine because I had never had to miss a meal in my life, but they were close to starving. Close to the edge. What about Hector? I asked. "Hector tries, but he is not a good provider. And there is no work in the Philippines, there was a very bad inflation. Hector lost his job at the Chinese market. He gets into an argument with his boss and—it's very stupid, we don't need to go into that. Something has to be done, someone has to do something, someone has to go out and make money to feed the kids, and my mother and my auntie and uncle. I took a course at night school in accounting, but . . . it wasn't enough to be proficient, and . . . no job opportunities, I didn't want to become a prostitute. That's what happens to a lot of women in Manila. A lot. But it also happens women go to another country to work. When she was the president, Cory Aquino says that the women migrant workers are the real heroes of the Filipino nation. I know I'm no hero, but I hear about the shortage of health workers in the States. We even thought of bribing the nursing school to get me a nurse's certificate, like a friend of mine did, but we don't even have money for the bribe. So it's up to me to do something, to come to the States and work, whatever I can, and send the money back home."

"Why did you leave Hector back there?"

"What, bring him along? Hector was only going to get in the way. He was not going to be any use here. We need him to stay back with the kids and help my mom. I came here to work. I thought I can be a chambermaid, a waitress, or a hospital attendant, I am not afraid to work hard, you know that. Someone I know puts me in touch with Gloria. I start filling in as a home-care attendant. Then I met you."

"And saw me as a means to an end."

"No! Those are your words. I don't think that way. I saw it as starting a new life. I could provide for my children, and I could start over again. With a kind man that I care for. Hector is supposed to stay back in the Philippines. But like a fool he shows up, he flies here even though I ordered him not to. Why? I don't know. He got lonely, he says. He says he couldn't manage without me. I was very mad at him when he showed up. You remember, you said something about it at the time. He and I had not been getting along even before I left, and then, when he comes here, to New York, it only makes things worse between us. But he's still my husband. I can't change that."

"And what about me? Am I still your husband, too?"

"Yes, of course. But I can't just toss Hector out in the street."

"You still love him?" I asked. It was a stupid question, one I had to ask.

She shrugged. "I don't know if it's love or habit. I love my children. I would do anything for them. I am not going to see them starve," said Rita. "You can't imagine, you're not a mother, you can't imagine what it feels like for a mother not to be able to buy her children enough to eat dinner every night, even rice, or new clothes, new shoes, new school supplies. I have been sending them money every month, and also sending the things they need. Christmas presents. Birthday presents. Easter outfits."

"Do you still have sex with him, since he came to America?"

"Yes. Sometimes," she said with a mixture of guilt and defiance. "He's my husband, what can I do? He expects it."

"You could divorce him."

"Hector doesn't want a divorce. He refuses. He says he will tell the police I'm married to two men if I try to divorce him. And then I'll be put in jail and I can't bring my children over. He will get full custody, and I don't want that to happen."

"You believe him? Would he really hurt his own wife and children?"

"I don't know, with Hector any fool thing is possible. He won't agree to a divorce, he says, and I can't take the chance. I want to get my children to America, to give them a new life—the two youngest, anyway; Entoy and Conrado are too old to qualify for alien relative visa. That's my one dream, my one goal in life."

"And you would even commit bigamy to do that?"

"For my children, I would, yes. Worse." She smiled grimly. "I didn't want to commit bigamy. You remember, I say to you when you propose to me, why can't we go on the way we were? But you insist we get married. What else am I supposed to do? I talk to my friends, I ask their advice, and they said I should accept your offer."

It made sense. My stomach ached, the blueberry pie was sitting on its ledge, refusing to digest. Everything suddenly fell into place, retrospectively, the packages sent to Manila, the arguments since Hector arrived on the scene, her reluctance to make love.

"So why didn't you tell me you had children before?"

"I was afraid that you won't want me. You will think I came burdened. I won't be able to give you all the love that should go to you."

"I see," I said. "You think I'm that selfish." My voice took on a weary, indignant tone, though I wondered whether she might have been right.

"I know I should have told you before. I was afraid! Please forgive me, Gordon. I know I did the wrong thing. I am such an idiot." She gave me a melting, teary-eyed, appealing look, which one would have to be hard-hearted indeed to resist. I put my arms around her, and then pulled away, gazing directly in her eyes.

"If you had been honest with me, Rita, I would not have rejected you."

"I know. I was stupid. But I was afraid! I know you are a kind man."

"Stop saying I'm a kind man. Right now I could kill you for sleeping with Hector, does that sound kind?"

"You can beat me if you like," said Rita.

"Of course I'm not going to beat you!"

"Go ahead, hit me."

It was getting late. In spite of the melodramatic turn the conversation had taken, or maybe because of it, as melodrama always makes me drowsy, I yawned.

"Do you want some coffee?" she asked.

"No thanks."

"I'm going to make myself a cup," she said, going over to the stove. "There must be some solution. Some compromise."

"What 'compromise'?" I asked bitterly.

"I don't know. You're a wise man. You'll think of something."

I was almost as mistrustful at hearing myself labeled wise as I had earlier resisted being called kind. In either case I felt diminished. My long-held ambition to act wisely and maturely had vanished for the moment. No compromise came to mind.

"Where were you planning to put the children?" I said.

"Here. In this big house. There is plenty of room. If you only can see how we are living back in Manila—"

"And how were we supposed to explain to our neighbors on the block where these children came from? Or who their parents were? Oh, you hadn't thought that far! I suppose you were planning to palm them off as your nieces and nephews, the way you fobbed Hector off as your cousin. And what are you planning to do about Hector? Install him here, too, in this 'big house'?"

"No. He'll stay in New Jersey."

"Oh great! So you can spend half the week with him in New Jersey and half the week with me? Why don't you just take your kids and live with him in New Jersey?" I was suddenly energized again, furious.

"It's not a good life. It's only one room. I'm not going to move them here from the Philippines just to have the same conditions, all of us squashed together in one room."

"Plus, what would the immigration officials say when they found out you were living with him, before our two-year trial period was up?"

"Do you want me to go live with him? I'll do it, if that's what you want," said Rita, bowing her head.

"No, no, I'm not saying that." I began pacing.

"What can I do? Please take care of me. Take care of my family. You are my only hope."

"Look, you can bring your kids over to live here, provided you promise to cut off all relations with Hector."

"I can't do that. Hector is the children's father. They love him. He's a good father, even if he has his faults."

"He's such a good father that he left them in the Philippines with your mother, a woman who is too frail to take care of them, just so that he could mooch off you."

"I know all that. But if you saw him with the children, playing with them . . ."

I threw up my hands. "I don't want to hear that. All right, he can see the children, but he cannot sleep with you."

"Yes, fine," said Rita.

"That's the compromise—understood?" She nodded. I didn't

know whether to believe her or not. But I was insistent. On that point I am firm.

MARCH 28

I don't know whether I've actually caught the flu or it's purely my emotional reaction to the revelations the other night, but the last forty-eight hours have been rough. I feel like pulling the covers over my head, or putting a bullet in my brain. I wouldn't know how to begin to give an account of my mental state. In a way, it surprises me that my reaction has been so extreme. At times I feel I'm close to going mad. My head is reeling, my stomach's in an uproar, I am filled with bile, a kind of acid reflux that floods my mouth, like soy sauce. My wrist is also killing me, because I wrote that long diary entry the other day. I overdid it. I have to cut back on these diary entries. My first impulse has been to curse Rita. I mean, to demonize her, and compare her to all the two-faced liars, schemers, Delilahs, and Mata-Haris in history. The problem is, Rita is not a femme fatale, not some man-eating gorgon, she is a woman in a bind, trying to do the best for her children. Alas—because it would be so much easier for me if I could write her off as a treacherous slut. As it is, I find myself in the impossible situation of admiring her even after I discover she's betraying me.

We were lying in bed early this morning at 5:00 a.m. (according to the digital clock on our night table), and I was staring at her body as she slept, that amazing, beautiful body of hers. One thing keeps nagging at me: if she's had four children, why are her breasts so firm? Whenever I slept with women before who had borne children, their bosoms were saggy, and sort of silky in texture. Not to say that was off-putting in any way, but still . . . Rita's breasts continue to exhibit a gravity-defying robustness. I guess I haven't had enough experience along these lines to generalize.

This morning I went out into the garden and tried to do some work there. Just some pruning, planning, getting ready to plant a few things in April. I couldn't concentrate, even at gardening, which does not take so much brain power. My head felt thick and listless, with a dull ache behind the eyes, which may in fact be a flu symptom. It was as though I were having an allergic reaction to my own toxic brooding, that obsessive regurgitation of the other night's conversation.

The nub of the problem is that I don't hate Rita. I love her, still.

But I am certainly not going to share her with Hector. That is out of the question. Forget it as an option. A man has some pride.


MARCH 29

One side benefit of the New Honesty. I learned that Rita's real name is Mildred. She did not like it, thought it prissy-sounding, so she changed it to something more "fun" when she was fifteen.

For a while she had everyone call her Lolita, then Lola, then she fixed on Rita. I am thinking of calling her Mildred from now on, just to bug her.

MARCH 30

On top of everything else, the pigeons have now come to roost on *my* house. When I opened the front door yesterday, still feeling fluish, I saw dismaying white splotches on the porch steps, like clotted glue, six or seven of these squirts, which revolted me. I looked up and sure enough there were three slate-gray, plump-bellied pigeons clucking away. I tossed some gravel up at them, gently, afraid of breaking a windowpane. They fluttered for a moment and then came back to their roost, surveying the street comfortably from the roof gutter, like duennas on the balcony in a Goya painting. I remembered back to the discussion I had had with my neighbor Lucia. She had said you couldn't put poison on the ledge, it was against the law, and spikes did not always work. I took to hollering up at the birds, "Go away!" "Get lost!" Just then Lucia came out of her house, chuckling, she had been watching me, no doubt, from behind her window curtains. "What's wrong?" she said. "These pigeons," I replied, "they're disgusting!" "I told you, but you wouldn't believe it was such a big deal. You thought I was overreacting." "How did you get them to leave your house?" I asked, crossing the street to continue the conversation. "They left. They left of their own accord. One day they were gone. And now you got 'em. Good luck!" "Did you ever try poison pellets?"

I asked, choosing to ignore her gloating. "Nah. They come, they
go. They're free agents. They do what they feel like."


APRIL FOOLS' DAY

Rita has been visiting Hector in New Jersey. There is nothing I
can do to stop her. I am not going to lock her up or tie her to the
bed like a jealous husband in *The Arabian Nights*. She is a free agent.
I have begged her not to have sex with him, and she says she doesn't,
but I don't believe her.

"I am going to need some more money," Rita told me this
morning. "My bank account is very low."

"How much?" I asked. I won't demean her, or myself, by
demanding that she account for her expenses. Still, I wondered
how much of this money would be going directly to Hector, who
has lost his job at the pizza parlor.

"I am going to need about five thousand dollars. Is that all
right?"

"I'll write you a check after I finish my coffee."

"I don't want to strain us financially. Do you have enough in
your account?"

"I have enough, don't worry about it," I said in a querulous
tone, more so than I had intended.

"Maybe I should get a job . . ." she said.

"Why not make Hector get a job?" I could not keep from saying. "What if he tried to find some work? Any kind of work, instead of lying around all day?"

"Hector? He's a good-for-nothing."

This is typical of Rita.

"He's a weak, foolish man," she'll say about him. "He's a good-for-nothing." But instead of such statements consoling me, they make me tremble inside. My experience tells me that women like their men weak and foolish—those are the ones they cling to. The reason is, women start off thinking that all men are big babies who don't understand the basics of life; so when they find a man who is weak in a clearly legible, predictable way, it reassures them, they know how to deal with him, and they invest their love long-term in that man. Also, weak, foolish men need protecting. I don't mean to imply that I am too strong or independent for her. I am sure that deep down Rita regards me as weak and foolish, too. But my weakness is less easy for her to minister to, perhaps because of the class or educational distance between us, or even my larger physical size, so in the end she'll stick with Hector, whom she has hectored all her life.

APRIL 2

My consultants on pigeon control have informed me there are several options besides poisoning, which is illegal (though I haven't ruled it out yet): spikes, nets, sticky gels, ultrasonic noisemakers, and electrified strips. Some people use fake owls, the equivalent of scarecrows, but I'm told this is only marginally effective. In all these approaches, you are merely shooing the pigeons away to another roost and making them someone else's problem. I am willing to do that, of course, but the reason I haven't yet eliminated putting out poison traps is that it seems less hypocritical than sending the problem elsewhere. On the other hand, I don't relish having to sweep pigeon corpses off my roof gutter, in plain sight of the neighbors. The ultrasonic noisemaker has a certain science-fiction appeal, and I much prefer it to electrified strips. I am still fantasizing hiring a local kid to pelt them with a slingshot, which would be the traditional peasant solution. My father would have probably opted for the ultrasonic noisemaker and Uncle Antonio for the slingshot. I asked Rita what she thought I should do. She said she didn't mind the pigeons being there, it would be a shame to hurt them. If I were a good Stoic, I would reason that the pigeons are external to my control, but what is in my control is my attitude toward them, which can change from opprobrium to acceptance.

APRIL 4

Rita was folding the laundry, and I sat next to her on the bed. I began looking for matched socks, and tucking one into the other, like a fish swallowing its mate.

"Do you still love me?" I asked Rita timidly.

"Of course, silly."

She seemed surprised that I would even doubt it. Looking at her tranquilly folding the laundry, I had the sense she was telling the truth. She did love me. She is a tender woman who probably has room in her heart for many men to love, I would think. But I wish she had not added the word "silly." It was as if she were talking to a child, reassuring him that there were no ghosts hiding in the closet when she turned off the light. That "silly" trivialized my anxiety, to which I have a perfect right.

What I wanted to ask her was: "Did you ever love me?" I refrained from asking that question, though it took some discipline in doing so, because I sensed it would offend her. I would be calling her a schemer or, worse, a prostitute, in the sense of a woman who used her body to get what she wanted. Besides, I did not want to ask that particular question because it would constitute a relapse on my part, with ignoble associations from the past, when I drove women away by too openly doubting their love.

The only other alternative is to let Hector come and visit her here, which is even less palatable. I would have to see his infuriatingly humble face with that poor excuse for a mustache, and watch them behaving like a pair of songbirds. But if he came here, at least I could keep an eye on them and make sure they didn't disappear into the bedroom.

APRIL 6

I am no longer certain that I could never accept sharing Rita with Hector. I am in uncharted waters here. Who knows how much my heart can be stretched to accommodate the woman I love? If I can consent to taking in her children, perhaps I can even look the other way when she sleeps with Hector, as long as she continues to sleep with me. Rita is a sublime female, a queen among women, why should she not have several courtiers? In the end, what

difference does it make if a woman sleeps with you and with someone else? In the past, I had sometimes been sexually involved with
women I knew were seeing other men on the side. I thought I had
no right to demand exclusivity, insofar as none of us can "possess"
another. But of course I wasn't married to those women. So is it
the legal paper that makes the difference in my mind? Is it that
age-old village fear of being publicly ridiculed as a cuckold? Or is
it that I really do love Rita, while I only partially loved those other
women, and so for the first time I am jealous? Why this reflex inside me that tells me it would be intolerable to share her? In an
ideal world, I would welcome Rita's children, and I would not
insist on exercising monopoly over her body. Why should it matter to me if Rita sleeps with that idiot? If I love Rita (and I do),
the proof of that love would be that I can forgive her everything.

What matters—or I should say what *should* matter—is that I
keep seeing her, continue to have her in my life, enjoy her presence as a free human being, coming and going at her will, however restricted our encounters may be. Lately, the circumstances
are that she cannot have sex with me. Okay, she says it "confuses"
her too much. She begs me to give her more time, and promises
that this will not be the final word. I should recognize the dilemma
she is in and help her by being understanding, not just thinking
about my own needs for once. What truly matters, in the end, is
that we respond generously and justly to human need. The only
way we can arrive at a better world is to act as if its utopian stan-
dards of conduct already existed. I want to act wisely. It has always been a dream of mine to act wisely and nobly, but I've kept

putting it off, thinking myself too young, or immature, to grasp such ideals as a practical matter. Now I am finally of an age when I can be governed less by drives than by reason. The older I get, the more wisdom becomes attractive as an end in itself. Wisdom counts more than happiness, in the long run, I believe. I can feel wisdom hovering just beyond my reach, fluttering above my head, I can almost taste wisdom on my lips, hear it whispering to me, though I can only make out every third word.

APRIL 7

The struggle facing me is whether I can perfect my love for Rita and take it to a different, higher plain. My love may have begun as lust, nothing wrong with that, love often announces itself first through the physical side of things, but once you have accepted that you can never own another person, and that sexual passion is transient (not necessarily because you grow bored with the other person, it could be circumstances outside your control, as in our case), then the question is, Can you transmute your love, through sacrifice, into a purer devotion? Can you take pure joy in the beauty and charm of the beloved without having to seek carnal satisfaction from her?

I once wrote in these pages that I worshipped Rita as a goddess. I had in my mind one of those goddess statues in India; maybe I was only pretending to worship her, maybe not. The point is: Is she any less deserving of worship if I can no longer, well, have my way with her? Don't misunderstand: I see very well that Rita is not a deity but an ordinary person, who has flaws and moods, who belches, farts, and so on. But I still see in her the incarnation of a divine spirit, what Goethe called the Eternal Feminine, it doesn't matter, call it whatever you want: strictly speaking, what matters in love, as in religion, is the quality of one's worship, not the objective merit (if such could ever be determined) of the revered object.

APRIL 12

I told Gabe about my predicament. He listened silently, like a Buddha, and then said with the slightest smile, "What did you expect?" These were not the supportive, empathic words I had hoped for from a friend. I asked him to clarify. "What did you expect?" he repeated. "You marry a woman about whose past you know nothing, a beautiful immigrant who needs a green card, a woman who shares none of your intellectual interests, so that you can never be sure what she is thinking, and all this makes her deliciously enigmatic to you, a mystery, when really she is just taking you for a ride."

"You never liked her."

"I liked her, but I didn't trust her. Again: What did you expect?"

"What should I do, Gabe? I am lost, really lost. I need your advice."

"If I were you, I would report her to the immigration authorities."

"I can't do that!"

"Then go on living with her, and learn to eat crow with every meal."

Gabe seemed almost amused—at my expense, I should add, for which I will never forgive him. Never! Of course, to be honest, I had already forgiven him, because every word out of his mouth could have been uttered by me, it was as though I were still at home, talking to myself in the mirror.

There is no more heartless statement in the English language, nor one more philosophically rich, I would wager, than "What did you expect?" I have been walking around ever since with these words buzzing in my brain. They are, strangely enough, my one consolation.


APRIL 20

"What did you expect?" I expected to be loved, I expected not to be loved, I always expect people to *like* me, and am not surprised when they do. After all, I am (for the most part) considerate, affable, unthreatening. On the few occasions when people have taken an instant dislike to me, I chalk it up to their eccentricity, or to the random distribution of malice in the universe. My mother loved me, but she was also very critical of me—which laid the groundwork for my seeking out women who would give me a hard time. I thought I had broken that pattern with Rita. She seemed to love me straight-forwardly, unquestioningly. Even as I continued to question my own innate lovableness, I saw, or thought I saw, in her eyes a shining approval of my being. Was I idealizing her? Certainly. What did I expect? I did not expect her to be wedded to someone else when she took her marriage vows with me, and I think that was a legitimate expectation on my part, not a sign of gullibility.

What did I expect? The heart, trained on disappointment, expands nevertheless to accept good fortune when it suddenly appears, and stoicism is cast aside like a temporary makeshift. Put an unloved bachelor next to a beautiful woman who seems to adore him and he will accept her adoration as a matter of course. What did I expect? I expected the worst, naturally, as I always do, but also the best, because I am not wise enough to understand the true nature of life. So I am always fickle as regards pessimism, and prepared at a moment's notice to abandon it for optimism, and vice versa. Were we not put on earth to experience joy? I think to myself when the sun is shining. Just because I have not encountered much joy in the past does not mean the fundamental stuff of life is bleak; it only means I have so far lacked the talent or knack to tap the unlimited joy that surrounds me, which others, the saddhus and satyrs who are gifted at the art of living, know how to appropriate. So I try on the possibility of happiness, like an oversized sombrero; and when, in the end, it doesn't quite fit, I shrug, and go back to my leaky umbrella. What did I expect?

I always expected to be disappointed, that is nothing new. The new thing I needed to learn was how to expect bliss. What achievement is there in stoical renunciation when one has never hoped, never experienced joy, or risked having one's heart broken? What did I expect? It takes talent to live without expectations, to be able to improvise in the face of any gift that comes our way. Of course

I feel like a fool for not knowing what was on the horizon. In that sense Gabe is right. But love requires taking a delight in not-knowing. It opens a space for play, which means not having a pre-conceived agenda. How could I love and, at the same time, expect?

APRIL 22

You could argue that Rita was part of my fantasy life—a part that had unexpectedly spilled into my real one. It was as though my desire had conjured her. Just as, in a dream, you meet someone who is extremely attractive, and the next moment she welcomes you into her arms, you may be taken aback, but you go along because why turn down good fortune, so I accepted Rita's love. We can live out our fantasies, it seems, for a while at least, and perhaps the wall between fantasy and reality is more permeable than we suspected, provided we relinquish, going into the game, any hope for understanding what is going on or what is just ahead, in other words, the whole concept of *foresight*. So the question "What did you expect?" becomes moot.

APRIL 23

I told Rita she had to leave. If she was going to continue to see Hector, she would have to move out of this house. I felt good that I had put my foot down. I have probably made the biggest mistake in my life, but that's not a new thing for me, making mistakes. Usually I err on the side of being too accepting. I have a tendency to adjust to whatever seat I am assigned on a plane, at a restaurant, my stubborn pride takes the form of seeing how obliging I can be. Not this time. We will see how it plays out.


APRIL 27

With Rita spending her days in Ridgewood, New Jersey, I have been having vivid dreams. Perhaps, sleeping alone, my unconscious is not interrupted by what would normally be the awareness of Rita's warm body next to mine, and so I slumber longer into the morning; also, I sleep longer because I am depressed, so there are more opportunities for dreams. Last night I dreamt that I entered a nightclub or a Latin disco. At a table toward the front, three women, too young, too foxy, too sexy, vivacious, and desirable to have been interested in me in real life, beckoned me over, and I came and sat down. They continued conversing amongst themselves in a vulgar, youthful lingo without addressing me. I began to suspect that I had been summoned because I was an older man with money, who would presumably pay for their drinks. I wondered if they even had plans to rob me afterward, should I become sufficiently drunk. I continued to sit there, listening to their chatter, on the off chance of learning something bitter about life, or else hoping against hope that I would get lucky with one of them—for instance, the brunette with the low-cut voile bodice who was gesturing brusquely across the table. The dream went no further, but when I awoke I thought of Rita as someone who had also been "out of my league," erotically speaking, and I thought of myself for the first time as a type, one of those pathetic older business-men who hang around young women, picking up their tabs.

APRIL 29

I had expected that I would not be able to teach well, my mind would be too distracted with sorrow, but in fact the opposite has happened. I became very eloquent in class last night, able to put into articulate words and syntactically complex, wholly formed sentences whatever vagrant thoughts brushed against me. I could tell my students were impressed. My sense is that I am going to get quite positive student evaluations this semester, certainly more so than the first semester, when the evaluations were mixed. I am finally acquiring the knack of working with undergraduates. I must speak to Gabe about the possibility of being moved from an adjunct to a permanent teaching line.

MAY I

I had a dream last night that I was stroking Rita, down below. Every time she was about to come, my finger would slip, I would lose my spot on her clitoris, and then I would have to start over from the beginning. I awoke both excited and frustrated—aroused by the thought of having had sexual contact with Rita (these days, it is only via dreams), and ashamed that I had not been able to satisfy her. I heard these words in my head on awakening: "You need to focus more," as though the whole problem in our marriage relationship were lack of focus. Was my dream-mind telling my waking one that I had lost Rita because our rhythms were fundamentally (if not erotically, then in some other way) out of sync? That I was not paying enough attention, it was my fault somehow, for not concentrating more? If so, is my subconscious not giving myself too much (dis)credit by believing that it had ever been in my power to bring about another, happier outcome?

MAY 2

I have lived alone in the past, I can live alone again. (Repeat this one hundred times a day.)

MAY 4

Fatalism and stoicism are not the same, though they overlap. To believe that everything happening to us has been preordained is fatalism. So a fatalist would say that I was destined to meet Rita and to lose her. In a sense, psychoanalysis starts from a fatalistic premise, by attempting to decode our current neurotic patterns through the causal clue of childhood imprinting, even if it holds out the nonfatalistic hope that those patterns can be broken through self-awareness. I am neither a fatalist, nor am I a believer that self-awareness can liberate us from our neuroses. I merely think (or thought) we can come to terms with our experience, with the cards dealt us, by accepting in a dignified, self-restrained manner what we cannot change. That is stoicism in a nutshell.

Epictetus put it this way: "What disturbs men's minds is not events but their judgments on events. . . . And so when we are hindered, or disturbed, or distressed, let us never lay the blame on others, but on ourselves, that is on our own judgments. To accuse others for one's own misfortunes is a sign of want of education; to accuse oneself shows that one's education has begun; to accuse neither oneself nor others shows that one's education is complete."

Applying that last set of distinctions to my present situation, if I were to blame Rita and Hector for the pain I'm in, I would merely be acting petulant, ignorant. If I were to try to trace my involvement with Rita to part of a lifelong pattern of choosing the "wrong woman" or "inappropriate love-object" (the psychotherapeutic model), I would be blaming myself alone, which is a step up from blaming others, but also a form of grandiosity (the clitoris dream), since I would be taking responsibility for events not solely in my control. If I blame no one (easier said than done), I am free to reshape my judgments on the events in question, so that what had seemed dreadful might appear in another light as . . . neutral? inevitable? comic? No, supportable. All I ask is to be reconciled to my lot, the way I was to the pigeons. "The good man's life," says Marcus Aurelius, is "the life of one content with his allotted part in the universe, who seeks only to be just in his doings and charitable in his ways."

## MAY 6

Can I *live* my stoicism? That is the question. It is one thing to have a philosophy, another to live it. Gabe claims that stoicism is at odds with the nature of being human and social. But since I am defi-cient in humanity and sociability, perhaps I stand a better chance of putting my stoicism into practice than others do.

In the past I had sought the Good by reading, going to con-certs and the opera, looking at paintings, and traveling to foreign places, where I also listened to music, went to museums, and col-lected books. I had sought the Good in culture and in philoso-phy. When I met Rita, I perceived the Good enshrined in a real person, and so naturally I wanted to wed my inner being with that exemplary model. It was not only that she was beautiful, I insist, it was her goodness as well that attracted me—her benevolence, her even temper, her humor, kindness, her capacity for content-ment. Even her conventionality, which aligned her with the majority—I am speaking of that love of puppies and Christmas and so on—was a sign of Rita's good heart. She exemplified the best of human nature, she was blessedly normal, a really decent person, and my desire to merge myself with her bespoke the wish to flee from those warped, antisocial feelings I had suffered all my life, and to . . . join the human race! I joked that Rita was teach-ing me to become a human being. But in the end the distance was too far for me to travel. I am not a human being, I am a freak. I deserve to be left alone, to live alone.

MAY 7

"All unhappiness comes from one's inability to give anything up." Who said that? Marcus Aurelius? Epictetus? The Buddha? No:

Coco Chanel. I read it in an article about the fashion designer years ago and clipped it. She collaborated with the Nazis during World War II—"collaborated" may be too strong a word, let's say she hosted and partied with the occupiers of her country, unable to give up her perquisites as queen of society. After the war, when she was cleared, thanks to the intervention of a friend in the Paris police force, she made the remark I have quoted. I find it pertinent to my situation. If Coco Chanel can attain such wisdom, I tell myself, why not I? I can choose to give up my exclusive claims to Rita. The question is, did Chanel then act in a disciplined manner according to this wise precept, or did she continue to flounder about miserably, even after knowing the cause of unhappiness, because she was still unable to give anything up?

MAY 8

I seem to be writing the same reflections over and over in these pages. I should try at some point to examine the reasons why my reflections keep circling back on these same intellectually threadbare homilies, these pathetic conundrums, without my being able ever to deepen the analysis.

MAY 9

Yesterday I received a phone call from Rita. She asked me to pick her up from Hector's place in Ridgewood, New Jersey. Her voice sounded controlled and formal, and, as is often the case these days, apologetic. Her voice is incredibly melodic, the notes go up and down like a mandolin, or like a certain kind of Asian music, Chinese or Vietnamese, I wish I knew more about such traditions, but in any case, I could listen to it for hours. "Yes, of course," I said, "give me the address. Are you planning to stay in Brooklyn for a while?"

"I don't know. Please, I just need you to do this. You're the only one I can depend on, Gordo," she said, dropping her voice.

"Yes, don't worry. I'll be there in an hour."

The phone call ended with Rita giving me a few directions. I drove through the Holland Tunnel and took the New Jersey Turnpike. The suburb itself wasn't hard to find, but the actual address took me awhile, because all the streets went one way and ended in cul-de-sacs. The street they lived on was unnecessarily wide, the houses on either side close together and shabby-looking, and altogether the impression was quite forlorn and dispirited, it disturbed me to see Rita reduced to such circumstances, and even more to know that I was partly to blame for her having to live this way. The house was aluminum-sided and painted a nasty green. I was about to ring the doorbell when I realized Hector and Rita would probably be in the cellar apartment, which had a separate side entrance.

I rang the basement bell.

Rita came to the door, her face brightening when she saw me. Pretty, as usual, very lovely, though there was something strained in her face, as though she had aged a little in the last week. Hector was in the background, grinning shyly, and he came forward and stuck out his hand, which was big of him, I suppose, or at least courageous. I could have decked him, after all. The ceiling was low, maybe only seven feet high, and made lower by the oil pipes suspended from it.

"Sit down," Rita said, gesturing toward the one semicomfortable chair in the flat. I moved toward the chair and banged my head on the pipes.

Rita said, "Please, have a seat. I'm almost ready."

I looked around, prepared to compliment the place, but I couldn't, it was too depressing. Ancient refrigerator, stove, bed, card table for eating, toilet, everything in this one square room. The walls had been covered with tarpaper and newsprint.

"Would you like some ginger ale?" Hector asked. "Or beer? We have several good kinds of beer."

"Just a glass of water," I said. I stood up to get it myself and banged my head again.

"Sit, sit," said Rita, "I'll get it." She ran the glass under the faucet for a long minute, to make sure it was thoroughly clean, and then filled it. From across the room I saw the glass had once been a peanut butter jar.

"Thanks," I said, and drank it quickly, grimacing at the brackish taste.

"So, how have you been?" asked Rita.

"I'm surviving. I'm happy to see you."

She nodded, and cast a worried glance at Hector. "I'll just be a minute," she said. Then she turned and addressed a stream of Tagalog to Hector, last-minute instructions, I assume, they didn't sound like endearments. He looked abashed, and smiled at me, as if to say: Isn't she the bossy one?

"Do you have any troubling finding this place, Mr. Gordon?" asked Hector.

"No, her instructions made it very easy."

"It's a nice area. It's good here because there aren't a lot of minorities."

"Rita, do you need any help?" I called out, immediately interrupting him, not wanting to hear any more of his prejudiced comments.

"I'm all right," she said from the corner of the room.

He rocked back and forth in a chair that did not look too stable. "Would you like some soda?" he asked.

"No thanks."

"The only problem with this area, it's hard to find work here. I can't do hard work, I'm getting too old for it," he said.

I stared at his contented boyish face and the hair falling over his eyes.

"In the Philippines," he went on, "the men stay home, watch the kids, because the women make more money nursing."

"You don't seem so old."

"Oh yes. In Manila I work too hard in a factory, a—slaughterhouse. I get aches and pains. I still paying for that job."

Rita dragged her heavy red suitcase forward, and I jumped up to take it from her. As I did so, I banged my head on the pipes a third time.

Hector laughed. "Everyone does that. You not the only one."

"Glad to hear it. Well," I added vaguely, waving with one hand as I grabbed the suitcase with the other, "sorry about this . . ."

"Me too. We Filipinos, we do not like to be left alone."

I wanted to say, "Who does?" but I was more or less struck dumb by his coming out with such a generalization at such a moment. It made me wonder if perhaps I had underestimated him.

MAY 11

It is good to have Rita back with me. Last night we made love, it felt whole, natural, simple. I am under no illusions that she will stop seeing Hector, but for the moment she is mine. I feel proud to have rescued her, if that is the right word, and regardless of whether she proves faithful to me, from here on in I cannot let her go back to that hideous basement apartment. The time for issuing ultimatums is past. I must accept Rita for who she is and what she does. I have the sense that I have been put on earth to protect her. As long as I have the means to do so, I will.

Brave words. Possibly they will prove mere bluster. But only by trying on postures and discourses that are wiser and more generous than our given ones, only by bluffing at being good, can we hope to achieve virtue. "Waste no more time arguing what a good man should be. Be one," says Marcus Aurelius.

MAY 13

Today is my mother's birthday. I have been thinking a great deal about her recently, not sure why. She seems very present to me these days. Very vital. I will have the thought, I need to visit my mother, and then remember, Oh, right, she's dead. But still I go on talking to her in my head. You see, I say, I did end up with Rita, that attendant you liked so much. And was that the right thing to do? . . . Did my mother really want me to marry? She sent me mixed signals. I wonder how happy her marriage to my father was. They always seemed reserved together, my parents, but that could just have been Castilian austerity, who knows what they were like when they were alone? My mother used to talk about an old beau she had in Madrid, several old beaux, in fact, there was one handsome doctor in particular whom she almost married before she met my father. She was going to school in Salamanca, and Papa was her professor. That sort of thing would be frowned on now. I miss my mom. I miss them both. The next one to die will be me. If only I could believe that I would meet up with the two of them after my death. How would I know where to reconnoiter with them? I imagine heaven, *were* it to exist, as a vast soccer stadium, with people trying to find each other, parents and children, spouses, pushing and shoving, although maybe some spouses would be in hiding from their other half, God would honor their wishes, there would be different sections for those deceased who wanted to find each other and those who didn't, and you would not discover until you died that in fact the person with whom you had imagined spending eternity felt differently about you.

MAY 14

Hector has overstayed his tourist visa and is now "officially" an illegal alien. I think he had intended doing this from the start, disappearing into the ocean of America. He relies on his nonentity camouflage to make himself invisible. Lately he has hatched a scheme with a Filipino pal who owns a garage, who will pretend to be employing him as a mechanic, and who will write him a payroll check every two weeks, which Hector will then cash and return the money. He's being paid on the books but not getting any dough, the opposite of being paid off the books. Clever, one has to give him credit for that. After five years of this charade he will be eligible for a green card. He has even gone so far as to acquire a fake mechanic's certificate, though he knows nothing about repairing cars. I feel like reporting him. Yesterday he came by to pester Rita and borrow some money from her. If you ask him why he has been without work for so long or why he has no money, or why his family is split up, he has one ready explanation: "Bad luck." He will refer to a fire that burned down the Chinese market that once employed him, or a boss who tried to cheat him out of part of his wages. Bad luck is his mantra, his deity. It galls me that I am the better man, yet he has the upper hand over Rita. (I must admit that he is fairly handsome in a conventional sense, handsomer than I am.) He even manages to lord it over Rita, to get his way and order her about. A paradox: you would think that with her being such a strong woman and he a weakling, she would call the shots. In life, I should remember, the weaker often tyrannize over the stronger. In the end she will fall back on the traditional role of fixing his meals while he watches television and drinks beer. I get the impression this is a common Filipino pattern, at least for a certain social class: the women are very strong, resourceful, hardworking, while the men idle about, drinking, gambling, and womanizing. Hector does not womanize, he is far too childishly dependent on Rita, but the rest of the stereotype holds true.


MAY 16

The big event around here is that Rita went to the beauty salon and had her hair cut off. Well, not all of it, but it no longer falls down her back, now it stops at about three inches below her earlobe. She said all that length bothered her in the heat, and summer is coming, but that can't be the whole explanation, she's been used to extreme heat in the Philippines all her life. I must say, she does look adorable this way. After I'd gotten over the initial shock, I began to appreciate the new, more gamine Rita. The hair bob gives her a much more sophisticated air, like a chic real estate agent or sales representative, I can see her in a Chanel suit and briefcase striding around Manhattan, knocking on office doors. I will have to put away my island fantasies, which were getting stale anyway. Now she will be more like Audrey Hepburn with breasts. Somehow this haircut, though, seems a declaration of independence on her part. I'm not sure if she's trying to assert distance from me, or Hector, or both.

Rita has been keen on initiating the paperwork to bring her children over. She no longer disguises the fact that this is her main agenda. We spoke to the immigration authorities, and what with the latest American distrust over immigrants and the worries about terrorism, it is going to take longer than she had hoped. My own feelings are mixed. Frankly I don't entirely relish the prospect of her children moving in with us. But on the other hand, I would like Rita to have her wish come true, it would help ease her mind and restore her to contentment, which she has not had for some while—I suppose since Hector arrived in the States. There is always the possibility, too, that I would get along wonderfully with her children. It would be like my having an instant family, without the anxieties of childbirth. I imagine I would make a decent father, not too stern, just firm enough. I could take them to the zoo, to the playground, to the movies. Or just go for walks around the city with them.


MAY 17

It seems there is a good chance that Nonoy, the youngest teenage boy, will come over here for two months during the summer on a tourist visa. He has to get back in time for the new school year, but he can live with us in June and July. The little girl would have to stay back with her grandmother.

Today Rita asked me for another few thousand dollars—five, to be exact. She was very sweet about it, not presuming, said she was "embarrassed" to have to bother me. I have had things too much my own way in life. It is time I learned to sacrifice and live more for others. I still don't accept personal responsibility for any imperialist immiseration of the Third World (though I do combine in my heritage the two colonial powers, Spain and the United States, that ran roughshod over the Philippines), but it does strike me that if I can help to rectify the injustices, the inequities, in this small way, by reuniting Rita and her children, I will have accomplished something good.

MAY 20

Oh, I almost forgot. The pigeons have departed. They did this of their own accord. One day they were no longer on my roof, they had migrated elsewhere. Is there a lesson to be derived from this? Maybe just the obvious one, that the universe is completely random and lacking in causality or purpose.

Today I planted a bed of dahlias in the backyard, I tied the lilies to stakes, I planted some gladiolus. I was outside puttering about for three hours. I had a sense of accomplishment. Now all I have to do is mark my students' final exams.

JUNE 10

Nonoy has arrived, Rita's third oldest. He is a handsome boy, as one would expect with that mother, small in stature, serious of mien, polite manners. Very polite, in fact, more so than a typical American kid his age. He does not simply go to the refrigerator to help himself, but always asks for permission first. "Mr. Gordon, may I ask you a question?" he will say, and then he will make the request. Rita says that he is good in his studies, and I should talk to him about what books he likes to read and what subjects interest him. She wants me to encourage him to stay in school.

He does not have any idea that I am married to his mother; he thinks I am merely the landlord, the owner of the house where they are staying. She begged me to go along with this pretense, and also (grrrr!) to let Hector move into our house during her son's stay, partly because Hector lost his job delivering pizzas and has nowhere else to stay, partly for the sake of appearances. "It's just temporary," she says, "but it would upset Nonoy too much to see his mother with another man . . ."

I do know. In the meantime, Rita and I are not to have sex.

J U N E 12

I took the boy into Manhattan to do some shopping. He wanted to visit Niketown, the fancy store with sneakers. It happens to be near the Museum of Modern Art, and I thought we would kill two birds with one stone. But alas, we ran out of time and never managed to make it to the museum. Instead, we went to a Japanese tearoom, the one in Takashimaya Department Store, for some tea, sushi, and dessert. I like that tearoom because it's quiet and you can talk. It has a tranquil spirit, with the Japanese waitresses discreetly removing dishes and rustling about in their kimonos. Maybe I was being too selfish in thinking of my own comfort rather than the boy's amusement, since he probably would have preferred a large noisy restaurant, the kind I hate. As it is, he sat there looking restlessly about, his knee jiggling constantly.

I wanted a quiet place so that we could have a talk and I could get to know him, as Rita had requested. She has this odd idea that if I was to have a serious talk with Nonoy, he could be made to follow in my footsteps and become a scholar. Or a professional of some sort, a doctor or lawyer. I eased into it by asking him what his favorite subjects in school were. He said Physical Education and English. Heartened to hear the latter, I asked him what sort of books he liked to read. There was a long pause during which he thought it over. Books about dragons, he said finally. He was obviously uncomfortable with this line of inquiry, so I switched to movies. What were his favorite films? He brightened up and said, *Jurassic Park*. He had seen it three times already and was hoping to see it again. What was it about the movie he liked so much? I asked. The dinosaurs, he said, especially *Tyrannosaurus rex*. Between his interest in dragons and dinosaurs, I predict for him a distinguished career as a reptilologist. (Is there such a word? What is the proper term for a biologist who handles reptiles?)

JUNE 18

I asked Nonoy if he wanted to go into town to see the dinosaurs at the Museum of Natural History. He seemed less than enthusiastic, so I didn't press it. The boy has been pouting a lot, sleeping late, moping about. He spends hours in the guest room watching television. Or else they play bingo, he and Hector, sometimes Rita as well. I have no idea why it distresses me so much to see them playing bingo in my living room. Rita makes her own kind of homemade pickles and they sit there munching the pickles and calling off numbers. I had associated the game with elderly church socials, but apparently it is big in the Philippines.

The other thing the boy likes to do is go to the park and shoot basketball hoops with his dad. In some ways he seems to get along better with Hector than with his mother. Rita is on his case a lot, scolding him for this or that (not sure what, as most of it is in Tagalog). She wants him to make something of himself: that seems to be the gist of it.

JUNE 19

The weather has turned summer-hot, and my garden needs a good watering every day. Today, around 5:00 p.m., I took the boy out to work in the garden with me. He seemed at loose ends, so it was not too difficult to entice him outside with an activity (and his mother's fervent approval). I taught him how to direct the water hose into the soil of the pots and flower beds, rather than from above, which most people assume is the proper way to do it but which only scorches the leaves. I also taught him to cut flowers properly, with a small knife at an angle, and together we compiled a very pretty arrangement of blue hydrangeas for the vase that goes on the dining-room table. (The hydrangeas have come out looking enormous this year.) I had him planting some seeds, weeding, and even extracting slugs from the marigolds. I'm very fond of marigolds, but they do attract slugs. The boy seems an apt pupil, and not afraid of manual work; he should make a good gardener.

JUNE 20

It was Father's Day today. I'm ashamed to admit that I have been having fantasies since yesterday that I am Nonoy's father and he is my son. Or that I might be able to adopt him someday. I really like the boy. The success of our gardening venture sent me sky-high, I can't wait to get out in the garden with him again. I'm also thinking of offering to teach him Latin. Just the basics, of course, but Latin is such a good discipline for ordering the mind. His vocabulary would improve, his memorization ability, his logical skills, his grammar, syntactical structure, everything, even math. I wish they would make Latin the cornerstone of all secondary education, the way they did in the prewar period. One can trace the deterioration of public discourse in this country to the expunging of Latin from the curriculum, along with the other so-called dead languages. They only become dead languages if you treat them as dead.

JUNE 22

Today I asked Nonoy if he would like to help me in the garden. He seemed very resistant this time. I wanted to know what the problem was.

"In the Philippines, only faggots are gardeners," he said.

"That couldn't be. You must be mistaken."

He insisted: "Only faggots and women."

I tried to remonstrate that gardening required physical stamina, agility, a knowledge of plants, it was an ancient art going back to the dawn of history, it belonged to everyone. He remained adamant. I was shocked at this sudden expression of hostility toward me which seemed to underlie his assertion. Where did it come from? We had been getting along so well.

What he said struck me as so foolish that I could only wonder: was it willed ignorance on his part, or a sign of fundamental lack of intelligence? The boy does not seem unintelligent to me. Therefore, it must be malice.

JULY 7

I am teaching a session of summer school. Gabe asked me to, and I felt I owed him a favor, because he has been so generous in assigning me those courses during the regular year. It's an awkward situation, having a friend as one's supervisor. But I know that he trusts and respects me in the classroom. We don't speak about my situation at home, he is very tactful, doesn't mention Rita, ever since I told him what was going on with Hector and he counseled me to report her to the immigration authorities. I have to admit that the counsel of others has always weighed heavily on me, I am so impressionable, I have never been able to forget a single scrap of advice anyone has ever given me. I guess it comes from the sense that other people are worldlier than I am. But who knows what Gabe would do if he were in my shoes? Sometimes I wonder what I really feel about all this. I vacillate between thinking my home life an intolerable nightmare and sanguinely accepting it. Asking others for advice must be a way to be told what I should be feeling.

The good part is that the summer teaching schedule is condensed and intensive, it gets me out of the house for hours every day, at a time when I am starting to feel increasingly ill at ease at home, as if I were *their* boarder.

## JULY 12

Yesterday evening Nonoy was doing some problems in a mathematics workbook, because he had failed math last semester and needs to take it over next year. I could tell he was very reluctant to apply himself to schoolwork during the summer vacation, but Rita had insisted on it. Hector was scratching his head, puzzling over the book, and Rita stood at the stove preparing dinner. I had every intention of staying out of their dilemma, when Hector said, "Maybe Mr. Gordon can figure it out."

I wandered over and asked to look at the book. Nonoy did not want to move out of the way, and Hector did not think to move.

"Can I please see the book for a moment?" I asked a second time.

"Damn! Can't you just look at it from where you are?" said the boy hotly.

"I suppose I can," I said. "Hm . . . It has to do with finding the area of a non-isosceles triangle."

"Duh! I know that," said Nonoy. "I'm not stupid! You must think I'm really stupid."

"I never said anything like that."

"Nonoy!" Rita called sharply, warningly, from the stove.

"Well, why he thinks he's such a brain that he can solve everything? This book is crap!" he said, slamming the workbook on the table. "That school too cheap to give us good books. That school all fucked up."

"Nonoy, watch your language," said Rita.

"It's true. That cheesy math teacher, he's prejudiced against me. I was doing okay in math, till I flunked that last test. But lots of other kids flunk math tests and they aren't left behind. It's not fair, I get all the bad luck."

By now he had worked himself into a lather sufficient to evade further study, while embracing his father's "luck" thesis. I started to leave the kitchen, intending to steal up to my study and read.

"Go ahead, Mister Brain, run and hide!" said Nonoy. "You're no help. How am I supposed to learn this stuff when the people who know it won't explain it to me?"

"I'll explain it to you," I said, returning to the table. I started to break down the problem into two parts, first finding the missing angles by subtracting the given one from 180 degrees, then multiplying, when he cut me off:

"Wait, you're going way too fast. Just because this is *easy* to *you*, you rattle off the answers like a know-it-all. I want to figure it out, I don't want you to give me the answers!"

"I'll try to do it more slowly. If the sum of three angles in a triangle equals one hundred eighty, and they give you $a + 79$ degrees, then you know in order to find the coefficient—"

"Coefficient! I don't get what he's saying. Dang! He talks like a book!" Nonoy protested to Hector.

I tried again, finding simpler terms and going over the material slowly during the next twenty minutes. Eventually Nonoy grasped the sequence of steps, but it was not a pleasant process for anyone. Nonoy was brimming with resentment, either because he thought I did not give him credit for having any intelligence and was oversimplifying the explanation, or because I was talking over his head and would not communicate properly on his level. Whatever I did was wrong. In the end he even refused to acknowledge that he had grasped the fundamental concept, which seemed odd to me, since I could tell that he did. The boy is not unintelligent, but he has too much invested in defending his underachieving, underdog status to submit to the humbling process of learning.

JULY 21

I came home from teaching the Introductory Latin course (there are no tenure lines open and available, Gabe told me) and there were Nonoy and Hector lolling on the leather couch in the living room, watching a basketball game on television. I had been looking forward to seeing the Metropolitan Opera repeat telecast of *Wozzeck*. Hector invited me to join them in watching the game, which of course I declined. They slapped each other high fives when their team made a basket; there were beer cans all around the coffee table. I stood watching them, paralyzed, not sure what to do. The thought presented itself to kick them both out of the room, but that would have been rude, and I did not want Rita to scold me for rudeness, so I decided to go off to my bedroom to watch the opera there, merely asking that they turn the sound down, since it was very raucous.

As I left the room, I heard the boy say, "Stupid old fart."

Hector immediately rebuked him for speaking that way. It was a horrible moment, all the more so in that I was forced to acknowledge Hector's protectiveness toward me. I went into the bedroom, fuming, and turned on the public broadcasting station. I found it difficult to concentrate on the music, so annoyed was I. After about forty minutes, however, I calmed down, and thought to myself, Well, the kid's right, I *am* stupid, clearly, for letting myself be used this way, and, from his perspective, I must seem old as well, ancient, probably. The "fart" part remains a matter of opinion. It is strange that Nonoy seemed so polite to me when I first met him, and that his manners could have deteriorated so swiftly. It must be partly my fault as well. He must be getting some signal from me that it is all right to treat me with disrespect.

JULY 29

I have found in life that the more intelligent person is often at the mercy of the less intelligent. During a verbal argument, the less intelligent disputant may contradict himself, use inconsistencies, resort to *ad hominem* or *non sequitur* with impunity, and if you point out the flaws in his argument, you are likely to find it an unsatisfying experience. First, the less intelligent person may not have signed onto the objective of fair, reasoned argumentation, and can mock the smarter person for using big words. Second, given the emphasis placed on emotion in our therapeutic culture, the smarter person may be accused of a cold, unfeeling manner when he tries to counter passionate utterances, however misinformed, with logic. Third, should the less intelligent person see a glimmer of merit in the smarter one's objections, he may as a last resort checkmate the smarter person by retorting, "Okay, I'm a dummy, you're the brain—I'm an idiot!" thereby trying to make the smarter one feel guilty for contributing to the less intelligent person's lowered self-esteem. Even if the smarter person will accept none of that guilt, one may still be stymied by the manifest irrelevance of the less intelligent person's buffoonish self-abasement. When the balance in an argument appears to be tipping against him, the less intelligent person says to the smarter, in effect, "Okay, you win—but is winning everything? Are you satisfied, now that you've made me feel so small?" Pointless for the smarter person to respond, "No, it was never about winning an argument but about trying to achieve clarity on the subject." He will not be believed. Thus the intellectual finds himself in a similar position to the professional boxer who is forbidden by law to use his fists outside the ring. With verbal arguments, it is custom, not legal statute, which prohibits the use of reason's weaponry in everyday life. All these frustrations have come to a head in my recent dealings with Hector, Nonoy, and yes, Rita as well. Even in the classroom—and one would think the academy would be one arena which tolerates intellectual rigor—I find students unresponsive or antagonistic if I point out the flaws in their thinking. They will say, "Well, those are my feelings about the matter, they're as valid as yours."

## AUGUST 12

Rita has given me a taste of domesticity and family life—a bitter taste, true, but a real taste nevertheless, and was I not naïve to think family life must be sweet, simply because, as a bachelor, I had idealized it? You pay in this life for naïveté. She *has* accomplished what I asked of her. Before I met her, my life was barren. Cultivated but barren. Now it is chaotic, hellish, furious, and fecund.

## AUGUST 24

Nonoy was supposed to return to the Philippines, but he hasn't gone back yet. I got the latest bill from the cable television company, with over a hundred dollars charged for pornographic movies. Apparently that polite kid has been sneaking off and watching porn in the guest room, simply calling it up by pushing the "Order" button on the remote. No wonder he was looking haggard and drawn. I spoke to his mother about the bill, and she made a geisha-like grimace, hand on face, and said she was very embarrassed. She offered to pay me for it, which means nothing, since all her money comes from me anyway. Meanwhile, I heard Hector chuckling in the background. He takes an amused attitude about the cable bill, as much as to say, Boys will be boys.

The other day I heard him say, "If we can just get our two older boys into the country, they can take care of us. I am counting on them to support us." The man is scheming never to have to work again.

I cannot seem to get Hector to move out. Short of calling the police, which would lead to Rita being evicted from the country, I am uncertain what to do. Meanwhile, Rita came up to me this morning and said, "You're the only one I love, Gordito. Don't get angry, please? Don't turn your back on me, you're my last hope." And she kissed me on the cheek. I didn't know what to make of that kiss, either.


SEPTEMBER 2

As we approach another Labor Day, Rita's latest scheme is that we sell the Brooklyn house and buy a place in Bloomfield, New Jersey, which has a large Philippine-American population. She says she feels more comfortable in a Filipino community, among her kind. We can get millions for the Brooklyn house in the current market, and buy a large three- or four-bedroom in New Jersey for one-third the cost, and bank the rest. I think she is also thinking her children will fit better in a Filipino community when they arrive, and there will be less comment from the neighbors about who their father is.

But how will I fit into all this? I refuse to leave the city for the New Jersey suburbs. Out of the question, I tell her. I would kill myself first.


SEPTEMBER 4

My fiftieth birthday today. I went into Manhattan to have dinner with Gabe, who was kind enough to meet me at the last moment.

He listened patiently to my account of the last few months, this time with manifest sympathy. He is the only one I have confided the whole story to, and indeed, who else could I confide it to, it is all embarrassing and humiliating and unbelievable. He advised me again to go to the INS and tell them everything. A harsh solution, I don't think I can bring myself to do it. I am not a snitch.

SEPTEMBER 6

Rita keeps bringing up the idea of selling the house, or renting it out at a high price, and moving to New Jersey. I wonder why I am being so stubborn. If it will make her happy, why is it so unthinkable? Do I care more about my identity as a city dweller than the happiness of my wife?

SEPTEMBER 7

I have more or less abnegated my conjugal privileges regarding Rita, for the sake of keeping peace in the household. The odd thing is that the longer I go without making love, the less urgent the whole business becomes. I conclude that sex is not as important as I used to think. Is it really necessary for a man's well-being? Are we not merely falling under the sway of modernity, the pressures and fads of contemporary psychology, whose very limited notion of happiness is sexual adjustment? The ancients did not require it, or the Christian mystics, the Hindus, the Buddhists, the Essenes. As recently as the late nineteenth century, celibacy was considered a respectable option for many, it carried no stigma whatsoever. Nothing says I have to keep having coitus, which after all gives but a few moments' pleasure and is sometimes too dearly bought for the trouble. It is not that sex is overrated, but that its pleasures are inherently the same thing over and over. And what is pleasure, finally, but a mental slant, an opinion on experience, as the Stoics teach? It should be possible, then, to find pleasure in not having sex, as well as in having it. To quote Marcus Aurelius: "Where another man prays, 'Grant that I may possess this woman,' let your own prayer be, 'Grant that I may not lust to possess her.'" Even if it were impossible to get rid of lust, the wise man could look back fondly on sex, without necessarily having to repeat the experience again and again. If worse comes to worst, I can play back memories of prior sexual experiences, not just with Rita, but with other women I've known. It is not even necessary to masturbate. The poetry of sexual memory lodges finally in the head, more than in the genitals. That quiet spiritual aura of repletion which good sex bestows in its wake should be possible to achieve, should it not, without engaging in the act itself, but by other means of attentiveness?

SEPTEMBER 15

Nonoy is going back to Manila today. That is the good news. The bad is that Rita's mother requires a complicated operation on her legs. "My mother has very serious arthritis," says Rita. "She already has liquid in her legs, and if she doesn't have the operation it can lead to amputation." Her mother has no health insurance, of course, so I had to wire the money, ten thousand dollars, to the Philippines. Because of these and other recent increased expenses, I am experiencing cash-flow problems. I could sell my entire stock portfolio, but that would be a one-time-only infusion. I need to bring in some more income. I have started looking for extra teaching work. The problem is that adjunct teaching does not pay well. My hope is that in time I will get a regular appointment at some local college or prep school, and in the meantime, I will beef up my employment résumé. All this is very mundane, the kind of grasping practical consideration that used to bore me when I would hear others go on in this vein. Now I see what they were up against.

I will be teaching three courses this semester, one in philosophy at the Free School and two in composition and rhetoric at a junior college in Staten Island. I told the junior college that I am "ABD," meaning I have completed all my graduate work except for the dissertation. I had to pretend that I was working hard on my dissertation and would have it done "in a year or less."

SEPTEMBER 20

Rita has just informed me she is pregnant. It is not my child, it's Hector's, she is sure, given the dates. Pointless to suggest an abortion, I did, but as a good Catholic she won't even consider it. Hers is not just a theological objection, either. "I need to feel a baby in my arms again," she says. She misses holding a baby. So now she is going to have her fifth child. I don't see how this is going to help her, being reduced to a baby-making machine, it will only chain her further to that lazy good-for-nothing Hector, and push them back into poverty. I am absolutely disgusted, I am fed up. She is apologetic about it all, but there are limits to how much I can help her, or want to anymore, for that matter. In fact, I told Rita that I was thinking about going to the immigration officials and blowing this whole thing sky-high. There are limits!

## SEPTEMBER 23

I can't take it, I'm going to go to the immigration authorities and tell them.

I write this sentence and stare at it, appalled. This temptation has been my constant preoccupation and companion since Rita told me she was pregnant. I went so far as to pick up the phone today and dial the USCIS agency, to speak to the examiner who had interviewed us (I still have his card). Then I couldn't go through with it. I imagined Rita being deported or locked up, forced to give birth to her child in a prison hospital. . . . If there was some way for me to get Hector deported, and not Rita, I would not hesitate. I still may go by the immigration office tomorrow and see if I can bring myself to tell them. This is what Gabe counseled me to do a long time ago.

How I wish I could have reacted more generously to her pregnancy news! I wish I could be like the man in Schoenberg's *Verklärte*

*Nacht* (or the poem that Schoenberg used as the basis for his score) who, on hearing that his lover is pregnant with another man's child, can say—wait, I have the lyrics in the CD notes:

> *May the child that you have conceived*
> *Be no burden to your soul.*
> *Look how the universe glimmers!*
> *There is a splendor all around,*
> *You are sailing with me on a cold sea,*
> *Yet a special warmth flickers*
> *From you to me, from me to you,*
> *Which will transfigure the child of another;*
> *You will bear it to me, by me.*
> *You have kindled the splendor within me,*
> *You have turned even me into a child.*

What I would give to be able to say, "Look how the universe glimmers!" "You have kindled the splendor within me." Such noble responses *could* transfigure a night of my soul's despair into welcome and plenitude. The point is not what happens to you but what you make of it, as the Stoics constantly assert.

I have to say, though, that mine is a different circumstance, the woman in the Dehmel poem had slept with a stranger, wanting a child to fill her empty existence, before she met her current love, whom she now exclusively adores, so it's easier for the man to be magnanimous. With Rita that's not the case, I have to put up with her bearing another man's child, and paying for it, while she continues to sleep with him. If it were possible for me to play the role of sole father to the child, to be Joseph to her Mary, I could accept and not find it ignominious. After all, I have sometimes fantasized being a father, though it was not high on my agenda, nor on Rita's, so I never pushed her in that regard, and I assume she was using contraception, I know for a fact she was using it most of the time we made love, the sense I got from her was that she wanted us to be a romantic couple in the first years of our marriage, not to be burdened by parental responsibilities, but now that she is going to have this baby, I could welcome it as my own, a roundabout way to fatherhood, were it not for the fact that Hector is still on the scene and will probably demand the paternal role. So this is not the same as *Verklärte Nacht*. How poorly high culture prepares us for the everyday blows of life!

SEPTEMBER 29

Rita is starting to show. The Italian women on the block have begun clucking around her, theirs being a true baby-centric culture. They ask her how she is feeling, does she have morning sickness, when is she due, whether she wants to know the child's sex beforehand, will she get the baby baptized, and, if so, at which church. Even Lucia has turned warm toward her. Rita accepts all their attention graciously, knows how to handle the role of the happy expectant mother. They congratulate me as well. Am I imagining it, or do I detect a trace of the dubious in their voices? They tell me all the equipment and supplies I must have ready when the baby arrives. I smile weakly, and pretend to be memorizing their tips.

OCTOBER I

Let us say I am being a patsy by not calling the immigration authorities. So what? Is one really a patsy if one consents to be taken with one's eyes wide open? You are only being taken advantage of if you think you are being taken advantage of. Otherwise, you are a Good Samaritan. None of which stops me from fantasizing revenge. Every day I play it out in my mind, the phone call to the examiner, my debriefing in person, how Rita would respond to the interrogation, and so on and so forth. I wonder, too, if I could be liable to arrest myself for not coming forward earlier, i.e., for deceiving the government and obstruction of justice. I could talk to my lawyer about that. He would have to be involved anyway at some point. As soon as I think of contacting a lawyer, my heart sinks. Odd, but I seem more terrified of involving the family lawyer than I do about spilling my guts to the immigration bureau. The immigration bureau remains an abstraction in my mind; the family lawyer, no. For now, I think it is enough just to threaten Hector with going to the authorities. He does seem to behave better when threatened. As with all bullies, you just have to stand up to him, then he backs down. Or else he is preoccupied with the new baby coming and knows it would be a bad idea to antagonize me at this moment, when they obviously will need my financial support.

OCTOBER 8

It was sunny but brisk today, windy, a perfect day to work in the garden. I have been planting a few bulbs for spring, moving some shrubs around, and trying to finish with preparations for winter before the first frost sets in. The temperature is supposed to drop this weekend. Still trying to decide . . .

OCTOBER 17

I am in a basement somewhere in New Jersey, I think. Last night, as I was putting the key in my door, several men with ski masks over their faces suddenly surrounded me on the porch. They put a gun in my side and more or less coerced me into a van parked in front of the house. I say "more or less" because there was a moment when I considered shoving them out of the way and making a run for it. I keep replaying that moment in my mind. I could probably have knocked one against the other and gained a few seconds' head start that way—but not much. Or I could have tried wrestling the weapon out of the gunman's hands and making a run for it. But I had no guarantee that he was the only one carrying a gun, and if I ran. . . . I did not fancy a bullet in my back.

In the van they blindfolded me. From their accents, I assume they were Filipino hoods, gangster friends of Hector's. I had thought of yelling, out on the porch, but none of my neighbors were in sight, and I was afraid, as I said, of being shot.

They spoke in Tagalog among themselves in a loose manner, and then would address me in English from time to time: "Don't worry," they would say, or "Just do what we tell you and you won't get hurt." All clichés from the international kidnapping manual, if such a thing exists. I could make out very little from beneath the blindfold, and I had a headache, and after a while I closed my eyes and dozed. I felt very tired. Spent.

They locked me in the basement and told me to rest, tomorrow I would have visitors who would explain everything. I assumed they meant Rita and Hector.

Fortunately, I had slipped this notebook into my leather jacket yesterday morning, and I always carry a few pens. At a moment like this, it is a great comfort to be able to record one's feelings and observations. The basement is uncomfortably warm and damp, the floors are made of concrete, there are steam pipes hanging low from the ceiling, making it necessary for a tall person like myself to duck or stoop. Just like in Hector and Rita's old apartment. This one is different, though. Or is it? I can't tell exactly, it could be the same place but redecorated. I don't think they will kill me. What would be the point? No doubt they will try to extract every last penny from me. And even if they do kill me, well, what is this great need to go on living? I have learned my lesson. I feel as if I had completed a proper course in human relations. I have learned my lesson: that everything always turns out badly. I am not afraid of dying, at least I think I am not. And it has been a good life—or let us say, a sufficient life. Just as even the greatest Mozart opera can pall by the last act, there begins to be a feeling of glut, satiety, restlessness, the wish to have it over with, this perfection of musical notes, so I too feel ready to leave this melodrama that my life has turned into. This encounter with destiny, necessity, Death, seems altogether too shrill and melodramatic for my austere taste.

Rita has been in to see me a few minutes ago. She claimed she had nothing to do with my kidnapping. She says she is horrified. It is all the fault of Hector, "that dummy, that clumsy idiot." She says he was afraid I would go to the immigration authorities—he just wanted to put the fear of God into me. She doesn't think any harm will come to me in the long run. She will go to work on Hector, and convince him to release me. But first I must promise to keep my word and not speak to the authorities.

I have no idea at this point whether to believe Rita or disbelieve her. She may well be the archstrategist in this whole affair. Or she may be telling the truth. In a way it doesn't matter. I have decided to let them have the house. If they would prefer to live in New Jersey, I can sell the Brooklyn house and let them keep three-fourths of the profits and retain only a fourth for myself. If I get out of this basement alive, I will find myself a cheap apartment to rent, either in northern Manhattan, near the Cloisters, or someplace like Hackensack. I can support myself by teaching as an adjunct. This may all be for the best. It will force me to finish my thesis and get my doctorate. I will support myself by the sweat of my brow. True, I will no longer have Rita, but I will have learned my lesson. In fact, several important lessons. I don't regret my marriage: I had times of sheer unadulterated happiness. I don't see why I should be pitied. For over a year I had the undivided love of an extraordinarily charming woman. Most men never come close to that. I wish her the best. She simply does what she has to do. She acts from a code of maternal logic, which has its own admirable consistency. I am the one who cannot be counted on for consistency. And if I am punished for it, so be it.

The hours drag by. They brought me a pizza to eat. It was not particularly good pizza, greasy, we get much better in Brooklyn, but I was famished so I ate it all.

I am not looking for happiness, I never have. Well, not true, in the first months of my marriage I was smug enough to think I had stumbled into it. But the main point stands: at this point in my life, more than happiness, I have learned to value peace and quiet, which for me means solitude. I cannot function well in the melodramatic turbulence which human entanglement brings. And if I manage to survive this crisis, to be released from this basement, I will see to it that I will go off somewhere and live by myself. Like Santayana in the convent in Rome. I value peace and solitude above all else. That is why I doubt I will ever marry again.

I need to conserve paper. While it is a relief to jabber on, what is the point if I keep repeating myself? I am terrified, I am shaking with fear. I don't want to die. But I tell myself: Whatever happens, one must never regret one's fate.

This is my third day here, I think. I am not entirely sure what day of the week it is. Friday, I believe. Rita comes every so often to visit and to reassure me. She is working out an arrangement. The sticking point is they need some guarantee that I will not turn them in after I am released. If I promise not to go the immigration authorities, and if I promise to sponsor her children's immigration, and to settle a reasonable sum of money on them so that they won't have to beg or live in the streets or go back to the Philippines but can have a roof over their heads and some financial security, and if I promise to let her live with Hector and her children in New Jersey, in short, to relinquish all possible claims on Rita as my wife, then I can go free and unharmed. If not, they will have to murder me. She says that originally some of them had wanted to kill me no matter what I agreed to, because they were afraid I would go to the police afterward and identify them and they would be caught. But she told them that, merely as a practical consideration, it would be very hard for her to inherit money from me if I were put to death, she would be a prime suspect, whereas she thought I could be absolutely trusted to adhere to my end of the bargain, and if by chance I did go to the police, they could kill me then. (She explained to me that she had had to appeal to their practical side, as they could not be counted upon to show moral compassion. She hoped I would understand.)

I said I was amenable to these stipulations. I would sell the house, I would settle at least two-thirds of the proceeds on her, and I would never bother her again. I had no desire to continue living on that block anyway, it held too many memories, and I did not want to keep explaining to my neighbors what was happening with all these strange people going in and out, and then suddenly they would all be gone and just me left behind, no thanks.

She begged me to understand that she had been perfectly contented living with me, and that it was only because that idiot Hector came to the States and spoiled everything that events had taken this regrettable turn.

I said I knew that. It was not her fault.

She said she felt horribly guilty toward me, regardless, because my life has been put at risk.

I said, Just get me out of here and all is forgiven.

Morning. Hector himself just came for a brief visit. I wouldn't be surprised if Rita put him up to it, he had that cowed look of having sustained a tongue-lashing. He wanted to assure me that I would not be harmed, that I would soon be released, probably by the end of the week, he just had to work out a few details, figure out a few problems. I have no idea what to make of it! The only way to describe his manner was apologetic, like that of an innkeeper who has botched a reservation and given you the wrong room, but the room you wanted won't be available until the weekend. He acted as if the whole thing were a misunderstanding, not a kidnapping. To top it off, he even said he hoped I would not be angry at him. No, I think his exact words were, He hoped I would not *stay* angry at him.

Anger is not the issue here. Terror, yes. I am frightened that they will take it into their head to kill me out of confusion; their very ineptness gives me most cause for concern.

MAY 4

Seven months have passed since my last entry. I offer no excuses. For a while I could not bear to look at this diary. Then I misplaced it when I moved. Today I found it, and its predecessor, in one of the cartons I had belatedly unpacked. Hence, this final entry, which should close accounts. When I am feeling stronger, one day I may be able to bring myself to reread these pages, but not now. Not for a long while.

I live on the Upper West Side, in a small garden apartment in a brownstone. The landlord lets me tend part of the garden. I am teaching all over the place, and trying to finish my doctoral thesis. I have thrown myself into work. Perhaps it is all for the best; I am now a functioning member of the workforce.

At first I could not be bothered with anything approaching romantic life. I worked, I read, I gardened, I took walks, I slept. But then I had dinner with my old friend Edith, and to my surprise she invited me to stay over. We have been seeing each other, in a manner of speaking, over the last two months; we get together about once a week, we are taking it slowly, she is very busy with academic affairs, having been appointed chair of her department, and I have many papers to grade, along with putting the finishing touches on my thesis. It is not a perfect fit, I am still a little wary of Edith, and she regards me as a troglodyte, but for now it seems to be all right, an appropriate alliance.

The last time I saw Rita, to deliver a check to her, she was looking as desirable as ever, but harried. Her thick lustrous hair, long again, it stops at her shoulders, just above the nipples, contained its first streaks of gray. Nonoy, little May, and baby Hector were clamoring for her attention, and she hopped to, like their servant. Grown-up Hector was not home, thank God, he was out delivering pizzas. Rita told me she had been applying for jobs as a nanny. She wants to go back to work. She hoped I would give her a good reference if called upon.

I had settled a sum of money on them several months ago, but apparently they mismanaged it, because they are once again at the bottom of the economic ladder. There is only so much I can do. Still, they are happy enough, in that they have achieved their main goal, which was to get a green card. (She, anyway, has one; his will follow in about four years.) In time, with patience, they feel confident they can bring all their children over from the Philippines and resettle them in the States. It's curious that that one purpose has so consumed them that they have no energy left over for other ambitions. But who am I to judge the proper degree of ambition for any individual?

There remains the question of whether Rita was complicit in the plot to kidnap me, or whether, going further back, she had planned it all in advance to dupe me, or was she merely a victim herself? I take the position that some thoughts do us no good to brood about. They are mentally unhygienic. If she was the mastermind, where does it get me? I am left with a cynical hollowness, and the substance of her love for me is reduced to ashes. And if she was not, but only an unwilling accomplice who did love me, and may still, I am not much better off. In any case, it is doubtful I will ever learn the truth one way or another. The truth is out of my control. All I can do is to try to attain a serene mental outlook on the whole affair and put it behind me.

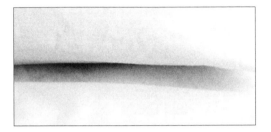

# Eleanor, or,
# The Second Marriage

*a novella*

*IT WAS THE* second marriage for both of them. Eleanor and Frank were determined not to repeat the mistakes of the last one. They were both, for the first time, making good money (he at a recording studio as chief sound engineer, she as a publicist for a book company). During the week they worked hard, gave each other room. On weekends they played: spent Saturday and Sunday mornings in a round bed covered with a satin quilt, then wandered around Smith Street or Atlantic Avenue in Brooklyn, looking for home furnishings and antiques. Frank liked to buy "monstrosities"—bits of armor, marionettes, old neon signs.

All the austerities of their first marriage, when Eleanor was married to a jazz musician and Frank had to support a family of four, they began to shed, at first self-consciously and then, one by one, like a striptease, with greater fluidity. They bought wine by the case, and beef by the side, ate steaks from a half-cow they stored in the large basement freezer, entertained frequently, giving dinner parties for their circle of friends, and usually had a houseguest staying in the top-floor apartment of a brownstone they owned and occupied in a quiet street on Cobble Hill.

This brownstone townhouse had been their greatest and most uneasy extravagance. The thought of putting up so much money in advance, of actually buying land, went against everything in their backgrounds. Did they really want to leave the heart of Manhattan and live in faraway Brooklyn? But the street was so lovely, with its flower boxes, gingko trees, and old-fashioned lampposts from the gaslight era, that they were willing to keep a tight budget, for years if necessary, to manage the mortgage payments and renovations. They agonized for a week (and would have taken longer if the agent hadn't made it clear there were other people interested), then said, Oh, why not?

What finally decided it was that there were enough bedrooms for Frank's two boys to stay over on visits, and also one for Cara, Eleanor's fourteen-year-old daughter from her first marriage. Cara was spending the summer at a riding camp but otherwise lived with them. Frank's two boys, Theo and Jared, lived with their mother, but Frank was very keen on having the boys regard the brownstone as their second home, one they might drop in on whenever they needed relief from their mother. The couple fantasized not only long visits from their children when they were grown, but also a steady flow of the children's friends, and their own contemporaries, a mixture of elders and young people, a benevolent richness and confusion of houseguests and family, to prevent that dryness of parasitic overintimacy that it was all too easy for married couples to fall into, as they knew well from their first-marriage experiences.

Frank was forty-eight; Eleanor, thirty-nine. Frank was on the short side. He had at one time wished he were taller. But he had a leonine profile, and shoulders befitting a longshoreman. He could be spotted in any crowd by that massive, powerful head that angled eagerly above the folds of his turtleneck sweaters. He had a fondness for lamb's wool turtlenecks inside dark blue blazers. His thick, healthy black hair, streaked with gray hanks, was longer than most men's his age, and it implied his continuing support for the anti-war movement, grass, sex, and rock and roll. He used to wear gold chains or amulets around his neck. But then it got out of hand: some of the younger people who worked with him at the recording studio began bringing him chains and necklaces as gifts, and he tried to palm them off on Eleanor as love gifts, but she wouldn't have any of it. Eleanor had her own austere taste in jewelry. She preferred a simple gold strand around her neck, which she never took off, not even while making love.

Eleanor's beauty had an efficient quality about it. She was full-figured yet trim. She filled out her clothes nicely. She had pinchable high cheeks that photographed well. When Frank had first known her—when she had been married to that crazy jazz musician Randy —she'd been a good ten pounds thinner and intimidatingly beautiful. People then were stunned when they met Eleanor. She had something wild about her; her hair was cut short as a boy's, years before everyone was doing that, and she rode a motorcycle to work. Frank had been attracted to Eleanor, like everyone else, but also a little scared of her. Then he heard some years later that she had been in a motorcycle accident. By this time Frank was separated from his first wife, Estelle. He wanted to send Eleanor a get-well telegram, but felt dishonest about it, knowing that his real motive was not so much commiseration as seduction. Frank kept hoping that Fate would arrange an accidental meeting between them. Fate refused to cooperate. Finally he got up the nerve to call her and ask if she would like to meet some night for a drink. She would. It was their first encounter in years, and Eleanor looked very different. First of all, her auburn hair was long. But there was something else. She had put on a little weight, and it suited her. Still, that wasn't it. Something else. She told him she had broken her nose in the motorcycle crash. That was it! He liked her face even better this way, it had more character. In less than six months they were married. They were both old enough to know what they wanted. Eleanor no longer wanted to be wild, it seemed. She had developed a crisp, cheerful, matter-of-fact voice. She dressed during the week for the office, stylishly, and on weekends grabbed anything at hand. Even in her frumpy weekend loungewear Frank saw her as sexy. But now it was the restrained sexiness of maturity, not that frisky, coltish wildness of the old bohemian days. Whenever she spoke about that period, she never said, "When I was married to someone else" or "When I was living the jazz life"; it was always, "When I had my hair cut short."

It was Saturday morning.

Each liked moments of having the bed all to him- or herself, so they took turns getting up first. This Saturday in July, Eleanor had been the first to take a shower. She heard someone in the kitchen. It must be Golo.

Golo was a Polish journalist in his forties, very handsome, amiable, who stayed at their house whenever he was passing through New York. Like many foreign correspondents, he had acquired the knack of being a perfect houseguest. He knew when to tell stories and when to keep quiet, when to be amusing, when to disappear for the day, and how to help out a little in the kitchen and make a bed with hospital corners.

He was valuable to Frank and Eleanor as a link with many of their friends scattered around the world, since he was always traveling and coming back with progress reports about people they knew in common. Besides, he had that Slavic touch of melancholy which is irresistible to established married couples, and makes them want to turn over an extra set of keys at a moment's notice.

"What are you doing, Golo?"

"I'm just . . . making coffee. I was looking for the—the . . ." His hands pantomimed the basket of the espresso maker.

"I'll get it."

"No, no."

"Sit down, Golo. It's no trouble," said Eleanor.

He obligingly sat down and glanced at the *Times* front page.

"Anything new in the world?"

"There is this story of North American Industries bribing a sheik in Saudi Arabia to get contract for some jets." Golo spoke English slowly, additively, like pushing abacus beads one alongside the other. "I am supposed to call my news service to find out if I am going to Washington Monday. I may do story about a guy down in Washington who works for Department of Labor, a typical bureaucratic functionary. But this particular guy is rumored to have contacts with CIA and he is thought to be the one who placed CIA money in different organizations for purposes of spying. My magazine wants me to do a profile of him. But I'm afraid he's a very dull guy." He laughed, and Eleanor laughed, too, turning away from the coffeepot to listen more attentively to Golo. "Or else he's a very hostile guy. I call him and try to reach him on the phone for days. Then yesterday the phone rings and I hear a voice saying, 'Hello, this is Mr. Clemmons's secretary. Mr. Clemmons is coming to the phone.' Then nothing. For two minutes. Silence. Then: 'Hello? Hello?'" Golo imitated a gruff Texas accent. "'Why you keep calling here? What you want?'—'Ah, Mr. Clemmons, I am calling from *Der Spiegel* News Agency,' I say in my most legitimate, conservative voice, and I am thinking if he could see me over the phone with my beard and jeans he would freak out. 'I was wondering if we could talk . . .' 'Whaddaya wanna talk about? I didn't murder anyone.' Just like that. I couldn't believe my ears. He sounds so much like a gangster. 'I didn't murder anyone.' I'm thinking, This guy has big guilty conscience. 'I didn't say you murder anyone, Mr. Clemmons, of course not, I am just a journalist who is interested in story about Department of Labor and I am wondering if we could have a chat.' So now he is getting accustomed to the idea and suddenly he becomes very friendly, almost too friendly. I have this picture in my head of a big angry guy with photographs of football players on the wall. You know that type of American that is proud of his dog?"

Eleanor laughed. "Yes. So what do you think you'll do?"

Golo scratched his armpit with one arm, like a monkey, and with the other he rubbed his hairy stomach under a blue cotton boating shirt. Then he lifted his eyebrows ironically, to her amusement.

They drank their coffee in silence. Eleanor looked through the newspaper.

"This is good coffee," said Golo.

"Want some more?"

"No thanks. I am going out. I am going into the city today. My plans are to visit the Bronx Zoo where they have the gorillas."

"What gorillas?" said Eleanor, already starting to smile.

"You don't know about gorillas? Everybody in New York I see is talking about these gorillas. The mother had a baby in captivity, which is very rare. And she takes care of the baby in full view of everybody. Astonishing. I went once already to see them. The old man, the papa, has his head in the mother's lap, and he is letting her pick his hair for lice, while the other hand he has stretched out begging people for food. He is getting it both ways!" said Golo enthusiastically, his eyes suddenly big as a child's.

Eleanor shook her head. It always surprised her when that enthusiasm whooshed out of Golo, who usually looked tired and hungover—and the curious things he chose to get excited about. Now it was gorillas.

"It could lead to a good story. I have to convince my editor, who is not big gorilla lover. Anyway, ciao, I will see you later, maybe around six or eight?" Golo stood in the doorway and waved, opening and closing his hand, like a sad mechanical gorilla.

"Get out of here!" Eleanor said, and went into the downstairs bathroom to shower.

"Golo's so funny."

"What's he doing?" asked Frank, leaning on his elbow in bed.

"He's going to the zoo to see the gorillas. He thinks he can get a story out of them."

Frank stretched his arms and legs under the peach satin quilt; he felt deliciously rested.

Eleanor was scratching a stain spot off her white terrycloth robe. With her hair falling in plaits, wet and freshly washed, she sat at the edge of the bed as if waiting for him to notice her.

Frank, whose mind had begun to work ahead on the weekend's activities, suddenly realized a comment was in order.

"You smell nice."

"You sound surprised."

"No, of course not, you always smell nice. —What do you say we go to that concert version of *Jubilee* tonight? The one that Barry's in?"

"Who is it by? I forget."

"Cole Porter." He was trying to sound casual, to mask feeling slightly guilty about his habit of needing to ensure a schedule of entertainments for the evening before he could throw himself into the day. He worried that Eleanor might take it as a sign of his lack of love: if they loved each other totally, they could while away the hours in each other's company without having to plan for outside entertainment.

"I'd like to go," Eleanor said. She roughed up his tufted hair. "You look wild this morning. Like some sort of wolf man."

"Awoooo!" He grabbed her around the middle and flung her onto the bed, though he had no intention of doing anything further. Actually, he had wanted to get *out* of bed, so it puzzled him why he had dragged Eleanor back onto the covers and was kissing her eyelids. Maybe he sensed from the way she had entered the room, just before, that she'd wanted to be made love to. It was hard to tell at this stage in their marriage where her appetites left off and his began. He peeled back her robe. He rubbed her smooth stomach, and she turned her whole body sideways and thrust against his with an urgency that disconcerted him, until he realized that she had merely wanted to press against his leg. That pressure reassured her and seemed to contain her nakedness in the open air, and she closed her eyes again, every so often flexing the muscles of her groin against her leg in tiny contractions. He was getting excited in spite of himself. He had wanted to dress, start the day—if he stayed in bed too long he would get a headache, and anyway, he wanted to talk to her about having guests over this weekend. He stared down at his uncoiling penis. Perhaps he was reading too much into her signals. She may have merely been making herself comfortable against his leg, and he was the one pushing for something to happen. She would go with whatever developed, sleep or sex, whereas he seemed to be the one who was always looking for closure, a release to this arousal. Perhaps it was true what they said about women, that their sexuality was more diffuse. Well, in any case, it always seemed to end this way, with his sliding into her.

He had entered her not quite hard; then he felt that peculiar secretion of hers, like an acid bath, gripping him gently, which always excited him. Bullish or tired, his body responded to hers; it had nothing to do with the will, it was a tropism, as sunflowers turn toward the window. She had that knack of seeming both sleepy and aroused, so that whatever he did would be acceptable. And so what he did was become a satyr. At the root of love was lust, thought Frank, no matter what moralists said about empathy. Lust was that place you kept coming back to. It was the rediscovery of tangy bones, and skin with a particular lemony smell, and muscle tone that was good to eat—cannibalism, that greedy wanting to eat the other person, the way you could sometimes get rabidly hungry for roast chicken.

He was in love with Eleanor's sex. And yet he knew that there was nothing extraordinary about her vagina in terms of its shape or the texture of pubic hair. He was a grown man, he had never felt that a woman's sexual organ had to have such-and-such configuration, narrowness or tightness of fit, or feel like cashmere mittens. Well, why then this infatuation? In some uncanny way he felt his penis belonged there. It was his nesting place, his cove; it made him think of Sailors' Snug Harbor on Staten Island, where he had once done sound for a concert when it was still a retirement home for mariners, and afterward he had walked its grounds, noting the lawns, the infirmary, the bungalows with white peeling paint, feeling the rightness of dying there, with the ocean so close by.

The phone rang as they were sitting around the breakfast table at noon. Eleanor was now in a loose-fitting cotton housedress, Frank had on a pair of brown Bermuda shorts and an old Hawaiian shirt. Eleanor answered it. "It's Theo. He wants to ask you something. —Sounds like a pot deal," she whispered.

"Hi, Theo. What's up?" Frank's voice instantly took on the grainier, pressured tone of an older man talking to his son.

"I wanted to know if maybe Heidi and me could come over later and you could try that business we were talking about."

"Sure. How much is it?"

"Hundred-eighty," Theo mumbled.

"Sounds reasonable. When were you thinking of stopping by?"

"Heidi has to pick up some art supplies first, so about three-thirty?"

"Three-thirty's perfect. We were just getting up," Frank said with a half-abashed, half-bragging laugh, as if to say, You know how it is, we've been in the sack all this time.

They hung up a minute later. His older son was not one for long phone calls.

"Theo's coming over at three-thirty."

"I gathered that," said Eleanor.

"I had an idea for tomorrow night," said Frank. Just then the phone rang again. "I'll tell you in a minute. —Oh, hi, E.G. What's up. . . . No, I'm awake. We got up awhile ago."

Eleanor began clearing dishes, rinsing and stacking them in the dishwasher. It took almost as long this way as when she used to wash them by hand, but Frank liked gadgets, and supposedly it killed germs better. Having set the dishwasher to "on," she stalked out of the kitchen with a watering can in her hand. Frank had the feeling he had offended her, but how? Meanwhile, E.G. was talking a blue streak. Eleanor came back, made an open-palmed gesture to indicate that this was taking forever, and Frank hurried to get off the phone. "Okay, you don't want to come into Brooklyn. So where shall we meet? —E.G. wants to go to Rudolfo's, you know, the place with the singing waiters."

Eleanor shook her head sternly. This time she was adamant.

Frank, interpreting on his end, said, "Rudolfo's is out of the question. The food is mediocre, and last time the waiter insulted Eleanor. She won't go back there."

"That's not why!" Eleanor made a fist. "Oooo—!"

"Wait a second, I'm hearing it from both ends." Frank chuckled. "Hey, why don't we try that French place, the Midi, right around Lincoln Center? . . . It's *not* too expensive, and besides, I don't want an argument. Just meet us at the Midi at seven-thirty if you know what's good for you." He tried to make it into a joke. "Oh, I almost forgot. What are you doing tomorrow night? I was thinking of having a few people over for Richard Preston, who's in town with that Sherlock Holmes show." Frank covered the mouthpiece and said to Eleanor, "If it's okay with you. That was the plan I was trying to tell you about."

Eleanor smiled mysteriously.

"What? Okay, bye, we'll talk about it at the Midi. Okay. So long." Frank hung up. He turned to Eleanor: "I get an earache listening to E.G. on the phone."

"What did he have to say for himself?"

"He started telling me about some date he had last night. He's been miserable such a long time, I mean ever since Ginny left him. How long is this going to go on?"

"It takes a good long while to get over a divorce."

"But I have the feeling he's starting to revel in this funk. And poor Ginny put up with plenty of his moping around before she kicked him out. He can be so charming when he wants to be, but he's beginning to get on my nerves."

I shouldn't wonder, thought Eleanor. You invite him everywhere you go.

"Anyway, is it all right?" Frank asked. "To have this thing for Richard tomorrow?"

"It's fine, honey," she said, patting his cheek patronizingly.

"You don't mind cooking? We could tell people to come after dinner, if you'd rather not cook."

"Don't be ridiculous, that always sounds so stingy. I can make something simple. I'll just look through my cookbooks."

"Are you sure it's all right? Tell me now, honestly, before I start calling everyone."

"If I said it's all right, then it is totally ALL RIGHT," she said, facing him with her hands on her hips. "Now don't ask me again. I'm perfectly capable of speaking up."

"Give me a kiss."

She put her arms around him and obeyed without a fuss. They kissed long and well. "You're a sex object, a boy toy," Eleanor said. "That's all you are to me."

Frank sat down happily and opened his black leather address book, bulging with address slips and held together with rubber bands. He ripped a sheet of paper from a nearby notepad and began making a list. "Golo. Theo and Heidi. Maybe E.G. will have a date. . . . David and Fabiano. Richard and his girl. Who else?"

"Oh, let's ask Mary if she can come," Eleanor pleaded. "I would love to see her again. I feel so bad about all that."

"Will you call her, or do you want me to make the call?"

"I'll call her."

"So, counting Mary, that's nine or ten, plus you and me."

"That's plenty. When are we going shopping for this?"

"We could do it tomorrow."

"I'd rather do it today and get it over with," said Eleanor. "Save tomorrow for cooking."

"We can go right now."

"But it's almost two o'clock and Theo will be over here in a bit."

"We can get the business with Theo over by four-thirty and send him packing," said Frank.

"Crudely put. Maybe it will be gentler if instead of kicking them out we ask them to come along."

"Are you kidding? Knowing Theo, I doubt it. I would think

a young couple had better things to do than tag along with us to the supermarket. I'll start making calls."

"I'll go look through my cookbooks."

Theo was sandy-haired, thin, with delicate features, taller but less robust than his father. At nineteen, he still had a boy's body. His facial expression looked sweet, sensitive, and a bit washed-out. Everyone who knew Frank and Eleanor took a liking to him, or pretended to. Some said in private that there wasn't much "there" there.

His fiancée, Heidi, had brown braids and wore patched jeans and gave the impression of a country girl who would be more comfortable in the woods with a backpack than in Theo's parents' townhouse. Under her loose Guatemalan peasant shirt, which was dingy from wear, she had large bones and rounded shoulders, which gave her an apologetic stoop. They were greeted warmly at the door by Frank and Eleanor and ushered instantly up the narrow brownstone steps to the second-floor parlor, a sunny room with a fireplace and burnished parquet floors, masses of plants, a white sectional couch (a Josef Hoffmann reproduction), and a wall of sound equipment.

"Can I get you something to drink?" asked Eleanor. "Some iced tea?"

"No thanks," said Heidi, gesturing to the bottled water she held in her hand, which she appeared to carry everywhere with her.

"How about you, Theo? Iced tea? Iced coffee, a beer?"

"A beer would do fine," said Theo. He grinned like a German shepherd that had been petted. Eleanor's vibrato voice saying his name always had that effect on him.

As soon as she had left the room, Theo took from his pocket a little silver box, whose lid had been painted like a Persian miniature, and placed it on the table.

"Did you just get back?" asked Frank.

"We got back a couple days ago."

"Vermont must be really beautiful this time of year." Frank turned to Heidi, in an effort to draw her into the conversation.

She smiled. "It was," Theo answered for her. Heidi rarely spoke much around his father or stepmother, though she had no trouble talking in other circumstances.

"I'll bet you're sorry to have to come back to the city."

"No." Theo started rolling a joint. "I liked it up there, but I like it here as well."

"Well, that's the best, of course. If you can feel comfortable wherever you are. . . . Where did you get this grass?"

"We brought it down from Vermont," said Theo.

"How would you rate it?"

"It's mild. It gets you there after a while. It's not the most powerful shit that will knock you flat on your ass in two tokes."

"Jesus, I wish we had some of that Michoacán you brought us."

"Ah, who can get Michoacán of that grade anymore?" Theo

said with a gentle smile, suddenly looking very old—older than his father, in fact.

"That was sheer heaven, that Michoacán. And this? You don't sound very enthusiastic."

"It's not that. I just don't want to push it on you."

Eleanor came back at that moment. "A born salesman." Frank laughed, looking up at her.

"Like father, like son," she went with the joke.

Theo shrugged at this characterization. It meant nothing to him if they bought it or not. He wasn't even making much of a profit.

"Want some, Ellie?" asked Frank.

Eleanor shook her head. Heidi took a drag and passed it on to Theo. Theo passed it to Eleanor, and this time she took a toke. Eleanor became rather sphinxlike around dope, Frank reflected. She would never ask for any, but would take it if it was handed to her in a certain oblique way, without eye contact. And yet she must have been around tons of it when she was married to that jazz musician.

"You stayed on a farm?" asked Frank.

"We stayed with friends of Heidi. They own a house."

"So this is home-grown, eh?"

"Home-grown," Theo nodded as his lungs filled with smoke.

Heidi picked up a puzzle with movable squares and began playing with it. Eleanor rocked back and forth in her chair, one long dark strand of auburn hair dangling over her eyes as she watched the two men, father and son, talking.

"I'm starting to have my doubts about this weed," said Frank. "Are you getting high? I have some body sensation, but not much of a buzz."

"It takes awhile. You can get very high from a few joints."

"But you have to work at it. What about you, Eleanor? Am I the only one that's not getting high?"

"No. I'd say it's rather mild."

"Mild! It's Wheatena!"

Everyone laughed. Then they laughed again; then they couldn't stop laughing; they shook their heads and tears rolled from their eyes.

"Must be doing something," observed Heidi.

"Oh, Heidi, you snake you!" Frank complimented her. Theo eyed her proudly for having made his father laugh.

"What do you think? Should I buy some?" Frank asked Eleanor.

"Do what you want."

"I don't know. How much is it?"

"One-eighty an ounce."

"How about if I bought two ounces for three-twenty?"

"Trying to finagle his own son!" Eleanor said.

"Well, he's not going to get many customers for this crap," said Frank, enjoying the role of the tough businessman driving a bargain. "What do you say? Two for three-twenty."

Theo sat silent, inscrutable.

"Three-thirty, that's my last offer."

"Three-forty-five," said Theo.

"Okay, okay," Frank said with a laugh. He went to his petty-cash box. "I only have fifties. Do you have the proper change?" He handed the bills to Theo.

"I do."

"Oh hell, forget the change. And do you need any extra money for expenses? Another fifty?"

"No thanks, Dad."

"Hit me while I've got it." Frank had seen that he had three fifty-dollar bills left in the box and was tempted simply to drop one in Theo's pocket. "You sure you couldn't use an extra fifty?"

"Positive."

Heidi let out a small grunt, looking uncomfortable.

"What?" Theo whispered to her. "You think I should take it?" She shrugged her shoulders.

"Take it, take it," said Frank, strolling over and placing the money in his son's hands. Theo took it unresistingly. Frank sat down heavily in an easy chair, pulling up his trousers at the knees, which caused his socks and a bit of his hairy legs to show.

"What about those Mets?" he asked his son.

Eleanor took Heidi into the bedroom and unfolded a new quilt on the mattress. She knew the way to get the girl talking: it was to show her things. The quilt had a half-moon in one box, a cradle in another, a bird in a third, a king's crown in a fourth, and so on. The connections between objects were not obvious, but one could sense a narrative behind them, like fragments of a lost tarot deck. It was all meticulous appliqué work; Heidi would appreciate it because she sewed quilts herself. Heidi also made her own jewelry, which she sold at street fairs and craft fairs—all in all, she was quite clever at making things, thought Eleanor. As Heidi commented on different sections of the quilt, sitting on the bed, Eleanor leaned over the girl and suddenly felt great affection for her.

Eleanor had two opinions about Heidi. On the one hand she could scarcely believe that this plain-looking, not very intelligent girl had ensnared a creature as rare as Theo. Maybe because the boy had grown up without a father around much, he needed a partner who was solid and practical. And Heidi seemed tenacious enough to hold on to Theo at all costs. On the other hand, she wondered if she was being unfair to Heidi. It wasn't easy for a young girl to grow up in this society, and Heidi was stronger-willed than most. She could even be fun to be with.

Eleanor was quite capable of judging a person in the harshest terms and the next moment taking that person aside with sympathetic engagement. Whether that made her saintly or hypocritical, it certainly helped in dealing with someone like Heidi.

In the parlor, the two men had finished their talk about baseball and were ready for more serious catching up.

"What you been up to, Pop?"

"Oh, I've been working on the new sound studio in Red Hook. Completely tearing the place apart and redoing it. It's going to be fantastic. State of the art. The only thing of its kind on the Eastern Seaboard."

"Sounds good," said Theo.

"And you? What are you up to?"

"Nothing as interesting as what you are, that's for sure. I've been . . . I haven't been feeling that well lately, to be honest. Been depressed. Can't seem to get it going."

"Going at what?"

"That's just it—at anything. Can't seem to get started."

Frank winced. "Do you have an idea what you'd like to start doing?"

"I have some vague ideas, wisps of ideas, too embryonic to talk about right now. My mind is like noodle pudding. I get a slight urge to do something . . . then it goes away."

"Of all these vague notions, tell me which one holds the most appeal."

"I'd like to transfer to another college and study oceanography. But, see . . . not even oceanography exactly. I'd like to combine music and oceanography and sound design, make music resemble waves."

"Like Handel's *Water Musick*."

Theo smiled ironically. "No, Dad, not Handel's *Water Musick*. I'd like to put microphones in the waves. And when the currents stirred up, the sound would seem to break in waves and you could produce music that also broke in waves." As he spoke, his right hand made a circular motion. "I don't know. It's probably a dumb idea. But I bet you could develop special microphones to record musicians playing underwater."

"No, it's not a dumb idea. There was this avant-garde composer I worked with once, Max Neuhaus, he made this piece in a swimming pool, and you could only hear the music if you stuck your head underwater. When you kicked your arms and legs, the thrashing sent off a sonic wave, a kind of humming underwater. The problem is, the more you got into the piece, the more your chances were of drowning."

"A victim of art appreciation," said Theo.

"Exactly. Like the siren calls in the *Odyssey*."

"And what about microphones to record underwater?"

"Oh, that's been done. You know that great record of dolphin songs?"

"I know. But dolphins are too operatic. I'm thinking something even softer. Like early Pink Floyd. I've been listening to old Pink Floyd albums and it's like holding a seashell to your ear. I curl up with my ear to the speaker for hours. It's about the only thing I can listen to these days without getting depressed."

"Why are you depressed?" asked Frank.

"It's a long story. I don't feel like talking about it. The whole subject bores me. There's nothing worse than having to listen to someone go on and on about his nothing life."

Frank took a drag of the marijuana, then realized he probably shouldn't have. He needed to clear his head for this conversation.

"You're not 'someone,' you're my son. So I'm interested."

"I've been boring the pants off of Heidi. Ask her. I've been murder on the poor girl. I sleep twelve hours a day, I find it hard to concentrate enough even to read a book. I'm really spacey."

"I was the same way. Don't worry about it. I was once in a depression that lasted for a year."

"Really? I can't believe you were ever depressed," said Theo.

"Why do you say that?" asked Frank, sensing an insult.

"You seem so—upbeat, so gung-ho, so productive all the time."

"Don't make 'productive' sound like a dirty word. But yeah, I've had depressions. I was flat on my ass for like fifteen months—more than a year. I never told you about it?"

"No. I would have remembered if you had."

Frank reconsidered. "You're right, I don't think I've ever gone into that period with you. The reason is that it involves my relationship with your mother."

"So?"

"So I don't want you to feel you're in the middle of one of our fights. Though I'm sure Estelle has told you about it dozens of times."

"No."

"She hasn't? That's odd."

"She doesn't bad-mouth you as much as you think. Look, if it's too painful to talk about, maybe you should just skip it," offered Theo.

"No, it's not too painful. It's not too painful to me, I was only questioning whether it would be too painful to you." Frank decided to make a present of his youthful depression to his son; he was feeling expansive. "It was shortly after I had graduated from college. I had my electrical engineering degree, and I thought I was hot stuff. But nobody else did. The job market was tight. I just couldn't get an engineering job. Here I was fresh out of college, with a young wife, I was expecting to support both of us. Naturally,

Estelle got a job right off. She had no qualms about a wife going to work. I didn't appreciate it then, but she was a lot more mature than I was. She understood that you had to go out and make a living, even if meant being a waitress or pushing dress racks in the street. I was more the spoiled prince. I worked in a travel agency for a while, but I hated it. Estelle was making good money as a buyer in a department store, and she encouraged me to quit my job and—and work on my microphones. I fancied myself an inventor back then. I had notions of running a custom-made sound-equipment factory out of our apartment. Of course it never happened. The brutal fact, which I'm still ashamed to admit, was that she supported me. Naturally she felt bitter when I left her ten years later, just when my career was starting to take off. She felt that she had carried me up to a point where she might be able to relax, and then sayonara, I'd 'used' her. But that's another story. During that whole fifteen months, she would go off to work every morning. I would wake up late and make myself coffee. Read the paper. I would bring out my engineering books and my spare parts and pretend that I was going to get started. Then I would feel sleepy. I would try to clear my brain. All that year I had the sense that my mind was never maximally crisp. It was woozy. I would wait for my brain to clear, and meanwhile, I wouldn't lift a finger. To wash a dish, sweep the floor. I *couldn't* lift a finger. But I took walks. That was my only exercise. I took long walks around the Bronx. In those days the Bronx was . . . most of it was composed of family neighborhoods, apartment buildings with two wings and a courtyard, baby carriages in front, pretty safe, pretty boring. I liked the fact that it was boring. Stimulation of any kind would have upset me. A sudden loud noise freaked me out. I didn't even go to movies. Just these long walks to the river and back, and then up to our two-room apartment, where I'd close the door, get back into bed. Not sleep. I would huddle—literally, like a fetus—under the covers for hours, until just before Estelle came home. What was the problem? I didn't know. Oh, I knew something was wrong, but that whole way we have now of looking at it and saying, 'Aha! This man must be bipolar or have manic-depressive syndrome'— that overview only came later. I had deluded myself into thinking that I was working on intricate formulations, solving equations in my brain, mulling things over, whereas in fact, as I've learned since then, it's impossible to solve creative problems when you're at such a low stage of energy. First you have to turn on the motor. Start with the practical. You need to work on something concrete, something small, and only in that way do you find the answers. But as I say, I had been deluding myself. And Estelle had enabled my delusions. This may sound very unfair, but I blame her partly, for giving me so much sympathy and support that it stifled me. She had such confidence in me, to begin with, as if she could see what I was going to become, and I couldn't, I didn't have nearly as much faith in myself. There were times when she backed me up, when it would have been more beneficial to have pitched into me. But in those days there was a different sentiment about marriage. We thought that two people who got married were supposed to stay close and fight the world together. We both felt we were up against a hostile world, so we prepared ourselves for a long struggle. You must understand that we were both political, and in left-wing circles 'struggle' has always been a positive term. There was the struggle against imperialism, against capitalism, against racism. . . . Eventually the struggle came inside our marriage. The only problem with that model was, it doesn't always fit love relationships. Love shouldn't have to be a struggle. At least that's what I think now. Love is a gift of grace, from up there. It's something that either happens or it doesn't. It's not just a product of labor and sweat. It's not always earned, either. Oh sure, there's labor involved, but best of all is when love comes for no reason at all, like a mystery. You can't *will* the damn thing into being is what I'm saying. With Estelle, I was always trying to browbeat myself into love. I tried to blackmail myself into loving her. Part of the deal was that we were supposed to be completely honest with each other. Honesty was supposedly the cure for all of a relationship's problems. It would sting, but it would heal, like iodine. So we'd analyze how we'd hurt the other's feelings, what we had done wrong, we would tell each other our hidden resentments, and always we would promise to do better next time. But what did all these so-called honesties matter when put up against the one big dishonesty I was always frightened she would find out, by looking into my eyes—that I didn't love her? I didn't find her that physically attractive. Honesty, yes, right, be honest at all costs, that was the goal—and not a bad goal. Up to a point. But you see, we were just babes in the woods!" Frank said, shaking his head and smiling at the memory. "We were kids, infants, and we couldn't see that all our closeness and intimacy was a kind of brother–sister act, orphans in the storm, huddled against the cold. We were scared, so we kept regular tabs on each other's mind and called it 'honesty.' Since then I've learned that a man and a woman living together have to give each other space. Ellie and I do. And yet, there are some aspects of that first marriage that I miss. Your mother's sympathy and warmth, for instance, spoiled me. She had—has—a rare capacity for giving emotionally. Ellie, on the other hand, never pretends to be that deeply sympathetic with my point of view. Eleanor makes herself separate. Eleanor is very private. When it comes right down to it, I've traded symbiosis for mystery. But to get back to the other thing—of course there were problems with your mother's sympathy. It became burdensome, I wanted to run and hide from it, especially since I felt I hadn't deserved it. How could she have such bad judgment as to believe in me? Couldn't she see I was a loser? The irony is that now I would be better able to accept her sympathy, it wouldn't feel like such a burden to me, because I'm much more successful, but now she probably wouldn't give it, for that very same reason . . ." He stopped, no longer sure where he was going with this.

"How did you finally get out of the depression?" Theo asked.

"We had you. And we had Jared. That made a difference. I knew I had to get out there and support a family. But I think that deep down I was still depressed. I went to work, I did my job, I built a reputation, we had friends, other couples with small children. We took vacations. But everything had a gray tonality, no real pleasure in it. Now that I look back, I have to admit that I was probably depressed for something like ten years!"

"Then how did you manage to get out of it?"

"By leaving your mother. That was the only way," Frank said grimly.

Theo nodded. But he was suddenly burning inside: he wished he could tell his father how bitterly he felt toward him for abandoning them. He knew his father had left because his mother had gotten fat. More than that, Estelle was an hysteric, a loud, unhappy, vulgar woman. It was bad enough having to grow up with her. That was what Theo really reproached his father for—that he left him to grow up in the company of that neurotic woman without any counterbalancing parental presence. Still, it had all happened such a long time ago, Theo thought, what was the point of holding on to resentments?

"How is your mother, by the way?" Frank asked.

"She's the same. She complains about everything. We fight. She picks on Jared, now that I've moved out."

"I gathered as much."

"Estelle's a loon—you know that. Her latest kick is to try to make me and Jared feel guilty for not spending enough time at the house. She threatens to call in the police if she can't locate us for a few hours."

"Try to be compassionate. Your mother had to raise you two by herself, it's not an easy thing."

Theo blushed. "I am compassionate with her," he said. "Too much so, maybe."

It was painful for Frank to hear this. He had been moved by his recitation of the past, and had almost wanted a compliment at the end, like "You told that so well" or "That was a good story." Instead, his son hit him with a wad of guilt. He searched for some way to bring the conversation back to its earlier level. "In any case, I don't think you should worry about not having a clear idea yet of your life's work. You're only nineteen. It took me a long time to figure these things out. And there are lethargies and depressions that can be extremely productive. Out of the vacuum comes direction. It's an Eastern idea."

"Yes, but you said earlier that the only way to find your true work is to start working. That you have to get yourself up to a certain energy level first. I don't think I'm anywhere near that level," said Theo, grinning self-deprecatingly.

"It takes time."

"I'm not sure I'll ever be at that level. I'm one of the laziest people I know. What worries me . . ." He was trying to frame in words his nagging fear of being, at bottom, incurably mediocre, while at the same time afraid to expose that side of himself to his father. "Ah well," he concluded with a smile. Frank returned the smile, as if they had reached some wry father–son understanding about the world's peculiar ways.

In fact, Theo had taken encouragement from the story of his father's depression. He had appreciated the generous gesture behind it, and he wanted to hold on to the strength that flowed from his father, identifying himself with him. At the same time, they weren't the same at all, Theo thought. Just sitting on the sectional couch, his father seemed so dynamic, a bundle of coiled power; where did this man get his fresh stores of energy? Even the terms his father had chosen to describe his depression were more forceful than the ones he would have used. His father's depression had been the Napoleonic sulk of a talented young man waiting to be called to power, whereas his, Theo fretted, stemmed from a wanness that might afflict him for a lifetime.

Heidi and Eleanor returned, and everyone went downstairs to the front entrance.

"Would you like to come shopping with us?" Frank asked tentatively.

"No, we've got to be somewhere for dinner," said Theo. "Thanks anyway." They opened the front door and were surprised to see the sky had turned dark gray. It would probably rain buckets. Frank went inside to get Theo an umbrella. As he looked around the little mud room near the backyard that held mops, the washing machine, shovels, and other equipment, he felt his chest tighten. Momentarily dizzy, he held on to the top of the washing machine.

Was he dizzy from the grass? Frank wondered, trying to calm himself. But he hadn't even gotten that high. He hated to think that it might be the beginning of a heart attack. He had never had one and didn't know what they were like. No, this was only a sudden waning of energy, like the lights in a house dimming momentarily.

It was curious, but he did sometimes get tired after a visit from Theo. The boy's passivity taxed his own overcompensating resources to the bursting point.

Frank handed the umbrella to Theo, and the young couple went off.

He decided as he walked upstairs to the parlor that he would not make a big deal about the chest pain to Eleanor. Maybe he would not even mention it. He hated to complain about his aches and pains and have her think he was becoming an old man.

Frank sat down on the couch, rubbing his cheek.

"Is something the matter? You look green."

"Ellie, I'm feeling kind of tired. I think I'll rest up for tonight."

"You should. You want to lie down in bed for a while? Can I get you anything?"

"No, I'm not sick, just tired. Maybe I'll read a little."

"Would you like an extra pillow?"

"No, I'm all right. Do you think you can . . . handle the shopping by yourself?"

"Don't worry. If it's too much I'll have them deliver."

"Thanks," Frank said weakly.

"You get some rest. Maybe we should call off tonight with E.G."

"No, no, no. I want to go to that. I just ran out of steam for a minute."

Eleanor kissed him on the forehead. "I'll be back in an hour."

He picked up the new issue of *Time Out New York*. He was alone in the house. The downstairs living room reflected the overcast sky outside; it had lost its sun. He yawned and his mouth had a corrugated cardboard taste that was oddly reassuring. He kept falling asleep on the sofa and opening his eyes to the darkening room, enjoying an afternoon summer nap, which was, all things considered, one of his favorite indulgences in life, one he too rarely permitted himself.

Frank woke around six o'clock and remembered to phone E.G., to tell him it would be better if they went to the concert first and had dinner afterward, since they were running a little late.

"Roast duck à l'orange, frog's legs provençale, Chateaubriand, escalope de veau . . ." Frank read aloud in a properly nasal twang. "I think I'll have the roast duck."

"I wouldn't order that, dear, if you're very hungry. It'll probably take an hour."

"What can they prepare faster?"

"The frog's legs, the quiche, almost anything."

"I'm going to have fried oysters and a steak," said E.G., putting down his heavy wooden menu. He had made up his mind first, which gave him the leisure, while the other two were deciding, to glance around at the copper pots hanging above the Midi bar, the blackboard behind the stairs with a menu of specials, and the young waitress with short skirt, black leotards, and a ponytail dashing here and there with several steins of brown beer in her hands.

"Hmm . . . I'll have the sweetbreads," said Frank.

"Sounds like a good idea," said Eleanor. "I know what I want—eggplant."

"You always have that."

"You know I like to eat the same things over and over. I'm very dull."

"Hardly," said E.G., before he could check himself. He was more than a little in love with his old friend's wife, and he tried to restrain himself from staring at her too openly, partly to conceal his true feelings and partly because he found Eleanor so beautiful it pained him to look at her.

The waitress came by and took their orders. As she walked away, E.G. muttered, "Pretty good legs."

"A little muscular, no?" said Frank.

"Probably a dancer."

"I can see it's going to be one of *those* nights," Eleanor said with a sigh.

"Now, now." Frank patted her thigh.

"Why don't you just ask her for her telephone number? She'll probably be flattered," Eleanor said good-naturedly.

E.G. shook his head. "If she's a dancer she's nonverbal, we'd never get along. Besides, she wouldn't find interesting what I had to offer—my brand of hot air."

"What happened to the other one?" asked Frank.

"Which other one?"

"Wilt Chamberlain."

"Oh, the six-foot-two one," said E.G.; his laugh came out like a snort. He was a stocky man in his mid-forties, medium height, whose sensual love of food coexisted with an otherwise skinny, ascetic soul. His eloquent brown eyes stared out from behind thick glasses. "Sharon. Yes, well, she went back to her old boyfriend, who beat her, but after all he *was* from Charleston, as she was, and in the end only one Charlestonian can understand another. Besides, his mother was dying and she felt he needed her more at that moment than I did."

"Understandable," said Frank.

"I have the sense she was using me from the start to make him jealous. She kept telling me how terrific I was, how sensitive, intelligent, gentle—all the wrong words. She even told me I was a fantastic lover, how no man had ever made her feel so much. Obviously she was laying it on too thick."

"It sounds like she really did like you," said Eleanor. "She may have been confused and afraid of you."

"Yeah, right," he snorted.

"You make it sound as though she purposely set out to deceive you," said Eleanor.

"No, I don't feel that way. She's a nice girl. It's just that—well, I think it's fair to say she misled me a little. The whole thing was doomed from the start. I knew it; I was much older than her. Why did I bother? To get laid, I suppose. No, that's not it entirely. I needed to have something more fulfilling in my life than my job. Some dream of romantic love. I'm beginning to think that lasting love is just a cultural delusion. —What did Kafka call it? 'A loneliness for two.' Once the fantasy wears off, the romance is kaput."

"But that's not always true," said Frank.

"Let me finish. I'll let you talk in a while. Do you know Karen Horney's theory of the monogamous ideal?"

"No, but I have the feeling you're about to explain it to me."

"Her essential idea is that romance is based initially on oedipal attractions or familial projections that disguise themselves.

After the first fantasy period of attraction is over, the couple starts to be confronted with the challenges of daily intimacy, and there begins to be activated intense feelings of an incestuous nature. The man feels that the woman is turning into his mother or his sister, the woman starts identifying the man with her father or brother. This in turn generates strong taboo feelings, a sexual turning off, and a sense of dread that enters the married life of couples after the second year. So it isn't boredom with the 'same old piece' that dries up the sexuality of married couples, it's the panicky fear of closeness."

E.G. signaled that he was finished.

"That's very interesting. I like that," Eleanor said.

"It's bullshit," said Frank.

"Wait a minute, let her speak. —This man has a passion for interrupting," E.G. said. "I don't see how you can live with him."

"You're the one who's been talking for half an hour!" objected Frank hotly.

"Why are you getting so upset?"

"Because you're talking bullshit! —All right, Ellie, why do you like his theory so much?"

"I hadn't thought of that connection before. It's interesting to put the emphasis on closeness rather than boredom. I hadn't heard it before, that's all," Eleanor said calmly. "Don't get so defensive."

"So do you think of me as your father?"

"Sure—Pops," she said playfully.

"Which is as it should be," said E.G.

"But we're already past our second year," said Frank. "Do you feel the 'dread' that E.G. was talking about?"

Eleanor paused, teasing, to build up dramatic suspense. "No."

"Do you feel we're happy together?"

"Yes. As happy as I reasonably can be."

"You're right, I'm a little defensive," Frank confessed. "I like to think that we're a fairly happy couple, and that we'll stay that way."

"But I think you *are* a happy couple," E.G. insisted. "I should have prefaced my remarks with 'Always excepting you and Eleanor.' You two might be the Last Loving Couple. They should put you in the Smithsonian or give you to the NIH labs, where everyone can study your urine and blood pressure."

"What I meant to say, in all seriousness, E.G., and at the risk of sounding a little ponderous and pompous here," Frank rejoined, leaning forward, "is that I think your theory is wrong. There are plenty of married couples besides us who love each other."

"Name one."

Frank reflected. "I think Ellie's parents love each other. They're both in their late seventies, and they seem to be very giving and loyal and tender with each other. Wouldn't you say so, Ellie?"

"I would say they've had their rough moments. But overall, yes, they do love each other."

"I think if you traveled around America you'd find lots of married couples like that. But I have another reason for rejecting your theory. It's not functional, it's not useful to me. Why would

I want to believe that love is impossible? It's a working hypothesis that defeats you from the start, like saying you're going to fail no matter what. Even if it *were* true, I would pretend that it wasn't. You understand what I'm saying?"

"I understand. I don't agree, but I understand," said E.G.

"Why don't you agree?" demanded Frank. Eleanor was watching them closely, like a tennis match.

"I would want to know if something is feasible or not before I ventured into it," E.G. explained. "That goes for building a bridge, falling in love, anything. And it's intellectually dishonest to say you believe in something even when you know, or suspect, that it's not true, just for practicality's sake. Look, maybe this doubt about love applies more to me than to anyone else. I didn't mean to engage in an abstract debate about the possibility of love. For *myself*, I will say that I've been feeling skeptical, that the cards are stacked against me from the beginning. And I'm getting very discouraged."

"Sorry to hear that," Frank said gently.

"*Very* discouraged. It's this kind of thing: in many cases a woman is trained to want a man she can look up to, whose intellectual or physical or even economic superiority she can admire. Despite all our current rhetoric about 'equality in relationships,' most intelligent, creative women I meet—which is the only kind I'm interested in, and maybe that's my problem—are quite uncomfortable unless they have a man they can look up to. They don't really want Equal, they want Better. Then they start going out with a man like that and they resent him. They feel like zero in comparison, like he's sucked up all the oxygen and they're suffocating. They want what he has—so they start to compete. The competition poisons the relationship. Someone has to win, but in either case, both lose."

Frank listened sympathetically. Now he saw part of where E.G.'s hurt resided.

"The kind of intelligent women I could have a relationship with," E.G. continued, "at this point in history, seem to be very angry, closed. They don't want relationships, they want to be 'free.' If you listen to single men and women talking these days, you would get the impression that it's the women who want one-night stands. They want detached sexuality. It's the men who want intimacy, who want babies."

"I think that's a gross overstatement," said Frank. "I know plenty of women who want commitment, and their men are shying away from it. I know what you're talking about, it is a phenomenon, but I just don't believe it's as widespread as all that. Maybe you're coming across a type."

"You don't know because you're not in the marketplace anymore and because Eleanor is very different from other women," said E.G. "Your wife is exceptional."

"I'm not that different," Eleanor replied, determined to nip E.G.'s embarrassing and too-revealing tribute in the bud.

"What do you mean?"

"Just what I said. I'm not as different from other women, or even from your stereotype of women, as you apparently think."

"And besides," said Frank, not entirely sure what Eleanor
meant, "what is the good of blaming women, or blaming one's
historical epoch? Again, it's not a useful attitude."

"Not everything can be useful," E.G. muttered.

"That's true," bridged Eleanor. "Do you want any dessert?"

"I'll have some. They probably have good pecan pie here."

Frank motioned the waitress over to their table. "One pecan
pie, with whipped cream on mine. How about you, E.G.?"

"On second thought, I'll have the peach cobbler."

"One peach cobbler," the waitress said. She looked at Eleanor,
who made a hand gesture indicating: I'll pass.

"Coffees . . . ? Three coffees," said Frank. "And the check,
please, when you get a chance."

"Are you coming tomorrow night for dinner?" Eleanor asked
E.G, with a dazzlingly persuasive smile.

"What is it about? You were telling me something over
the phone."

"We're having a few people over. Richard Preston's in town,
doing a play, so I thought I'd throw a dinner for him," Frank said.

"Who's coming, besides Preston?" asked E.G. testily.

"Nice people. My son, his girlfriend, Golo—"

"I could do without him."

"You don't like Golo?" asked Eleanor with wide eyes.
"How odd!"

"Nothing odd about it."

"Oh, and Mary's coming," she remembered.

"She said she would try to make it," said Frank.

"I hope she does," said E.G.

"You old lecher! She's half your age!" Frank ribbed him.

"No, it's nothing like that. I just happen to think Mary's a fine girl."

"Mary is a lovely girl," Eleanor said firmly, "and a fine person."

"How's she doing now?"

"She's working at a friend's jewelry store."

"No, I mean, *how's* she doing?"

"Oh, I think she's going through a rough period," Eleanor said, and settled into a faraway look. The subject seemed painful to her.

"What was it that finally caused her to leave your house, if you don't mind my asking?"

"She was getting room and board and a small salary to take care of Cara," Frank answered for Eleanor. "And when Cara went off to riding camp for the summer, there was no point in her staying."

"But is that the only reason?" prodded E.G.

"No, I think there were some deeper issues than that, Frank," Eleanor said. "I think she felt she was getting under everyone's feet. Especially my big feet. It was never clearly settled what her duties were, and so sometimes she felt I intruded into her domain and sometimes I felt the same way. We had left it a little too vague. She resented, I guess, being something of a servant."

"But we never treated her like a *servant*, I don't think," interjected Frank.

"Still, I'm reporting it the way she saw it, honey," Eleanor said, and turned again to E.G. "Mary is a very feeling person.

She takes things deeply. And about some of our disagreements I must say I think she was perfectly right. And also, I think she wanted to feel more independent, not under our scrutiny all the time. We were like surrogate parents for her. She seems much happier working in her friend's store. She's quite talented, our Mary is. She'd studied to be a harpist, you know, and had gotten to the point where she was auditioning for orchestras. But I don't think she knows what she wants to do. Whether she wants to go back to Paris or to live here, or stay with friends in the country, or go back to graduate school. It's very hard for young people these days to find a clear path. She's a bit confused. It's too bad. I miss her terribly."

Mary was early, around 5:30. She saw Eleanor toiling in the kitchen and, without thinking, gave her a hand. The two worked alongside, picking up easily where they had left off. Eleanor could have run a tony restaurant if she'd wanted; Mary had always been attracted to the logical, unfussy way she organized the ingredients and the work flow. A look at the oven, a space cleared to make salad, water boiled for rice, the sauces readied, all done with a minimum of hysteria. By now the "simple meal" had grown into a banquet. Each guest was to have his own Cornish hen (nine of these little birds were basting inside the oven); there were hors d'oeuvres to nibble, and a zucchini vegetable terrine, wild rice with cranberries and scallions, hot biscuits and sun-dried-tomato bread, Greek olives, chutneys, mesclun salad, an array of cheeses, blueberry pie, and Kahlua mousse for dessert.

Mary went to work on the salad. She was tall, well proportioned, and might have, if so inclined, carried herself off as a beauty, but she chose to camouflage her good looks in baggy pants and an oversized T-shirt. Her scowling black eyes and sharp chin cleft made one think of a Roman statue of an empress, with harsh bulging eye sockets from whose mouth one expected water to gush. By temperament, she was less ferocious than her physical appearance suggested. She found a bag of tomatoes and started slicing them.

"How's your mother?" asked Eleanor.

"She's fine."

"And your sister?"

"She's great. She's going to Paris tomorrow," said Mary.

"I bet you wish you could go with her."

"I wish I could go to Paris, period. Not with her. I traveled with Annie once through Greece, and it was a killer." Mary looked about for some dill. "Who's coming to this thing?"

"E.G., of course."

"Oh goodie. I love E.G., he's such a funny man."

"Careful. I think he has a crush on you."

"Nah, not E.G.," Mary said cheerfully. "We straightened that out long ago. We kiss each other when we meet and we joke about someday having a 'thing,' but that's just theater. He's like an old friend."

"Do you think underneath he's gay?"

"Wow! You surprise me when you say that. I don't know. What makes you think so?"

"I *don't* think so," said Eleanor, backtracking. "It was just a speculation. He does have a lot of bitterness toward women. Last night we had dinner with him, and you should have seen Frank and E.G. Now that's an interesting pair."

"In what way?"

"Oh, they love each other, that's all. They get jealous and upset. Sometimes I think Frank takes his relationships with men more seriously than his ones with women. Pours deeper feelings into them."

"That's often the case."

"It is. And I'm glad he has intense feelings for his male friends."

"E.G. might be the same way," said Mary.

"Yes, but I get the feeling E.G. could go homosexual one day. Whereas Frank I doubt ever could."

"Frank's not the least bit gay."

"Frank could use a little gay in him," said Eleanor.

"This salad dressing could use a little more oomph. Where's the balsamic vinegar?"

"Behind you."

They chopped away in silence.

"Who else is coming?"

"Theo and Heidi. Richard Preston, if he can make it. He's got to do a TV interview to promote his show. Oh, and Golo! Have you met Golo? He's staying in your room now."

"No. Maybe I have," Mary said, reconsidering.

"Well, you would remember him if you did. You don't have to do that, dear. I can finish up."

"No trouble. What's he like, this Golo?"

"Golo? He's very sweet. Curious about everything, and funny. Knows a lot of the same people we know. And on top of that, he's handsome as anything, in a Rudolf Nureyev, Eastern European sort of way."

"I *would* like to meet him," said Mary.

"You will. But he does have a girlfriend in Berlin."

"Serious?"

"They're living together. I don't know if it's serious. Would you call that serious? Hard to tell these days. He's from Poland and travels a lot, he's a freelance journalist."

"That settles it. I don't get along with newspapermen."

"But Golo's hardly your typical newspaperman."

Frank came into the kitchen. "I heard voices. I know Eleanor talks to herself, though it's usually not in two different voices. So good to see you, Mary." He threw his arms around her and rocked her back and forth. "You look wonderful."

"You like my T-shirt?" she said dubiously.

"It's smashing."

Just then the doorbell rang. Frank advanced to answer it with a gregarious, anticipatory grin. He opened the door and said radiantly, "Why it's Richard! Richard and—"

"Sara. We just popped by for a bit. Gotta do a show, you know."

"Come in, come in! Ellie, it's Richard and Sara!" he shouted toward the kitchen with wonderment, as if it were a miraculous surprise instead of the perfectly logical outcome of phoning people and asking them over.

"Richard!" said Eleanor. She gave him a hug and, more tenuously, embraced the newcomer. Richard's date had the whitest skin imaginable, with brown nail polish, brown lipstick, and a dark plum silk blouse and brown satin skirt and high leather boots that looked uncomfortably hot for the summer weather. She was so pale she seemed as if she might faint any moment.

"Sit down at the kitchen table," Eleanor directed, and introduced Sara to Mary. But there was no need to introduce Richard Preston, since he was an internationally renowned English actor, comic and monologuist, presently touring the country in a one-man show based on the writings of Sir Arthur Conan Doyle.

Every dinner party needs a star. Richard Preston was it, and he had already arrived, so the main anxiety of the evening was over.

"Can I get anyone something to drink?" asked Frank, rubbing his hands together.

"That's like asking a sick man if he wants to go to hospital," Richard said, perhaps quoting a line from an unknown play. "Of course I'll have a drink. Never turn one down."

"Gin and tonic, wine, sherry, cognac, beer . . ."

"Gin and tonic'll do fine."

"You're staying for dinner, aren't you?" said Eleanor.

"I've got to leave unfortunately around 8:30. Must ply my trade. Must practice the art," he said self-mockingly. "But we should have time to grab a bite. What do you think, Sara?"

"You can go. *I'm* staying for dinner," Sara replied pertly, with a British accent. Everyone laughed. Eleanor thought the girl could use a meal: she looked emaciated.

The doorbell rang again.

"Well, Theo! And Heidi! So glad you could make it," said Frank. "We're all still in the kitchen, the meal hasn't started yet."

"Hi, Theo," said Mary.

"Hullo, Mary," Theo said, giving her a bashful smile.

Eleanor put her arms around the couple. "Well, you haven't changed a bit since—yesterday. And Richard Preston I think you know."

"'lo, Richard."

"Here, have a seat," said the actor, offering his own.

"Don't get up. We need more chairs, Frank."

"Maybe we should all just move to the living room. This kitchen is getting a little crowded."

"No, not yet, they'll just have to come back in ten minutes to pick up their food."

Theo left with his father to fetch a few chairs.

"You look very spry tonight, Missus," said Richard.

"Well, I've had a few. That's what comes of cooking with wine. —Oh, there's that darn doorbell again."

"I'll get it," said Heidi.

"No, I'll answer it," said Eleanor, speeding to the front passage.

Behind the door, leaning against the wall with bunches of fruit (bananas, grapes, strawberries) in a brown bag, was E.G.

"How thoughtful," she said, eyeing the bag's contents.

"Am I fashionably late, I hope?"

"No, just in time. We were just getting ready to start the meal."
Eleanor stopped to listen to the sound of a key turning in the lock.

"Everyone arrives at the same moment. Go inside, this must be Golo," she said, giving E.G. a push, remembering his antipathy for their houseguest.

E.G. wandered into the kitchen, holding aloft a bunch of grapes, like the severed head of John the Baptist. "Hello, everyone. Where shall I put this?"

"I'll take it," said Frank.

There was a long silence. "Hey, E.G., don't you say hello to me anymore?" called Mary from the corner.

"I said, 'Hello, everyone.' That automatically included you. And besides, I couldn't squeeze through all these chairs."

"Sorry," said Richard, politely pulling his chair out of the way. Mary stretched out her arms, and she and E.G. mimicked the movie ending of lovers rushing into each other's embrace.

"Missed you!" she said.

"At last, at last!" he cried.

All eyes were on this extended embrace, which looked fairly realistic.

"Well—excuse me!" Eleanor mock-gasped as though she had come upon an indiscreet love scene. "Get a room! People, this is a dear friend of ours, Golo." She completed the introductions all around, for the last time.

"Am I late? I'm sorry," Golo said with a sheepish smile.

Much ooh-and-aahing and applause met the nine stuffed hens as they arrived from the oven, in two black-and-white speckled oven pans. The kitchen table quickly filled with gravy boats and carving platters. The guests were asked to walk around the table and fill up their plates.

"Help yourself," said Eleanor, "it's all self-service here."

"We won't have enough room for everything," worried Mary.

"We'll make room. Take off the biscuits, nobody's eating them."

"Can I help?" asked Sara.

"You can help by filling your plate and eating, dear. Everyone, after you've gone around, take your plates into the living room and I'll be there in a minute. You'll find lots of wine, juice, iced tea in the living room. Mary, did you bring out the club soda?"

"There's so much!" said Sara.

"It's like Christmas feast," said Golo.

Sara turned to Golo. "That's a lovely jacket. I love that herringbone. Is it pure wool?" she asked, feeling a corner of the material.

"I think so. I got it in London. Do you know about clothes?"

"That's how I make my living," Sara said briskly. "I design for three London boutiques."

"Very nice," said Golo appreciatively.

"Heidi also makes clothes," said Eleanor.

"Do you?" Sara turned around to her, looking her outfit over quickly to see if there was anything she might compliment. There wasn't. "We should get together sometime and go shopping. I heard of a fabulous shop on the Lower East Side. They have floors and floors of fabric, notions, buttons, ribbons. You know it?"

"I used to go down there a lot," said Heidi. "But not in the last couple months."

"Oh? Why not?" asked Sara. "Has it gotten too expensive?"

"I just don't have the time." Heidi shrugged.

The first to enter the living room with full plates were Richard, Sara, Golo, and Frank. They took the sectional white couch around the low Noguchi table. Theo sat across the room, using his lap and the geometric-patterned rug for a table surface.

"Why don't you come closer, Theo?" said Frank.

"No, I like it here."

Mary plopped down unceremoniously next to Theo.

Heidi and E.G. had been lingering in the kitchen with Eleanor, but eventually she joined her other guests in the living room and the two kitchen stragglers had to as well.

"It's delicious, Ellie," said Richard. Everyone echoed his opinion.

"I'm glad," said Eleanor.

"That zucchini dish, and the salad—everything."

"Well, that's Mary. She made the salad. Take a bow, Mary."

"But especially the fowls. Super!" Richard pronounced with gusto. "What did you use for stuffing? It's the best stuffing ever."

"Oh, just some old herb stuffing. Cornbread, onions, celery, sausage, a few cut apples, a few odds and ends."

"It's terrific, Eleanor," said E.G. "You're an amazing cook."

"Can I bring in seconds for anyone?"

"I'm stuffed!"

Eleanor took orders for refills and started to leave. There was a lull as everyone finished their food.

"Oh, that's lovely, isn't it?" said Sara, wandering over to a framed drawing of a dragon on the wall.

"Come back here, Ellie. Sara is complimenting your dragon," said Frank.

"It is so lovely. And here's another one, a rhinoceros."

"That's by Dürer," said Frank.

"Oh," said Sara, embarrassed. "Well, I like the one by your wife just as much."

"What's all this?" said Eleanor, returning from the kitchen.

"Tell her, Sara," said Frank.

"I was just saying that I think your dragon drawing is lovely, and that I like it just as much as the rhinoceros."

"Well, thank you. I'm not sure I would agree," Eleanor replied. "I did this as a favor for a book designer. It was a medieval bestiary, and it came out pretty well, I thought."

"Yes, I'll say!"

"You are a woman of many talents," Richard said roundly.

"I can do a few other things besides cook—much to E.G.'s surprise, I'm sure."

"I know you can," E.G. said gloomily.

"Just teasing you," said Eleanor, dimpling.

"How about you, Golo? Refill?" offered Frank, pointing to his glass.

"Of course."

"Are you still thinking of going out of town?" he said, pouring more wine for Golo.

"Yes, I have to go to Washington, D.C., this week to interview CIA guy. And then to Cha—Chappaquiddick, because the magazine wants me to do anniversary story on the bridge where Senator Edward Kennedy's secretary drowns, Mary Jo K—K . . ."

"Kopechne."

"Kopechne. Sounds like good Polish name. I will interview old-timers from the town, Chappaquiddick. I think it could be an interesting assignment."

"Better than the gorillas," Eleanor said.

"Better than gorillas." Golo laughed.

"What gorillas are these?" asked Richard, already a little drunk. Golo told the story of the gorilla family in the Bronx Zoo, acting out the parts with zest, and everyone had a good laugh.

"Well, I think I'll set up the projector," said Frank. It was his habit to conclude dinner parties with a screening of one of his 16mm prints. He insisted that DVDs on television would never replace the magic of celluloid projected as a beam of light.

"What are we seeing?"

"The Marx Brothers in *Animal Crackers*."

"I was afraid of that. I detest the Marx Brothers," said E.G.

"Oh, you old grump, the Marx Brothers are hysterical," Eleanor said.

"They're anarchic," said Frank.

"I'm not an anarchist," said E.G., crossing his arms over his chest.

"But their language is very clever, wouldn't you agree?" Richard said.

"The Marx Brothers are just not cinematic," E.G. explained his position. "Their camerawork is dull, they're vaudeville actors transported to the screen, and if I wanted to see theater I would go to the theater. Language don't make motion pictures."

"I don't know, he has a point," said Golo. "I enjoy Marx Brothers pictures very much as a boy, but they're not so interesting as cinema."

E.G. ignored Golo's support. "What else do you have around besides *Animal Crackers*, Frank?"

"I have *The Gold Rush, The Magnificent Ambersons, Gold Diggers of 1933, The Maltese Falcon, Flying Down to Rio* with Fred Astaire. I have lots of stuff. *The Grapes of Wrath* . . . I have a beautiful print of *City Lights*."

"Let's take a vote. I vote for *City Lights*," said E.G. cheerfully.

"I don't know if it's fair for me to vote, since I can't stay for the whole show," said Richard. "Still, I say *The Magnificent Ambersons*."

"It's a great movie," said Frank, "but it's such a heavy film. I'm not really in the mood, it's too hot for *The Magnificent Ambersons*. And we've eaten too much."

"I vote for *City Lights*," reiterated E.G.

"Now, you see, Chaplin's never been a favorite of mine," said Richard. "'The Little Fellow.'"

"What don't you like about Charlie Chaplin, Richard? I'm curious to hear," said Eleanor, leaning forward in a flatteringly receptive way.

"Chaplin always strikes me as sloshing in self-pity and sentimentality. He is the quintessential *little man*, and like most men of short stature he derives a spurious sympathy by mixing up his sense of inadequacy with identification with the underdog. But he has no true use for the underdog, because it's self-aggrandizement he's after. You can see it from the way Chaplin the filmmaker directs Chaplin the actor—or I should say, Chaplin the actor directs Chaplin the director. You know what W. C. Fields says about him: 'Best damn little ballet dancer I ever seen.' I'll take Buster over him any day."

"That's an old argument. The Brits are always touting Buster over Chaplin," said E.G.

"You don't think Buster Keaton is the screen's greatest comic?" demanded Richard.

"I'll bow to no man in my appreciation of Keaton," replied E.G. "All I'm saying is that Chaplin is great, too. You're confusing sentiment with self-pity. Chaplin has sentiment, and that's the lifeblood of art."

"Well, I haven't seen his films in a number of years," said Richard conciliatorily. "You may be right."

"Let's vote, shall we? Secret ballot." Frank tore a brown paper bag into pieces and handed them out.

"Oh, we must have something better than that!" said Eleanor.

"This'll do fine. List your first choice first, and your next two choices after that. Whichever gets the most first-place votes wins."

"What are the choices again?"

"*Animal Crackers, The Gold Rush, City Lights, Flying Down to Rio, The Magnificent Ambersons, Gold Diggers, The Grapes of Wrath* . . . and *The Maltese Falcon*. I have others, but those are probably the best. An usher will be around to pick up your ballots shortly."

"How did you get all these films? I think that's fantastic!" said Sara.

"It wasn't difficult. Some are in the public domain. The others —you can buy duped prints from small dealers once you get on their lists. I always had this fantasy as a boy of having my own movie theater at home. So about ten years ago it occurred to me that I could still realize my boyhood fantasy. I went out and bought a good old Bell & Howell projector and some bootleg 16mm prints, and now I have my movie theater. See?"

"That reminds me of something Freud once said," E.G. offered. "He said that if a man stumbles on his vocation later in life, he can be content, more or less. But he can only be truly happy if he realizes a fantasy that was hatched in childhood."

"And you think it's true?" said Golo.

"God, I hope not!" Richard injected with a roar, and everyone laughed with him.

While they were tabulating the votes, Mary turned to Theo, who had said no more than five words all evening.

"What's up with you these days, Theo? You're so quiet tonight."

"I'm on vacation from college. Maybe permanent vacation."

"How come?"

"I'm thinking of dropping out," he said softly. "I don't want to talk too loud about it because it might upset Frank." Mary nodded and slid closer to him. "I was also thinking of transferring to another school. To study oceanography."

"I didn't know you were interested in oceanography."

"It came to me recently. I've always liked the water. And I figured it might be possible to combine a music major with oceanography," he said with a self-mocking shrug, though it was beginning to sound more real to him each time he told another person. "You played the harp, so you would understand. That's very ocean-sounding."

"But I quit because most of the orchestral music written for harp is garbage."

"Oh sure, I just meant the dynamics."

"The winner—da da!—is *City Lights*," proclaimed Frank.

"I've seen it," murmured Theo.

"Me too," said Mary.

"Want to smoke something?" he said in a whisper.

"Love to. Where shall we go?"

"Upstairs. My room. I'll go get Heidi."

Heidi was in the bathroom, so the two went upstairs by themselves.

Theo felt around for the light switch. There were more potted plants than last time near the windows, an overflow from the ones in the parlor. Theo sat on the bed and took out his silver box with the Persian-miniature lid and rolled.

"This is like old times. I used to get stoned in this house a lot," said Mary.

"You too, eh?"

"Sure. Many's the time I would put Cara to bed and come up here. These plants, they could look prit-ty strange, giving me the eye."

"Mmm."

"I miss this old house."

"Why'd you leave it?" asked Theo.

"You really want to know? You want the truth or the sanitized version?"

"The sanitized version. No, just kidding."

"It's a long story. Part of it is the lifestyle. I mean, look at all this." Mary waved her hand around. "I don't fit into all this. This isn't my life. Dinner parties, cases of expensive wine, scarfing till you're stuffed like a pig. So much waste! I lived here for a solid year and I couldn't believe the wastefulness. And then every time Frank gets a whim to buy a new gadget or car or something for the house, he has to have it. So self-indulgent. Oh, Frank may still feel he's a good guy politically and sympathetic with the poor, but the fact is, they live very luxuriously. Their politics are miles apart from their daily reality, and their lifestyle is—what can I say?"

"Nouveau riche," said Theo.

"Right!"

"I feel pretty much the same, I'm put off by all this. Though to be honest, I like central air conditioning and certain comforts."

"Don't get me wrong. A beautiful American bathroom—all the fixtures, sparkling clean—the height of civilization. Who wants to take a crap in an outhouse? That's not what I mean. It's the hypocrisy that bothers me. You want to know what precipitated my leaving? I got into an argument with Frank about politics and religion, and I couldn't stand the piggy positions he was taking. And after that he expected *me* to apologize. Did he really think I was going to alter my views just to continue living under his roof? Those wounds never healed. I still have a lot of esteem and respect for Frank. —What am I saying? I love Frank. Your father is one of the kindest, most wonderful people in the world, and I'm not shitting you now. Frank has helped me, practically saved my life, numerous times. But Frank has another side. He likes to get people to work for him for nothing, and to take all the credit for himself. When he did that CD recording of Victoriana, he needed someone to help with the producing. I did all the research for that recording and I wasn't on salary, mind you. I did it because he said he couldn't manage it alone. I busted my—pardon me—ass on that record. Do you think he would see to it that my name got on the credits? No way. All it says is: Produced by Frank Bauman."

"That's . . . cruddy."

"Of course it's cruddy. And it didn't only happen once, it happened several times. It pisses me off. And another thing that irritated me was that I was supposed to take care of Cara in exchange for room and board. But in addition to babysitting that thirteen-year-old brat—don't get me wrong, I love Cara. She's one of my best friends, I'm happy to say. But she does, let's face it, have some issues. She's very mixed up emotionally, as who wouldn't be, having grown up with two fathers and the whole bit. And she can be very whiny and theatrical and manipulative. But I'm good with her. I'm stern. What bothered me is that I would say no to her and then she'd go over to Frank or Eleanor and they would say yes, dearest, sure thing. Frank spoils her rotten. And she's none the happier for it, believe me. But all I'm saying"—Mary paused to take a long drag from the joint—"all I'm saying is that looking after Cara was a job in itself. On top of that, I was expected to help out in the studio with Frank and help Eleanor with the meals and cleaning the house. Although Eleanor never asked me to. I just couldn't stand to see her doing *everything*, working a full-time gig and dragging around the house like a maid and Frank never lifting a finger. I'm not talking feminism here, because I'm not sure I am a feminist. . . . you know? But in this particular case, it's only decency and common sense that if you see this woman being dragged down by a thousand chores, the thing to do is give her a hand. But will Frank? Noooo. Except very rarely, and that's when other people are around and he wants to create a good impression. You see what I mean?"

"I do see," said Theo, nodding sagely. He was floating away, into the avocado plants. He was very stoned. His head was weak with understanding all sides, Mary's, Eleanor's, Frank's, and the saddest of all understanding, that everyone has his point of view and there is no way of reconciling them all. At the same time, he was captivated by Mary's capacity to sustain, even when high, such a long, indignant speech with logical rhetorical connections. He could do little more than listen and be carried from one of her sentences to the next, hoping that she would continue talking for a great long while, or at least until his divided, fragmented attention had managed to focus on one strand.

There was a competition in his brain, like two bands in a Charles Ives composition marching down the same street from different directions. Alongside taking in Mary's entangled outpouring, an idea had begun to come to him, but it was so complex he was not sure he would ever be able to grasp it. He kept almost reaching it, but his pot-clouded thoughts yanked it away. He wanted her to see at least a part of the idea. It involved an odd pain, and his depression, and a swelling around his heart; it involved her in some hopeless way that made him ache with the inevitability of her misunderstanding him. He imagined himself a Pagliacci clown singing an aria to a woman whose back is turned to him and who would certainly laugh at him if she knew a word of the foreign language he was singing in, or thinking in. But what if the idea was really quite simple? If he were to take the square root of all this fog and attempt to call it something—not even pin a label on it, but turn it into an action, a gesture, which symbolized in shorthand the whole ratiocination process. . . . There was that comfort about gestures, that they could stand for complete idea systems. That was their vitality—their primitive reassurance. Theo suddenly knew the idea was that he wanted to kiss Mary.

"It's almost out," she said, looking disappointedly at the joint.

"Want to smoke another?" he asked, feeling very cunning.

"Thanks. See, they like to pretend in this household that both partners have their careers and respect each other's work. But take another look. Have you noticed how, in a crisis, it's always Frank's career that counts? Eleanor drops whatever she's doing and comes to his aid. Deep down he considers her career as something frivolous, something to humor her about. But as soon as things get hectic around here, the household revolves around him. It's *his* schedule, his needs, his meal times, not her meal times. So what does she do? She comes to me and complains. I told her, 'Listen, woman, it's not gonna do you any good to complain to *me*. Tell him!'"

"Of course," said Theo. After all, what she said made perfect sense.

"But she won't. That's what's so screwy about Eleanor. I think she's afraid of Frank."

"Oh, I don't know," Theo objected mildly. She had a very sweet shape underneath that T-shirt, he thought. If you could get past that scowl—that gorgon's face of anger—if you could kiss the mouth and smooth away the bitterness, kiss that cleft in her chin, kiss the lips and make them blossom like plums, radishes, rose petals, nipples. . . .

"All right, you're right, she's not actually *afraid* of him. But she is afraid of hurting his fragile ego. Of upsetting that hairline balance that enables Frank to function at a very high level, under incredible pressures, in spite of being a fairly insecure man."

Why are you telling me this? Theo thought suddenly.

"And don't get me wrong," said Mary. "I think your father is a *prince*. I love Frank and always will. If he happens to be wrong in this particular situation, it's as much Eleanor's fault for letting him get away with it."

"Certainly." He must be out of his mind, the idea was crazy. Heidi could come into the room at any minute. He could just see Heidi inserting herself into the middle of this mad idea, like a dream where someone is watching you have sex. But he could no longer contain himself. "I have to kiss you," he said, getting up off the bed and standing over her chair.

"What?"

"I just have to kiss you." He kissed her on the forehead. Then, knowing this would never satisfy his urgent hunger, he kissed her full on the mouth. Mary let herself be kissed, and even let his tongue roll into her mouth, because she was enjoying it.

"You are something else," Mary said, laughing. She pulled her head away a few inches and examined him.

Now he wanted to lick her breast. How was he going to manage that? He could feel Heidi creeping up the staircase, any moment she would be standing in the doorway like a Velázquez maid of honor. He had to hurry. He wondered if he could get Mary's pants off, here on the couch. If not her pants, then her T-shirt.

"I have to kiss you again."

Mary laughed at this transparent stratagem. "Not again!"

"Yes. One more time." He pressed his mouth against hers. Then he eased his hand under her T-shirt, till he could touch her breast. He felt something like an electric buzz go through him.

"I think that's enough," Mary said.

Theo kissed her gently on the cheek.

"Boy, there's no stopping you once you get started."

"I want to make love."

"Uh . . . don't you think they'll start to get worried about us? We should really go downstairs."

"I guess so." He looked hurt.

"I think we should go downstairs."

"All right, okay. You don't have to keep saying it," Theo replied, offended.

"You're something else," Mary said, smiling.

"What's *that* supposed to mean?"

"It means I really like you."


They were watching the end of the second reel of *City Lights* when Theo crept into a space on the rug near the white couch where Heidi was sitting. He smiled up at her. Heidi had a numbed expression, but he thought she did not look very happy.

When the second reel ended, Eleanor brought out the coffee and dishes of pie and Kahlua mousse. Richard and Sara had already left. The party seemed much quieter without them. Watching a movie in the dark, after several glasses of wine and a heavy meal, had also had its internalizing effects.

Frank threaded the third reel while the others were having their dessert and coffee. It was an old manual-threading projector, and he would not have had it any other way. He liked standing by the Bell & Howell's side throughout the screening, in case a spring popped or the film started unspooling on the floor. It gave him a marvelous feeling of capability, this active vigilance, like a sentry who guards the sleeping camp. He knew all the projector's quirks by now and kept a pair of pliers, a screwdriver, and a rudimentary splicing kit under the film stand, just in case.

"I'm about ready," he said.

E.G. hit the lights.

Now Charlie was in the boxing ring. All hoped he would win. He was ducking, rubber-bouncing off the ropes, his opponent was getting tired. Then, inexplicably, Charlie lost. A groan went up from the living-room viewers. That wasn't supposed to happen in a comedy, he was supposed to win. Then Charlie bumped into the drunken millionaire again. Now the robbers came. Now the lights in the millionaire's mansion went out; it was like a stage set with everyone knocking into furniture. Expressionistic lighting. Now Charlie is falsely accused of being the robber and is arrested. He escapes. Gets the money to the blind girl. Finally he's arrested for good this time. Dissolve. The girl can see; she has a job in a florist's. She keeps looking at every man who comes into the store, trying to find her anonymous benefactor. She assumes it's someone handsome and rich. She has a pretty dress on, her mother has a job, the whole family is thriving. Charlie comes by, fresh out of jail, his bum's outfit shows he's down and out. The neighborhood kids tease him. He chases them away. The girl stops her work in the florist shop to watch this silly tramp. Long shot: Charlie on the street corner, stumbling, the girl behind him, watching from the florist window, laughing. He turns around. She runs out of the store to hand him a flower. He doesn't want it, he sees it's her, starts backing away. His pride is hurt. She insists. Chaplin once said that the long shot was good for comedy, the close-up for tragedy. He goes in for a close-up; it's the most heartbreaking close-up in film history. She recognizes him. "It's you!" Charlie smiles.

Frank turned on the lights quickly, to see who was crying.

Eleanor's eyes were red and tearing, E.G. was snorting into a Kleenex, Mary stirred woodenly in her chair, Golo was solemn-faced, Heidi looked expressionless, Theo, subdued.

"Not a dry eye in the house," Frank declared with satisfaction. "That ending always gets 'em."

"Christ," said E.G. "Whew!"

"Would anyone like more coffee?" asked Eleanor.

"No thanks. We gotta get going," said Theo.

"Glad you could all make it," said Eleanor, walking her guests to the door, "especially on such short notice."

"Dinner was delicious," said Mary.

"Hey, don't be a stranger. Come back sooner next time," Eleanor scolded her.

"Good seeing you again, Mary," said E.G. "Sorry I didn't get more of a chance to talk to you."

"Sure glad to see you, E.G."

"Nice to see you, Mary," said Theo, with a meaningful edge, but not too meaningful.

"Same here. Take care, Theo. Bye, Heidi. Bye, Frank. Bye, Ellie."

Everyone said goodbye to each other and went home, leaving behind Frank, Eleanor, and Golo.

When the guests had all gone and Golo had settled upstairs, Frank was in a bad humor. Eleanor guessed it at once. First she left him a wide berth, going about her business, cleaning up. Frank sat at the coffee table with the tin of grass in front of him, wondering whether to roll a joint. Maybe it would relax him. It was the old story, jealousy. Eleanor had kept leaning over E.G. and touching him casually. She must have known he had a mad crush on her.

What nonsense! thought Frank. How do I let myself get into these states? It bothered him that he could still feel jealous of his wife and yet nothing that he did would ever make Eleanor jealous in the slightest. He decided to roll a joint, hoping that it would have an aphrodisiac effect on him. He wanted to make love with Ellie before going to sleep; it would chase away the bad feeling and help him to sleep better.

"Do you want some?" he asked, as Eleanor entered the living room.

She lowered her eyes, nodded yes. He handed her the joint.

"It's just that I don't like seeing you flirt with E.G. so much," Frank began *in medias res*, as though she had been a party to his prior musing.

"Was I?"

"You could barely keep your hands off him. Every time I looked over, you were accentuating a point by putting your hand on his arm or his knee."

"I guess he does bring out that touchy side in me," said Eleanor. "The more he withdraws or sulks, the more I get the urge to reassure him with a pat."

"You can't leave well enough alone."

"You think that's it?"

"Yes. Your belle-of-the-ball instinct," Frank said bitterly.

"But if you understand it so well, why does it bother you?"

"I guess I'd better get sulky, too, so that you can make a big fuss over me."

"But that's what's different about you. You're not pouty or sulky. I've had enough to do with men like E.G.—poor wounded weak guys who were full of hostility toward women. I may feel maternal affection for him but I *love you*." She looked him straight in the eye. He was trying to pull his glance away, because he knew she was right and soon he would have to relinquish his anger in the face of her reasonableness.

"But sometimes it bothers me that you're on such good terms with all these ex-lovers of yours," he said doggedly.

"I'm on good terms with them. Right. I did sleep with lots of men before I met you. I slept with them partly because they didn't mean anything to me. What happened with them in bed and what happens with you are like two different acts. You've no reason to be jealous of my past. Because there's nothing back there that can threaten you or compete with you."

"I do love you to pieces, you know that."

"And I love you, more than I believed it was possible to love someone. I ask myself what it is—the difference between what happened in the past and with you. I think it's that your body trusts my body."

"It surely does. We fit together beautifully." Frank got up from the couch, with the intention of leading Eleanor into the bedroom.

"But listen. I just want to say this," she stopped him. "Not every man is like you—confident enough in himself to love a woman. In the past, sometimes I would sleep with a man and get the feeling that underneath he loathed me. Loathed my body, because it was a woman's body." She shivered.

"Don't even think about it," said Frank.

He squashed the burning joint in the ashtray. He was not high, but he had that dark tenderness toward her that would do just as well.

It was a hot night, even with the air conditioning, and they couldn't sleep. After their lovemaking, Eleanor moved far over to her side of the bed. Frank felt something restless in her. He woke just as she was putting on her nightgown.

"Where are you going?"

"I want to clear away some more of the dishes. Kitchen's a mess. I don't like leaving it that way."

Frank kicked the satin quilt off his legs. "I'll keep you company. I can't sleep either."

"No, don't!" Eleanor admonished, adding more gently, "it will only be a half-hour's work. You keep sleeping."

"But I can't sleep. Maybe it's the wine. I'll go with you. I won't get in your way."

He put on his plaid robe and followed his wife into the kitchen. "Can I help?"

She shook her head. "You know I have very particular ways of doing things in the kitchen." He heated up some old coffee, sat at the kitchen table. She stacked the dessert plates in the dishwashing machine. He had the feeling she was unhappy. He tried to guess what it was. It happened often after a party that she would get the blues: a letdown after all that preparation and cooking.

"Is something bothering you?"

"I'm a little sad." Eleanor pushed a strand of hair from her eyes.

"Why?"

"Oh . . . different things. The discussion we had before upset me."

"Which discussion? You mean the one about you and E.G.?"

She nodded. "It bothers me that you can still be so jealous."

"I'm sorry. I shouldn't be, it's ridiculous."

"It means you don't trust me. Even after all this time, you think I'm going to betray you. You have this funny idea about women that we're all two-faced and we're going to two-time you."

"Do I? I was unaware I felt that way," said Frank with skeptical amusement. "But go on."

"Yes, you do, Frank. You're always thinking that women will reject you. I don't understand where it fits into your character, which is otherwise so secure. What its *function* is for you."

"I hate to sound ungallant, but I was the one who walked out on Estelle."

"That's my point! You're so sure women will reject you in the end that you don't allow yourself to take your relationships with them all that seriously. And so you push them away first. You beat them to the punch. Your walking out on Estelle doesn't disprove my point, it confirms it."

"I don't understand. Where is all this coming from?"

"I've been thinking a lot about this side of you lately. It's just something that bothers me," she murmured hesitantly. "I'm probably making too big a deal of it."

"Sit down. I don't like having to converse when I'm looking up at you. It's bad for my neck."

She walked over to the kitchen table and sat down reluctantly.

"*What* bothers you?"

"Maybe I'm just being paranoid."

"Maybe. But what is this paranoia about?"

Eleanor sighed. "Let's not get into it."

"No, I want to get into it. We haven't had a talk like this in a good long while."

"You're right," she said, suddenly energized. "Okay: I'm suspicious of you."

"What are you suspicious of?"

"I'm suspicious of you for a lot of reasons."

"Name one."

"Well, I've named one. I'm suspicious of you because you're so jealous. And because you're possessive of me in an old-fashioned way that I don't exactly find flattering. I'm suspicious that you'll use your mistrust of me as a protective shield against loving me. I'm suspicious because you don't trust me."

"Do you trust me?"

"No."

"Well, then!" Frank said, smiling. "What can you expect? But go on. Why don't you trust me?" He felt himself infinitely trustworthy at the moment, and therefore on firm ground.

"I think you don't always tell the truth. You're very secretive. You don't say what's going on inside you. You leave it for me to guess."

"I thought I was generally pretty explicit."

"About some things you are. Others you keep to yourself. You can be very indirect," said Eleanor. "For instance, you never tell me when you stop loving me. You just clam up. I think you're terrified of my finding out, so you try to finesse it with gracious small talk."

"Wait a second. You don't really expect me to make a speech every time my love for you dips five percent below the norm."

"That's not what I meant. But I would rather you said it, those times that you felt you were temporarily out of love for me, instead of leaving me to guess."

"Okay. In future I will. Anything else you don't trust about me?" Frank said, more brusquely than he had wanted to, feeling rather like a boss entertaining a workers' grievance committee.

"I think you lie. I think you lie about other women. If you were having an affair, you wouldn't tell me," she said.

"Now who's being jealous?"

"But it's true, isn't it? You wouldn't tell me."

"I might."

"I don't believe you," said Eleanor.

"This is terrific. I'm being accused of lying about a hypothetical situation which has never even occurred!"

"Have you made love to anyone else since we've been married?"

"No. Not once."

If it was reassurances of his fidelity she wanted, he knew he was in a strong position to give them. "Not only haven't I slept with any other women, I haven't really been tempted. I've got my work at the studio to think about, I don't have time to fool around. I'm not the kind of guy who can divide himself between two or three women at the same time. I'm too 'unidirectional,' to use a microphone term. You're the direction I've chosen for life. Besides, my sexual desires are satisfied by you, so I don't need to look elsewhere."

He had expected that bold affirmation to clear the air. But there was still an occluding feeling suffocating him. It was not exactly a repeat of the chest pain and dizziness earlier in the day; this sensation was more vague, intuitive. He looked at Eleanor's face, as at one of those trick drawings where one suddenly sees another shape leering behind the first, a skull instead of a lady at her vanity table, and had a chilling reverse perception. He thought that she was trying to get him to ask her the question she had asked, and that this reciprocity, and not any mistrust of him, had been the motive behind her whole line of questioning.

Frank's heart pounded. He felt a kind of stage fright. "And what about you?" he said, barely able to speak the words. "Have you made love to anyone since we got married?"

Eleanor was silent for a too-long moment. "I don't think I have to answer that."

"Well, you have answered it, then," he said grimly.

"No, I haven't! Just don't jump to conclusions, Frank. You have a way of putting words into people's mouths and then attacking them for what *you* said."

"All right, I won't assume anything."

"And I don't like that habit of yours. It's bullying."

"Okay, I won't put any words into your mouth."

He sat back, giving her more space. He looked at the hairs on his arm, scratched his nose, glanced at Eleanor, drank cold coffee from his cup. He felt like an actor stalling with bits of stage business, while the main actor was being gotten ready in the wings. Waiting like that, he began to feel his nerves calmer and his breath flow more evenly. Then he wondered whether Eleanor would ever speak, or whether she was trying to slip out of it, hoping the question would evaporate in the silence.

He cleared his throat. "Shall I ask you again?"

She shook her head. "I want to talk about it. This is very hard for me."

"I can imagine."

"Give me time. I feel I need a lot of time for this."

"You can have all the time in the world."

"Frank, I'm afraid of you."

"No reason to be afraid."

"I *am* afraid of you."

Frank turned around, as if to see a ghost or gorilla standing in back of him. "I never knew I was that terrifying."

"It's not funny. I'm afraid of your anger. It's really frightening when you let go of your temper."

"What are you talking about?"

"Ever since that time you hit me in the face—"

"That was three years ago. Come on, Ellie, haven't you gotten enough mileage out of that one slap?"

"It's easy for you to be sarcastic, you're stronger than I am. You can use that strength whenever you want. There's nothing I can do to stop you from beating me up any minute."

"But I don't beat you up every minute."

"But you have hit me, and you could again. The potential is there, don't you see? I'm afraid of you!" she said, almost bursting into tears. "Mary herself noticed it and commented on it once."

"Come on, Ellie," Frank said. "I'm not going to hit you! You're being melodramatic. I have the feeling you're exaggerating this fear you have of me to get out of talking about the other thing."

"No, I want to talk about it. Give me another minute." She got up and ripped a paper towel from the roll, daubing at her eyes briskly.

"I'll make a deal with you. No matter what you tell me, I won't strike you," said Frank.

"I don't really care if you do or don't." Her tone was suddenly numb, flat.

"Well, I won't."

"I had sex with a man," said Eleanor.

"Go on."

"That's it. I had sex with a man."

"Do I know him?"

"You don't know him."

"What's his name?"

"I don't think it's very important."

"I'd like to hear it, though."

"But his name would mean nothing to you."

"Then it won't hurt to tell it."

"Why? So you can find him and—beat him up?"

"You really do have this misconception of me as a violent bruiser. No, the reason I would like to hear his name is that it would set my mind at rest that it's not someone close to me, Theo or someone like that."

"It's not *Theo*. God, you must think me a monster."

"I just don't know," he said coolly.

"Well, I would never do anything to hurt you like that."

"You know, I can't help thinking that just a little while ago you were assuring me that I had nothing to be threatened by or jealous of. You lied to me outright."

"I didn't lie to you."

"How is that not a lie?"

"I had sex with someone, but I didn't make love to him."

"Oh come on! That is the shabbiest verbal trick—"

"Shhh! Keep your voice down." Eleanor looked toward the ceiling and Golo's room.

"You didn't make love but you fucked him! When was this?"

"About a year ago."

"And that was the only time with this man?"

"There was one more time," said Eleanor.

"When was that?"

"What difference does it make?"

"If it was last week, it makes a big difference!"

"No, it was around the time of the first one. Around a year, ten months ago."

"I'm afraid to ask anything more. Those were the only two times? Each time it goes up another number! How can I believe you?" demanded Frank.

"If you don't believe me, what's the point in talking with me?" said Eleanor.

"You don't exactly inspire confidence with your manner of delivery."

"Oh, come off it, Frank. You have your lies, you have your secrets. You don't tell me everything."

"Like what?"

"If I knew what your secrets were, they wouldn't be secrets."

"Great. Back to that baloney. I—I just can't take it anymore."

"Then stop it."

"This is not my idea of fun."

"Nor mine," shot back Eleanor.

"What was the man's name?"

"Why do you want to know?"

"I want to know, so that, if I met him a cocktail party, not to invite him home! No, you really want to know why? Because the human brain can deal with certainty, however horrible, better than uncertainty. What's most frightening is to have phantoms, doubts, to suspect everyone."

"That's true. So you really think it would be better if I told you?"

"Yes. The known is always easier to deal with than the unknown."

"All right," said Eleanor. She lit a cigarette.

"Since when have you started smoking again?"

"Just tonight. You smoke enough grass. Don't start nagging me about that."

"Sorry."

"It was Jack Sullivan, he's an editor at my office. He's married, too."

"How did it happen?" asked Frank.

"It was a late night at work, everyone else had gone home. Do you want details? Positions?" she said sarcastically.

"I do want details. I don't know what I want. In a way I want details because my mind is swarming with so many images that at least the truth would limit me. But I don't want to know positions—I'd rather not. Was he a good lover?"

"He wasn't bad."

"Aieee!"

"You asked me. He was a moderately good lover, nothing special. What's that got to do with anything? It was nothing to brag about."

"So what attracted you to him? I mean, was it his looks, his physique, did he have a big cock?"

"You know that doesn't matter to me. Why are you being so hostile?"

"Why am I being hostile? *Why?* I assume there must be some reason why you fucked this man. I was only surmising: maybe he had a big one."

"He had an average-size penis," Eleanor said, with a wry smile.

"Why were you turned on to him in the first place? Was he young? Did he have good looks?"

"He has fairly good looks. But that wouldn't necessarily make me want to screw someone. In fact, he's very cold. He's a cold son of a bitch and he has no feelings. I don't think he's a very nice human being. He's Irish Catholic, and that interested me in a way, because he's very moralistic, and he thinks most people aren't worth two cents. He's judgmental. He's cold. That's all."

"Sounds like a lovely guy."

"He isn't. And I don't think I could make you understand why I went with him."

"Try."

"It was something that—seemed bound to happen. We both felt it. Not good, but inevitable. And the circumstances were peculiar: the fact that I was so angry at you, that it was raining hard that night, and the two of us were left alone in the office . . ." She fell silent.

"Why were you angry at me?" said Frank.

"For a number of reasons. Let me talk for a while. You've been cutting in on me, and I want to say this straight. Promise not to interrupt?"

"Okay."

Eleanor took a deep breath and began to talk.

"I have a dark place in me. It's when I lose hope. It feels very empty and hollow. I don't feel my body as real, I feel smoky. All brittle and black. I'm trying to describe a certain kind of despair. You don't know about this place, because you don't have it in you. But Jack had it in him, and we recognized it in each other immediately. A cynicism. A hopelessness. 'Nothingness' is the word I'm looking for. You're not a nihilist—for you life is a matter of working hard, and if you work hard you'll get rewarded, in an ever-forward progression. That's what I love about you, that you do have hope, that you're optimistic. But I can't always feel that way. Sometimes I have utterly closed-off moments, where I'm empty and I seek—oblivion. Self-annihilation. It's not suicide, because suicide would imply a belief in action. But in this place there is no belief, all belief has died. That's the rule of the place, that's the—ticket of entry. When I went with Jack, it wasn't because I thought of that as a positive action that would break the cycle. It was because I thought all my actions were equally futile, and so why not? What difference did it make? Nothing made a difference, no matter what I did. I felt abandoned. I felt that you didn't love me anymore."

"But that isn't true, I never stopped loving you."

"You said you wouldn't interrupt. Whether it was true or not, whether it was just my 'paranoia'—let's say it was my paranoia. Only I know it wasn't, entirely. I went around for weeks wishing that I was going crazy, because a sick mind was preferable to the conclusion I was reaching. But there's a reason why paranoia is called the most realistic of all mental illnesses. And there was a reason for my suspicion in the first place. First there was the business of your not taking me to Santa Barbara. —Just let me finish. I know you think it's petty of me to harp on that, but that trip was very important to me. You were stubborn. You knew I wanted to go and you wouldn't take me. I had the feeling that you wanted to have some fun on your own, to get a vacation away from me. Well, that's all right. But why the hypocrisy? When you went to Santa Barbara, I had the awful feeling I was being cast aside. I don't know if you've ever felt that bereft, being left by someone, but it's much easier to do the leaving than to be left behind. I hated myself for telling you it was all right, when it *wasn't* all right, and buying you a pretty leather bag to take to the airport, when deep down I resented you like crazy. What the hell was I doing buying you gifts? What was I thinking of? And there were other indications. I would say 'I love you' and you wouldn't answer. Or you would say 'Thank you.' But you wouldn't say 'I love you' back. You were being scrupulous. Maybe you didn't feel so much love for me at that moment, and I know you have a horror of lying. But when you stopped saying it, or said it grudgingly, infrequently, I became desperate. I had thrown myself into this second marriage.

If this didn't work out, I mean, I couldn't stand another disappointment. Suddenly I was frightened because I saw how much I had gone out on a limb. I had been falling in love with you, but you weren't falling in love with me to the same extent. Instead, you were still cautious. You wanted me to be hopelessly in love with you, you wanted bottomless devotion, like any narcissist, but you weren't prepared to match it. You wanted to remain detached, so that you could always walk out, like with Estelle. You wanted to be loved, sure, but you didn't want to have to love. And I was angry about it. I was furious. I wanted to get back at you any way I could. I think I chose the wrong way. You can despise me for it all you want."

"I certainly don't despise you."

"Well, good. I'm glad. But that isn't what I was going to say. What I did, I did because I loved you too much, in a way you'll probably never feel. I pity you. Because you're always holding back. Maybe you're putting that love into your work, I don't know where it's going, but I know you're sure as hell holding back with me. At least my hostility was overt, I put all my emotions right on the table. And you can scorn me for that, you can beat me up, you can despise me if you like. But at least I took an action. It happened to be the wrong one. Whereas you never do anything wrong like that. All you do is imply, infer, make innuendoes. It's maddening! You leave me to guess at the undertones. I feel like a mole half the time, groping around in the dark. 'What did he just say? What did he mean by that?' I feel like I'm in a Henry James novel, trying to piece together some awful truth. Sometimes I even get the feeling . . . that you want me to sleep with other men. That you set it up for me, psychologically, to confirm your notions of women. That I was obeying your wishes by being unfaithful."

"What an excuse."

"I don't expect any sympathy from you. I have just one more thing to say. I know the way your mind works. You have a dirty mind—you think I did it for lust. Like that I'm a scarlet woman. No. I'm satisfied with our sex life. I told you you were a good lover, so don't twist this around to feed your sexual insecurity. That's not why I did it."

"Then why did you do it?"

"It was nihilism, pure and simple. And maybe I was curious. I *am* curious about other people's bodies—aren't you?" Eleanor asked.

"Yes. But I don't act on that curiosity."

"Neither do I, most of the time. Sometimes I have acted on it, though."

"Sometimes you have," Frank said sardonically. "Are you finished? Can I ask a few questions?"

"I'm ready."

"For the record, you fucked this guy Jack twice."

"Something like that. Once was a blow job."

"Twice is no longer a one-night stand done as animosity against me. Twice is already an affair, a relationship that has a life of its own."

"Call it whatever you want."

"Are you in love with him?"

"No. Haven't you been listening to anything I said?"

"Do you plan to sleep with him—sorry, 'have sex' with him—again?"

"No. It's all over."

"Good. That's something to be grateful for. Now, about these innuendoes. I'm sitting here listening, and I'm feeling pangs of guilt because, you're right, I don't always love you. I even feel neutral toward you at times, or plain irritated. But I'm also thinking that over the months and years, on average, I do love you pretty consistently. And you've got to believe me on that. Do you?"

"I . . . would like to believe it."

"Good. That's a start. Now about these 'undercurrents.' Did it ever occur to you that one of the reasons undercurrents stay undercurrents, and don't coalesce into actions, is that they aren't strong enough to? When I was married to Estelle, she didn't need undercurrents to know that I no longer loved her. It was right on the table, as you say. I couldn't get a fucking erection!" said Frank.

"Men can get erections even when they're filled with hostility and rage," said Eleanor.

"Touché. Good point. The point I'm making here is that the law doesn't condemn a man for his thoughts but for his actions. If there's one thing I've learned in life, it's that deeds are what count. Not undercurrents. Now you're trying to hang me for undercurrents! If I wanted to be mean to you, I wouldn't do it with undercurrents, I would be flat-out mean. The way you were. I draw a distinction between thought and act, between fantasizing cheating on someone and actually cheating."

"You're talking very legalistically. Do you want me to say I'm guilty? Okay, I'm guilty. I'm sorry. I really am sorry!" she cried.

Frank looked down at his balls, peeping through the robe. They looked so dejected, so silly. He would have to leave this woman, he thought. He no longer wanted to live in a world where a wife could be sweet, make him cinnamon toast one minute, and have sex with some other man the next. He felt as if the marriage had already died, and there was no point in raging and throwing chairs. Everything was already ruined between them, the careful life he had built for himself shattered, he would have to move to another city, he would leave all this, purely to stay alive. She had tried to kill him by insinuating herself into the closest of trusts and then dealing him this blow. She'd tried to poison him with a diet of lies. And he would stand up to it; he would not have a heart attack. He would survive. She looked so innocent sitting there, in her nightgown. Not at all the kind of woman you imagine betraying you. Almost bland, in a buxom, wholesome way, with little swellings on her face. How dare a woman with little swellings on her face torture him like this? (As if you had to be a perfect beauty to twist a man in knots, he thought.) Maybe that was the problem: he had taken her too much for granted and she had needed to go out and find reassurance of her seductive allure. But how could there be any married love without some taking each other for granted?

"What are you thinking?" she asked.

"I'm thinking, This is a nightmare. It just goes on and on."

It was 2:25 on the big walnut kitchen clock.

"Do you want to go to bed?"

"I can't. I'm fully awake," said Frank. "And I was also thinking: It's true what they say about women, you know? They *are* devious. The one thing I don't understand is why you would keep it a secret so long. Every minute you were with me you were lying to me, this past year, there was a secret between us like a barricade. Even now you probably wouldn't have told me if it hadn't come out in this accidental manner. Or if I hadn't asked you directly. The deception could have continued for years! You've shown no sense of responsibility for keeping our relationship honest."

"It's not true that I feel no responsibility. As for this past year, it doesn't wipe out everything good that happened between us, if that's what you're saying."

"The thing I can't stand, even more than that you had sex with someone else, is the lying. So you went to bed with someone outside the marriage, these things happen all the time. Who am I to inveigh against such a commonplace? But all that lying to me!"

"I did intend to tell you," Eleanor said. "I've been planning to for some time."

"Then what kept you?"

"I didn't think it was a good time, since we were having all that trouble with Cara. It was still too raw. I've never believed in honesty at all costs, you know that. People can be very sadistic in the name of honesty. You can do serious damage to another person's psyche."

"Did you think I would crumble?"

"You can take things very hard sometimes. You can be very unforgiving."

"Of course I take things hard! But I don't die from it. I survive."

"At least now you know. Maybe this will bring about a good change," she said wistfully.

He would not acknowledge that possibility yet, or even that he had heard her last statement. There was a dish of candy on the sideboard behind him. Frank took a nougat from the dish and started unwrapping it. A piece of yellow wrapping clung to the nougat, and he had to scratch it off with his fingernail. It seemed to take forever. "Want one?"

"No."

"I don't understand nougats," said Frank, "why they wrap them this way. It takes so damn long to get to the meat."

"I need a drink," said Eleanor. She stood up and started into the living room.

"Are you coming back?"

"Yes, I'm coming back!" she said.

He held his forehead with his left hand. His right eye ached, and his glands felt swollen, the way they did when he was coming down with a sore throat. It could have just been the lateness of the hour. He felt as solitary as a birch tree. The world kept trying to peel the bark off him, but he would remain standing, isolate and private, the way he had been before he met Eleanor. Everyone would blame him, because everyone always sympathized with Eleanor. They would say he had walked out on her. No one would understand. And he would tell no one the reason. He had a fantasy of himself as a chivalrous knight bound by honor to silence about his lady's treachery. Of course he would also be protecting himself by remaining silent. The cuckold is a comic figure.

"Frank?" said Eleanor, returning with her drink. "What are you feeling?"

"My throat's a little swollen."

She looked at him sympathetically. "Do you want a Valium?"

It amazed him that she could put him through this torment one moment and the next minute start to nurse him. "No, I want to feel this pain. It's unique."

"That's silly. But suit yourself."

"I'm tired. Do you want to get some sleep?" he said.

"I should be tired, but I'm wide awake."

"Me too."

"I thought you said you were tired?" she said.

"Mentally wide awake, but physically wiped out."

"I get it," said Eleanor. "I know what, let's go for a walk."

"It's already past three."

"I need to go outside and see the night. Let's take a little walk. Please?"

"Sure," said Frank.

"It'll just take me a minute to change," said Eleanor.

Frank put on an old jeans shirt and some lemon-colored beach slacks and sandals. Eleanor met him at the door, in a white blouse and wraparound corduroy skirt, her hair tied in a ponytail, like a teenager, or Audrey Hepburn.

They headed toward Montague Street. It was a muggy night. Small groups could be seen moving down the broad thoroughfare, night owls coming home from parties, teenagers dallying on the street-corners. It was hot and a lot of people must have had trouble sleeping. The street was covered with that steamy mist or fog that hits the city on humid nights and swirls around the lampposts. Only something like the purple fluorescent night-lights in a plant store window punctured this fog. Manhattan was barely visible across the river: a few skyscrapers, like giant, smudged gum erasers or bits of charcoal, shone in the soupy night. Frank and Eleanor passed a twenty-four-hour Polish coffee shop that served breakfast at all hours. The acrid coffee smell pinched at him, and he was tempted to go in and order corned-beef hash and coffee, not so much for the food as for the company, to get rid of the band of marital dismay pressing down on his chest and exchange it for the grubby common humanity of the graveyard shift. But they kept on walking; they needed to walk, though where to, finally, remained unclear. A breeze came off the river. They followed it, moving toward the Promenades.

Eleanor took his arm. "Nice night, isn't it?"

"Yes, it is nice."

She looked, Frank saw, rather fetching, alas: more relaxed than she had looked in months. For her, the trial was over. Just beginning for me, he thought. He had to admit, though, that everything at this hour came at him with acute forlorn beauty: he experienced the surrounding environment so deeply, the sounds, the wooden boardwalk under their feet, the mist, the lights on the river. How strange that this heightened sense of things should be triggered by such misery! He had been jolted into seeing these tureens of fog, the whole gritty sauna of a New York summer night, in the crack between one epoch of his life and another. He would have to leave Eleanor—that much was certain. Or maybe he wouldn't leave her. He felt a resentful tenderness toward her; he had misjudged his wife badly, but that was no reason to discard her. Maybe the point God was making was not that the Eleanor era was about to close but that the era in which he would finally learn how to forgive and accept was about to begin. In another few years he would be fifty, then sixty. There was no point in turning out one woman after another because of some crucial mistake on their part, and then scrambling, at seventy, when one really needed a helpmate, to find a companion who would put up with him.

They came to rest on a wooden bench with wrought-iron arms. A gay couple walked by, then another. The night and the Promenade belonged to gays at this hour. A lone gay man walked quickly down the main rut of the boardwalk and looked around swiftly from side to side. He had on a green-and-blue-striped beach shirt and his skin was outrageously tanned. He looked at Frank and Eleanor, then kept walking with his head proudly erect.

Frank thought of the vacation to the Virgin Islands they had planned to take in a few weeks. If they were still together. He let out a sigh.

"What are you thinking?" Eleanor asked for the second time, breaking the silence.

"I'm thinking . . . where do we go from here?"

"Yes."

"And I'm thinking about the lights on the river. I'm thinking about gay men. I'm thinking about a lot of things."

"Where *do* we go from here, do you think?"

"I don't know. What do you think?" asked Frank.

"That all depends. If you want to, we can get a divorce."

"I'm not thinking about it," he lied.

"Do you hate me?"

"No."

Eleanor laughed ironically. "Do you love me?"

"Yes, unfortunately."

"Bad habit, eh?"

"A dumb stupid habit. When I look at you, I feel so—fond of you, I just want to put my head in your lap. Or give you a big squeeze."

"Put your head in my lap."

Frank arranged himself clumsily on the bench. His head felt like a lead pipe, stiff, tense, muffled against the corduroy skirt that covered her groin. She brushed the hair away from his widow's peak with a practiced motion. He tensed as she did, because it exposed how much of his hairline was starting to recede. But Eleanor liked to see him that way, with his brow left candid and open. She continued to comb his hair back with her hand, gently but persistently, as if it were her intention to force him to accept himself as he was, or was soon to be.

"Do you think we could make a go of it?" she asked.

"I think we could." He lifted himself up on one elbow to speak to her. "We've both made our share of mistakes. That's obvious now. The question is whether we can break the destructive pattern. We're not kids anymore. We're getting older. You can't just throw away a marriage because you've made some mistakes."

"But that's not enough of a reason to keep the relationship going, because we're feeling middle-aged," said Eleanor. "I refuse to do it on that basis. That's what got us into trouble in the first place. The idea that you were 'settling' for me, as if you were making a big compromise."

"But don't you think marriage involves a set of big compromises?"

"Yes. But not at the core. At the core you have to choose someone and mean it."

"I chose you. I choose you." Frank took both of her hands solemnly in his. Mentally, he knew the odds were still about 50–50 that he would split.

"I don't believe you."

"Well, that's your problem."

"No, my problem is that I chose you but you didn't choose me. At least not to the same degree," Eleanor said with analytical calm.

Frank was silent a few moments. "No, the real problem is that you can't believe I love you."

They were stalemated.

A tugboat hauling a flat barge with oil barrels was moving down the East River from the Bronx. They saw its wake churning up white foam as it traversed under the Manhattan Bridge and then the Brooklyn Bridge, and slowly passed alongside them. Two men were on the tug, coiling rope around a black cylinder.

"Okay, I believe you," said Eleanor.

"Let's go back."


Morning approached. She bent over him with her gold chain tickling his face. Her breasts were blue-veined against the darkened window shade, and there was that serious look in her eyes.

Neither touched the other, as if they were afraid it would be interpreted as a presumption. Then Eleanor lay beside him with her hand under her chin.

"Lie on top of me," Frank said.

He started to go to sleep with her still lowering down on him. Her body felt wonderful. He was floating from half-thought to half-thought, and it would have been torture for him if anyone had demanded he give an accurate accounting of these fragments. Meanwhile, there was the reassuring pressure of her breasts, her legs.

She seemed sound asleep. Then her leg twitched against him, the way a dog does who is having a bad dream.

"What?"

She woke up and started speaking like an oracle:

"I had a dream that I wanted to sleep with someone else. I just had the urge, don't ask me why. It was the idea more than anyone in particular. But then I asked you if you could pretend to be another man and sleep with me. And you said you would. And so that's what you did, and I woke up feeling that everything was going to be all right."

Frank was not sure it would be that easy.

Eleanor closed her eyes again and started to drift off.

"Was it nice, making love in the dream?" he asked.

"I don't know if we actually made love in the dream. All I know is that I woke up with a feeling of incredible relief."